COURTED BY BEASTS

EVA CHASE

THE HEART OF A MONSTER

BOOK 2

CHAPTER ONE

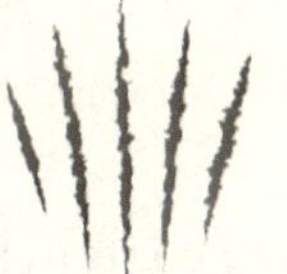

Quinn

Monsters surrounded me. In the faint glow cast by the distant streetlamps along the edge of the mostly vacant parking lot, their claws, spines, and searing eyes glinted eerily. The massive beast crouched on the hood of our sedan leered at us through the windshield as if the tint in the glass didn't obscure his vision at all.

After being swarmed by hordes of shadowy creatures multiple times in the past, maybe I should have been getting used to this scenario. No such luck. My heart hammered in my chest, my fingers curling against my palms tightly enough to dig my fingernails into my skin. I jerked my arm through the strap of my messenger bag automatically—it held my medication and other essentials—but my whirling mind couldn't see any way of escaping this time.

Dozens of the creatures prowled around the car on all sides. The leprechaun who'd apparently led them here, the man one of my protectors had considered a friend, was still staring at Torrent with a tight, pained smile.

Our luck had run out. Our one sort-of ally had turned on us. The vest of silver and iron beads I'd commissioned to stop the shadowkind creatures from tracking me down didn't do me any good when they already knew exactly where I was.

Where the hell did we go from here?

Torrent turned his head toward Crag. Whatever communication passed between the tentacled man and the gargoyle was totally silent. Beside me, Lance hopped up nimbly into a crouch on the seat, flexing his vicious dragon-shifter claws.

The huge fiend on the hood raised a fist to smash right through the windshield, and the men around me sprang into motion in an instant.

Torrent hit the button to activate the car alarm. The sudden blare echoed through the vacant lot, startling the beast on the hood in mid-punch. Creatures all through the horde surrounding us flinched, heads jerking toward the nearest buildings in an instinctive fear of discovery.

At the same moment, Crag dove into the shadows of the car and re-materialized practically on top of me in full gargoyle form. His bulging arms yanked me against his immense chest. He grunted as my vest smacked against his stony skin, and I realized that coming into close contact with the metals toxic to shadowkind must be hurting him, but he didn't hesitate. Without missing a beat, he threw himself into the door shoulder first.

The car door burst right off its hinges. We hurtled out into the night, the flap of Crag's wings sweeping us up over the heads of most of the throng. I shifted in his embrace, hugging my messenger bag and adjusting my position so as little of my vest was outright touching him as possible. I had to make myself as easy a burden as I could.

But our enemies had come prepared this time. They'd seen how the gargoyle had carried me to safety before. Several winged bodies launched themselves after us, most of them smaller, but a couple were nearly human-sized and one was almost as large as Crag's gigantic form. My pulse stuttered.

The wind warbled past us as Crag soared higher. My pale hair whipped around my face. Hisses and shrieks rose up from below, where the car alarm had cut off. Torrent and Lance would be fighting for their lives—they couldn't just leap into the air and take off. Would they be able to escape all those attackers?

My chest ached at the thought of abandoning them, but our own escape was looking more precarious by the second. The effects of the silver and iron in my vest must have been tiring Crag, because the other flying beasts were catching up. A rasp had crept into his breath. I wanted to fling the vest right off me, but I didn't have the room to maneuver without risking his hold on me.

A creature that looked like a barracuda melded with a bat shot toward us. Crag clutched me firmly with one arm and swung his other fist at the thing. With a crunch of fracturing bone, it tumbled down through the air, the smoky substance shadowkind had for blood pluming up in its wake.

Three more of the smaller shadowkind lunged at us from different sides. Crag's wings whooshed as he spun and flipped, dizzying me. His heel shattered one thing's skull, his thick fingers snapping another's spine. The third flitted past him, aiming its curved talons straight at me.

I didn't have time to think, only to react—but I knew what the most powerful weapon I had on me was. I managed to fling out my arm, snatching the creature's wing and yanking it even faster so that it slammed right into my vest.

The thing's skin outright sizzled with the contact with the noxious metals. It screeched and shoved away, and Crag bashed its head into a pulpy mess.

He was still breathing hard—and the larger creatures had almost caught up. He pushed his wings faster, careening over the tops of the Jacksonville buildings with the city lights glinting through the darkness from below us, but the monstrous forms tore after us just as quickly. One of them made a low, guttural sound it took me a second to recognize as a chuckle.

"Stay still," Crag muttered, the only warning I got before he plunged into a dive. He shot between two high rises and swerved around a condo building. If anyone was up at this way-too-early hour of the morning and looking out their window, they'd have gotten quite a view.

I craned my neck and spotted two of the monstrous figures still on our tail. My throat constricted.

"You could land and put me down," I said over the rush of the wind. "You'd be able to fight better if—"

"No," Crag said gruffly. "That would give them the chance to snatch you. They're not getting you, Softness."

His emphatic insistence and the affectionate nickname sent a bittersweet pang through my chest. The three shadowkind men who'd rescued me from more murderous examples of their kind a week ago had already been through the wringer to protect me. They'd fought battles, gone on the run, even defied the boss they'd all spent decades working for.

They'd dedicated themselves that much to me... but what if the decision ruined them?

Yes, they were monsters too, but in the past week I'd discovered that they were so much more than that. The thought of Crag with his brutal protectiveness—or Lance and his playful wildness, or Torrent and his curt determination—being cut down on my behalf wrenched at me.

The slightly smaller of our two foes, a beast that looked like a winged, scaly jaguar, hurled itself the last short distance toward Crag. Its claws raked across Crag's shoulder as the gargoyle swiveled. Smoky blood streamed from the gashes.

Crag lashed out with his own clawed hand. He shredded the edge of the creature's wing, but the thing only bobbed before regaining its balance. The other flying fiend had almost reached us.

Crag pushed away with a heave of his wings and kicked out with both of his powerful legs. He caught the scaly beast in the face with one foot, cracking open its snout. It still managed to snarl through the gush of smoke, but the pain turned it wilder—and more reckless. It sped at Crag, who whacked it to the side and crushed its neck between his heels.

By then, the largest creature was on us. It sprang too quickly for Crag to reorient himself in time, and the sound of ripping flesh made me flinch. The gargoyle listed to the side with a snarl resonating through his clenched teeth. My stomach lurched.

This creature was way too big for me to help in the battle, though. I couldn't hope that contact with my vest would do more than briefly irritate it, and trying to strike out at it myself would only put my limbs in Crag's way. As he whipped around in the air, I held myself as still and small as I could, my pulse thundering through my head.

Our last opponent didn't let up for a second. It swung a fist here and swept out a taloned leg there, its sinewy body contorting this way and that to evade Crag's blows. He dipped lower, still favoring one side, and a deeper terror gripped me.

The beast had injured his wing. He was having trouble just keeping us in the air. Maybe he'd *have* to come down to earth.

I wasn't totally sure that was a bad thing, but Crag seemed determined to hold us aloft as long as he could. He struck out at the creature with his legs and the arm that wasn't holding me tight against him, even battering the thing across its oddly pointed head with his good wing.

The fiend just gave another of those low, unnerving chuckles as if this was all a game to it. As if it wasn't the slightest bit worried about the outcome of the battle.

A chill coursed through my veins. Crag spun, and the creature leapt in the opposite direction. With another tearing sound, Crag grunted and dropped even farther. Smoky blood hissed from his wounds.

He beat the creature off as well as he could, but it wasn't a fair fight while he was clutching me, dealing with the pain of my vest and his failing wing. The beast landed a strike to his head, scraping its claws right through one of the pointed gargoyle ears Crag had told me were a vulnerable spot and slamming its spiked tail against his side. More smoke streamed up, and almost all of it was Crag's.

Tension wound through my torso alongside a prickling sensation that spread out across the rest of my body. *No*. I couldn't let this happen. I had to do *something* to save the man who'd given so much to protect me.

If I didn't, we were both going to die.

A now-familiar fluttery wobble of energy ran through my chest. It seemed to cast a bubble into the base of my throat. My heart thumped, propelling a quiver through my blood that I could almost taste, like something electric crackling all through my flesh.

The thing lunged at us again, and my mouth popped open. I expected to scream or cry out.

Instead, a shout burst from my lips: a string of syllables that meant nothing to me but that rang from my mouth with a sense of urgency and purpose I couldn't explain. The electric energy surged out of me with that sound.

The fiend jerked backward as if I'd slapped it. It shook its head, its muscles tensing, but its wings were already whirling it around. It took off in the opposite direction like a shot.

As Crag plummeted into an alley even darker than the quiet street beyond, I stared after our attacker. The gargoyle didn't say anything about the weirdness of what had just happened, but he didn't have to. Nausea coiled around my gut.

Did I really need to wonder what had happened? The

heart now beating fast but more steadily in my chest, the one that'd been transplanted into me nine years ago after a childhood virus had ruined the one I'd been born with, had come from a sorcerer's daughter. We'd already suspected that some of the magic those rare mortals could use to control the shadowkind had carried over to me with it.

And I'd just drawn on that power without even understanding what I was doing. In whatever language had come to me instinctively, I'd ordered the fiend to leave... and it had.

Maybe I should have felt triumphant, but I couldn't summon excitement from beneath the sick feeling in my gut. That power might have saved us just now, but technically it made me an enemy not just to the monsters that wanted to capture me but to the men who'd protected me as well.

Crag's feet hit the ground in a landing much less graceful than usual. He was still streaming smoke from multiple wounds. The second his grip on me loosened, I dropped to the pavement and swiveled toward him, groping at my bag. Was there anything in my first aid kit that could help a being made of stone and shadow?

"I'll heal," the gargoyle said in his gruff way, but he couldn't hide the thread of pain in his voice. In the thin light that seeped from the street, I made out the imprint the beads on my vest had burned into his muscular chest, turning the gray flesh nearly black. A fresh wave of nausea swept through me.

Then the little bit of illumination we had dimmed even further. A sedan had pulled up to the curb just outside the alley—but not ours. The black one we'd used for the past few days was ruined now anyway. This one was silver.

As I braced myself to run and Crag grasped my shoulder, a figure wavered into being next to the car, having skipped the need to open the door. Crag's former boss, Rollick—the one hostile shadowkind I'd thought we no longer needed to worry about—rolled his shoulders and aimed a knowing grin our way.

CHAPTER TWO

Quinn

As Rollick strode into the thicker shadows of the alley, Crag wrapped a protective arm right around me, his wings fanning out on either side of him. The other man stopped in his tracks and raised his hands in a gesture of peace.

"Don't strain your wounds more than you already have, Crag," he said in a smoothly assured voice. "I'm not here to threaten her. You need to listen to me."

Everything about the guy radiated assurance. When I'd first seen him on the dock a couple of days ago, I'd thought he looked like a movie star who'd stepped right out of the screen in full cinematic glory, and that impression hadn't diminished. And that was true even though I had even more reason to distrust him now than I'd had before— partly because it'd become clear that he wanted to grab my heart for himself just like our other enemies did... and partly because I doubted he trusted *me* after I'd stabbed him while making a run for it.

I still had no idea what monstrous attribute he brought with him into his mortal guise. Other than the aura of power that tingled off of him over my skin and woke up another quaver of energy in my heart, he looked completely if stunningly human. He smiled again with a flash of those white teeth and ran his fingers back through his tawny hair, leaving it perfectly ruffled. I saw no hint of the injury I'd given him. The cut from the silver-and-iron dagger must have healed already.

"You can't have her," Crag rumbled, hugging me close. "You're not setting one finger on her while I'm here." But the fact that he hadn't taken off into the air didn't bode well for his ability to do so. How long would it take *him* to heal?

How well could the gargoyle fight off Rollick in his current state if he couldn't flee? Torrent had said that their former boss was a very powerful demon.

"Well, I suppose that depends on how you look at it." Rollick stayed where he was and tipped his head toward the street. "Would you really rather *that* mob got their hands on her? They're already heading this way—they saw what direction you flew in. You'll have trouble outrunning all of them in your current state."

The monstrous horde was on the move—which meant they weren't fighting my other shadowkind men anymore. My pulse stuttered.

"Are Torrent and Lance all right?" I blurted out.

Rollick blinked and focused on me rather than Crag for the first time. One eyebrow arched. "If you think they're going to save the day, you've greatly overestimated what they're capable of."

My jaw tightened. "That's not what I was thinking about. I just want to know that those creatures didn't... didn't kill them."

I couldn't stop my voice from wobbling. For a second, the demon in man form looked outright puzzled. Then he shrugged. "I'm not sure about the welfare of my mutinous employees. They are very adept at getting out of jams. I've only seen your other pursuers from a distance. I wasn't looking to get up close and personal."

We didn't just have to worry about the horde tracking us down on their own, it occurred to me. I hadn't enslaved the being I'd used my sorcerer magic on, only given him a single command. How long would that stick? He knew exactly where we'd been—he could lead the others right to us the second he snapped out of the spell. Which he might already have, for all I knew.

I eyed the man in front of me, tucking my hand around Crag's arm so I'd be ready to help him carry me as much as possible if he determined we needed to take off. Could I use that power on Rollick to give us a chance to escape?

I had no idea how I'd summoned enough energy to begin with. It wasn't crackling through my body the way it'd been in that moment. Maybe if he came at us and provoked enough desperation, that would trigger the same reaction. But I didn't know how to generate it on my own.

And who knew if it'd even work on a being as powerful as my men had suggested he was? They hadn't believed they could defeat him in a fight even three against one.

"How are you even here?" I asked, for the sake of

drawing out the conversation—and giving Crag more time to recover from his wounds. "Torrent saw a photo of you back in L.A."

"Oh, I did go home," Rollick replied. "Quite the trick the bunch of you pulled with that body in the park. It actually convinced me. But I have eyes all over the place. I got word that shadowkind had amassed in Miami and then headed north, and I knew that meant there was still a prize to be had here. So I flew straight back, and I've been cruising around keeping watch for you for the past couple of hours."

My skin prickled uneasily at his words. "I'm not a *prize*."

He gazed at me steadily. "To a whole lot of my monstrous brethren, you most certainly are."

"And to you?" I shot back.

"I recognize your value." His gaze lifted to meet Crag's eyes again. "That doesn't mean I'm going to hurt her."

"You wanted her heart," the gargoyle growled. His wings extended and contracted at the edges of my vision, and I could tell the damaged one was still barely mobile. More smoke was coursing off the ragged tears in its leather surface. Shit.

"Yes, well, I happen to think that heart is much more useful while still in the body currently harboring it." Rollick aimed a wink at me, as if we were all having a grand time here and not in a life-or-death standoff.

"What do you want, then?" I demanded.

He paused as if considering his answer and slung his hands in the pockets of his fitted slacks. "You're a piece on a very large playing board, one you don't even know the half of. I prefer to hold as many pieces as possible. But I meant what I said. I don't intend to harm you, certainly not to kill you like some of those lesser shadowkind might if given free rein. I can help you figure out what to do with all that unexpected energy inside you."

My pulse hitched again, but this time it wasn't with fear. He might know how to deal with the sorcerer magic lodged in my heart? How I could control it or even get rid of it? The memory of the strange word that'd reverberated up my throat and the way the creature I'd aimed it at had fled came back to me again with a chill.

I might not know how to turn it on at will, but the power was getting stronger, more active. I hadn't used it on purpose. What if I accidentally turned it on one of my men next? If all three of those men had even survived the latest horror show I'd dragged them into.

But Torrent hadn't believed that Rollick would protect me. He'd defied his boss specifically to protect me from *him*. The demon in front of me could be lying through his teeth, and I'd have no clue.

I wet my lips. "Why shouldn't we just walk away? What are you going to do if I don't agree to go with you?"

Crag shifted his stance behind me, drawing himself up even taller as if in an attempt to look as threatening as possible.

Rollick considered both of us calmly. He folded his arms over his well-muscled chest. "You can't fly right now," he said to Crag. "We both know it, or you'd already have jetted off. I don't *want* to fight you, if only because I'd rather not traumatize the girl by having her see what I'd have to do to you, but I will if I need to. There's no one watching here that I need to hide from. You'd be taking on the demon."

I kind of wondered why he hadn't launched into battle already. He had to be pissed off at Crag for disobeying him and then tricking him. Was he really that worried about my emotional well-being? It seemed unlikely. But then, I got the impression Rollick played a long game on that board he'd talked about. Who knew what his full motivations were?

We could still run for it. I curled my fingers tighter around Crag's thick forearm, prepared to let him heft me up so he could charge off down the alley. At the same time, my back pressed more firmly against his chest, and I felt the faint flinch he couldn't suppress at the feel of my vest.

Could he even run fast enough to outpace Rollick the way he was now? What would Rollick do to him if we forced him to give chase?

The gargoyle's head twitched, his attention seeming to shift to something beyond the alley. A low growl escaped him. He didn't say anything in front of Rollick, but a chilly certainty washed through me.

Crag had told me that he could sense the presence of other shadowkind when they were close enough. The ones hunting us must be nearby—maybe no more than a few blocks away now.

"What guarantee do I have?" I asked abruptly.

"Quinn," Crag protested, his arm tensing around me. "You don't have to—"

"Guarantee?" Rollick interrupted, cocking his head.

"That you won't hurt me," I said. "You could say

whatever you want, and then as soon as I don't have Crag guarding me, you'll be ripping my heart out."

Rollick's mouth twisted slightly in what looked like genuine distaste at the thought, but it could have been an act. He contemplated the question for a moment. Then he raised one hand and flicked his fingers. A spread of black claws shot from the tips where his fingernails had been an instant before. They were only half as long as Lance's talons but equally vicious-looking.

He poised the claws over his other arm where bare tanned skin showed beneath the rolled-up sleeve of his dress shirt. "I'll give you my demonic oath. You come with me and do as I say, and I'll defend you from bodily harm to the best of my ability."

Crag went rigid behind me. I glanced up into his monstrous face, searching for affirmation of Rollick's claim in his angular gargoyle features.

"It would be binding," Crag confirmed. "That kind of oath—he wouldn't be able to break it unless you failed your end."

I dragged in a breath. Maybe it would be okay, in that case. I couldn't really expect the demon to offer that kind of promise without getting something in return. And if I disagreed with his demands, hopefully by then we'd be in a better position to flee.

All of us. As the idea took hold, I raised my chin. "I can agree to that as long as you swear the same for Torrent, Lance, and Crag." Assuming the first two were still in one piece.

Rollick stared at me for a second, appearing taken aback for the second time since this conversation had started. He recovered quickly. "Also dependent on your cooperation," he said.

"Of course."

Crag bowed his head close to my ear. "This isn't necessary. I'll fight if I have to. The others will catch up."

Even as he spoke, a roar rang out what sounded like no more than a block away. The hairs on the back of my neck stood on end.

He might be right, but we didn't know when Torrent and Lance would reach us. We didn't know how close all of our other pursuers were. Torrent had at least used to trust this demon, enough that he hadn't run away when Rollick had first shown up. That was more than I could say for any of the other fiends who'd attacked me.

I could go with him, see what he could tell me about my powers, and ensure our safety at least temporarily, or send Crag into a battle I doubted he could come out of alive and end up in Rollick's clutches anyway, with no agreement in my favor at all.

"We'll find Torrent and Lance before we leave," I added. "They're coming with us—if they want to." I didn't know how they'd feel about the deal I was making, but I couldn't exactly ask them ahead of time. "All right?"

The dawn light that was spreading through the streets glinted in Rollick's dark blue eyes. "You drive a tough bargain, mortal. But I'll accept in the interests of getting us out of here."

He dug two of his claws into his flesh, carving a swift sigil that released tendrils of smoky blood. "I will defend the human Quinn Moody and the shadowkind Torrent, Lance, and Crag from bodily harm to the best of my ability, after first seeking out Torrent and Lance, so long as Quinn complies with any requests I make of her. This oath will remain binding until either of us violates the terms or for ten days, at which point we may revisit it."

I hadn't expected that last part and wasn't sure whether it benefitted me or not. But there was a bit of relief in knowing it wasn't an eternal contract no matter what either of us did. I didn't love how open-ended the phrasing about Rollick's requests was, but another snarl carried from down the street even as I absorbed his words.

We didn't have time to debate whether he should include an addendum. If I didn't like what he requested of me, I could simply not do it, and our deal would be broken.

Rollick stepped back toward the car and opened the back door like a chauffeur, his confident demeanor erasing any impression of servility. Chest tight, I squeezed Crag's arm and tugged him with me toward whatever our future held now.

Please, oh please, let me not regret this gamble.

CHAPTER THREE

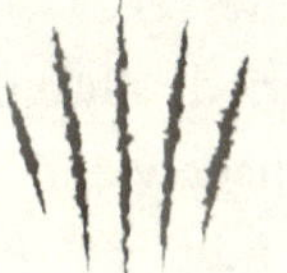

Quinn

It was clear from the moment Rollick's private jet arrived in L.A. that the demon *really* didn't want anyone knowing that he'd brought me back to the city with him. First, he made me wait on the plane while he checked out the car he'd had brought to the tarmac and the surrounding area. Apparently he didn't trust any of his underlings all that much. Or maybe he was being extra cautious now that three of them had recently turned on him.

As soon as he'd vanished near the doorway, I turned to the three men *I* trusted. My heart leapt with relief all over again taking in Torrent and Lance, looking not particularly worse for wear. We'd managed to find them fairly quickly on the streets of Jacksonville with Crag helping with the search, and they'd escaped the onslaught of enemy shadowkind with no major injuries.

I hadn't been able to express my relief all that thoroughly yet, because Rollick had kept us apart and in view during the flight. He'd insisted that I sit at one end of the cushy leather seating area and his three former employees stayed at the other while he lounged in the middle of the space, periodically glowering at them.

All three of the shadowkind men moved to join me where I was waiting near the door, and I immediately motioned them even closer. Lance hooked one hand around my elbow, careful as usual not to let his ever-present claws do more than graze my skin. Normally his touch sent tingles through my body, but right now my insides were too knotted up to feel anything except anxious.

"Tricksy, tricksy," the dragon shifter muttered, his violet eyes even wilder than usual beneath the fall of his erratic dark brown curls. He cocked his head, and I couldn't stop my gaze from shooting to the new scar that marred the smooth, golden-brown skin at the crook of his neck. A scar he'd gotten during the battle earlier this morning—he hadn't made it out completely unharmed. "We could make a run for it while he's distracted."

He glanced over at Crag, who'd come up behind him and set a hand on my shoulder. The gargoyle was back in human-like form, nothing hinting at his true nature other than the rocky jut of his jaw, but his otherwise bronze-toned face had taken on a grayish cast to match it. I didn't think he'd fully healed from his own wounds, although it was hard to tell how badly his wings were doing with them invisibly tucked away.

The gargoyle ran his other hand over the sheen of black

hair on his skull and ducked his head. "I'm not sure of how far or well I could fly yet."

We all looked toward Torrent, the de facto leader of the trio, who'd come up at my other side. Seeing how drawn his pale face was beneath his scruffy dark red hair, I swallowed hard and reached out cautiously to slide my arm around his torso, just above the spot where his two supporting tentacles emerged from his waist. I'd have hugged him more tightly if I hadn't wanted to give him enough distance that the silver-and-iron vest I was still wearing wouldn't touch even his clothes.

My growing understanding with Torrent had been a lot more tumultuous than my connection with Lance and Crag. I wasn't sure how he'd react to the choices I'd made.

"I think we should wait this out and see how it goes," I said before he could speak. "We're safe under the deal I made for ten days at least. If we go against it, who knows what he'll do to any of us. Crag needs time to recover, and it could be a good thing to find out what Rollick knows about my heart. It seems like he realized there might be something important about it before any other shadowkind did, considering he sent the three of you to watch over me way before I got attacked."

Torrent gazed down at me with his pensive sea-green eyes. "I agree," he said. "There's too much we don't understand about this situation. It'll be easier to determine how to tackle our enemies while we have fewer of them— and access to Rollick's resources. He can't break the deal he made. When the ten days are up, we'll be much more prepared for whatever we need to do."

He raised his hand to my shoulder and leaned over to

brush a kiss to the top of my head that brought a larger lump to my throat even as it reassured me that he wasn't pissed off with me. All the same, I felt the need to say, "I'm sorry. It seemed like the best out of a bunch of bad options. I didn't even know if you were still alive... or if you would be for very much longer if I didn't make a deal with him, now that he knows you all tricked him."

"It makes sense," the tentacled man said. "I wasn't there, but I don't think I'd have wanted you to choose differently." He frowned in the direction of the door. "He's been good to me in the past. He's more generous and fair-minded than the majority of shadowkind I've met, even if that isn't saying a lot by your human standards. The fact that he offered the deal at all... Maybe we did simply misunderstand his intentions."

He didn't sound as if he totally believed that was true, but I was glad he thought it was possible.

"If he asks anything of you that you feel is unreasonable, do what you can to get out of it and get to us before he can turn on you," he added firmly.

Before I could say anything else, Rollick blinked into being in front of the door. He waved his hand in my direction. "Quinn, come with me. The three of you, assuming you're sticking around, make your way through the shadows and don't show yourselves until we reach my private rooms in the hotel."

Lance let out a little growl, but when both Rollick and Torrent shot him a warning glance, he pecked my cheek and grudgingly faded into the shadows. The other two men did the same. Clutching the strap of my messenger bag where it was slung across my chest, I tramped down the plane's boarding stairs.

The silver sedan waiting outside looked a lot like the one Rollick had driven in Jacksonville. He motioned for me to get into the back. I found an oversized suede purse sitting in the middle of the seat.

"Put everything in there on," the demon told me as he started the engine. "Mortals are always snapping photos and plastering them all over the internet. The last thing we need is one of the beings who's got his sights on you spotting you in an image from the hotel."

When I unzipped the purse, I understood what he meant. Inside was a knee-length, high-collared silk dress with a billowy cut that I could tell would fit over the vest to disguise it, a wig of long black hair, a make-up bag, and a pair of sunglasses with large, round panes that would hide half of my face.

"Am I going to have to be going incognito the whole time I'm at this hotel of yours?" I asked as I quickly tugged the dress over my vest, the tank top I had on underneath, and my jean shorts.

"You'll be staying in my private suite," Rollick said. "Once you're settled in, there won't be anyone around to see you who shouldn't. You'll even be able to take off your very creative anti-shadowkind armor without any beings sensing your presence. I had the building constructed with a layer of silver and iron a few floors below the penthouse to discourage uninvited visitors and ensure no one could exert unwelcome influence on my living space or my guests."

"You thought of everything," I muttered.

He chuckled lightly. "I haven't stayed alive and well for as long as I have by leaving my fate to chance."

I studied the back of his head, the short fawn-brown hair framing his ears with just the slightest trace of a curl. "How long *have* you been alive?" I knew from past conversations that Torrent had been in existence for several hundred years, and I'd gathered that Crag and Lance both had at least a couple of centuries under their belts. There wasn't much that killed shadowkind other than being pulverized by another monster.

"Long enough to have watched nearly every civilization your kind has created rise and fall," Rollick said, as languidly as ever. "Get yourself together now. It's your life we're protecting here."

Right. I peered at myself in the little mirror that came with the make-up palette and dabbed on red lipstick when we were stopped at a streetlight. Then I smudged on some bronzer to give my skin more of an olive tone. There didn't seem to be much point in bothering with my eyes when they'd be concealed behind the sunglasses anyway. It wasn't my typical style for my occasional nights out, but I wasn't looking to find a quick hook-up today.

I managed to get the unfamiliar wig cap over my long hair and tugged the wig over that. When I looked at the mirror again, I barely recognized myself. That seemed like a good sign.

As I put the supplies away, I turned my gaze to the world beyond the window. For a few minutes, all I could do was stare.

We'd driven into the city proper. In some ways, Los Angeles wasn't that different from Jacksonville. Palm trees stood here and there along the streets; the roads were clogged with cars rumbling and periodically honking at each other.

On the other hand, everything was so much *bigger*. The skyscrapers loomed taller, and there seemed to be a gazillion of them. The streets were wider. I felt abruptly very small.

But even as the intimidated part of me shrank back a little, the architect-in-training took the sights in with an expanding sense of awe. Imagine designing a soaring high-rise to stand among *these* giants. Would I be able to come up with something that would strike the same awe I felt in people who were used to living someplace like this?

My fingers itched for my sketchpad. I almost pulled it out of my messenger bag to see what I could come up with on the fly, but taking full stock of my surroundings seemed more important. I wouldn't be able to become any kind of architect if I ended up a prisoner of shadowkind—or a worse sort of victim—for however much longer my borrowed heart would keep beating.

I thought I spotted a sign for a nearby train station. There was a police station... not that cops were likely to be much help against shadowkind attackers.

The buildings were starting to look increasingly posh. I saw more and more people on the sidewalks snapping pictures with their phones and consulting the street signs—tourists. I'd have been following our route on my own phone's map if Rollick hadn't demanded I hand it over the second I'd accepted his deal. I guessed it made sense that he didn't want there to be any chance that I'd give away my location, but its loss left me even more uneasy.

It wasn't much longer before Rollick pulled the sedan

into a driveway outside a tall, white-washed hotel with vivid purple trim. He drove past the curved section out front and over to a secluded side door that looked like it'd be mostly used for deliveries, where he parked to the side of the lane.

"The door will be unlocked," he said. "Go in and follow the hall until you can first take a right. You'll find an elevator there. Get on, and once you're inside, I'll enter the code to get us to the right floor. I'll be with you the whole time in the shadows."

I wasn't sure if that information was supposed to reassure me or threaten me, but I wasn't inclined to argue anyway. I was in this situation now, wherever it led me.

Clutching my messenger bag, I eased out of the car into the sweltering summer heat and hurried over to the door. It didn't look like there was much of anyone around here to notice me anyway, but Rollick was clearly being extra careful. I slipped inside and couldn't help sighing as a blast of air conditioning washed away the heat.

Forward and then to the right, he'd said. I hurried onward over a hall runner that was thick and velvety even in the maintenance part of the hotel. Muffled voices carried from up ahead. I passed what must have been a kitchen area where dishes were clinking and savory cooking smells wafting from beneath the door.

My mouth started to water. I'd had a snack in my bag to pass for breakfast, but it hadn't been all that substantial, and it was almost lunchtime.

When I reached the next hall, where a solid door stood between me and the front section of the hotel, I turned right as instructed. The elevator was just a few steps farther. It opened immediately when I pressed the button. I stepped on, jabbed the Door Closed button, and flinched when Rollick popped into being next to me.

"So jumpy," he said in a lightly teasing voice, and leaned past me to flick his fingers over the display next to the door. He angled his body so I couldn't see the code he'd entered. Was it a general code or only required to go up *to* his special rooms, not to return to the public floors? If I managed to get back to the elevator, maybe I'd be able to get out of the building if I needed to.

When the demon pulled back, his arm brushed mine, but he stepped to the side to give me a little space. "No need to worry. I think you'll find your new accommodations very adequate."

The elevator rushed upward, and my stomach dropped. It pinged and opened to a small vestibule.

"My office," Rollick said, indicating the door across from us. "You won't bother with anything in there." He led me over to a small staircase, the door to it opening at a press of his thumb against a digital pane. I wasn't opening *that* on my own without cutting off the digit to bring along.

The private staircase only descended one floor. We emerged through the next door into a suite as grand and luxurious as I'd expected from the demon.

The deep maroon carpet hugged my feet. Black leather sofas and armchairs stood in a cluster by a gas fireplace. A vast flatscreen TV stood in a tall entertainment unit near the corner. Built-in ebony bookshelves filled the opposite wall, packed with a diverse assortment of volumes from aged linen spines to garish modern paperbacks. A scent that was both sweet and faintly smoky laced the air.

At the far end of the living room, floor-to-ceiling

windows looked out onto a broad terrace with a view of the ocean beyond. There were doors in the walls on either side of the stretch of windows, both of them open. Peeking past one, I found a bathroom as big as my bedroom at home, with a huge jacuzzi tub as well as a glass shower stall and double sinks, everything mottled black-and-gray marble.

Across from the bathroom lay a bedroom with an immense bed I had to think was some size larger than a king surrounded by an ebony wardrobe, vanity, and small matching desk.

I halted in the doorway between the living area and the bedroom, my skin prickling. "This is where *you* live. Where am I supposed to sleep and everything?"

Rollick propped himself casually against the back of one of the armchairs and aimed one of his warm grins at me, as if we were friends having a companionable discussion. "You have free run of these rooms, including the terrace—it's totally private. I don't *need* to use any of the facilities here."

Right, because shadowkind didn't require sleep any more than they did food.

"If I feel the need to indulge other urges of mine, I can do so elsewhere," he added, his grin widening. "If you're not interested in enjoying those benefits of my attention too, that is."

Did he mean—*oh*. My face flared, and I hugged myself instinctively. "Um, no, I think I'll pass, thanks." Sure, he was possibly the hottest guy I'd ever seen, but he was also a potentially murderous demon who'd been threatening to bash one of my actual monstrous lovers into oblivion earlier today. I did have standards.

I'd only just finished speaking when all three of my lovers wavered into being near the door. However they'd traveled here, it hadn't taken them much longer than Rollick's driving. Lance started toward me at once, his gaze intent on me and a smile flashing across his ferally gorgeous face, but Rollick held up his hand.

"Hold on," he said. "We need to discuss what I'm going to do with the three of you."

My spine stiffened. "You swore not to hurt them."

The demon shot me a baleful glance. "I do remember that." He patted his arm where the small sigil still showed faintly, pink against his tanned skin, and turned to the three shadowkind men. "Let's be clear: I'm not happy with any of you over your little rebellion. But I suppose the worst you did was follow my orders *too* well when it came to protecting her. That and your long history of service are the only reasons I haven't yet decided to eviscerate you."

Torrent's mouth tightened, and Crag appeared to suppress a wince, but the gargoyle spoke up anyway. "We'd like to continue protecting Quinn, if—"

Rollick waved whatever else Crag would have said away. "Yes, yes, I'm sure you would. But I think you're enraptured enough as it is. A little distance to clear your heads would do you some good."

"We're not just letting you take her—" Lance started to hiss.

Rollick snapped his fingers. "That's *not* what I'm saying. You want to be useful to the mortal? Wonderful. Then our ends are aligned. I want to know everything you can find out about who the beings after her are and how we can foil their plans. And finding that out requires you be out *there*, not hanging all over her in here."

Lance shifted on his feet, but he couldn't seem to come up with a firm argument against the request. Rollick had played his cards well, I had to admit. I suspected that knowing they were working toward my long-term safety was the *only* thing that would have kept the three men from insisting on staying near me.

"It's okay," I said, even though my lungs constricted around the words. "I'll be all right. I want to know how we can defeat those monsters too. That matters more than... just about anything." As much as I was aching for the comfort of their arms around me.

My gaze slid to Rollick. "What about me? *You* wanted me for some reason. What am I supposed to be doing while I'm here?"

Rollick met my gaze with an unconcerned expression. "I haven't made a definite decision yet. I don't believe in committing to action without seeing what I'm working with." His dark blue eyes skimmed down over my body, making me feel abruptly naked despite the three layers of clothing I had on.

I hugged myself tighter. "Can I get my phone back? And my computer—I need to give my parents some kind of story, and if I could keep up with my classwork—" Torrent had thought to take my school backpack with him from the car when he and Lance had dodged the attacking beasts, not wanting them to find any clues about my full identity, though Rollick had confiscated that item too.

The demon gave his head a slow shake. "I'll bring up your other bag, but I'm holding on to your devices. No contact with the outside world. These rooms *are* your entire world for the time being."

"I need the alarm on my phone to make sure I'm taking my pills on time."

Rollick studied me for a moment and then reached into his pocket. He pulled out the phone and flicked open the small compartment at the base. "Fine. Then I'll take out the SIM card so it's basically just an alarm clock. You can forget about getting the WIFI password."

Oh, come on. An automatic protest tumbled from my mouth. "But—"

He lifted his eyebrows. "Do you really want to see what'll happen to your family or your schoolmates if the fiends after you catch on to those connections?"

My voice died in my throat. No, I didn't. We didn't know how much the other shadowkind had figured out about who I was beyond the energy my heart gave off, but Rollick had managed to determine my full name and address. The more I interacted with anyone outside of the four men in front of me, the more likely I'd put everyone I cared about in danger.

I closed my eyes and girded myself, tamping down the niggling anxiety. I'd already given my parents a story that'd cover my absence for a week or two. If I fell a couple of weeks behind in my classes, I could make that up when I got back. The important thing was making sure I *could* go back eventually.

"Okay," I said. "For now. Open to further negotiation later."

Rollick chuckled softly, the sound sending a quiver over my skin that wasn't entirely unpleasant. "Negotiation is one of my favorite pastimes. I look forward to your counter-offer." He handed over the partly disabled phone and nodded to the room around us. "Make yourself at home. I have to inform my disgraced employees of their first missions."

Then the four of them vanished, leaving me alone and adrift.

CHAPTER FOUR

Quinn

It took me a long time to decide what to do with myself in Rollick's suite. I knew he'd said he'd gone off to talk with the other men, but I couldn't shake the feeling that he might be watching me from the shadows, observing me for whatever purposes he hadn't wanted to share yet.

I wandered around the living room restlessly for several minutes and then remembered he'd said I could take off my protective vest.

The seamstress who'd created the unusual piece of clothing for me had done a fantastic job considering that she'd only had a matter of hours to pull it together. The thin silver and iron beads, a mix of round and rectangular, weighed a lot less than I'd imagine full chainmail would but deflected the shadowkind's ability to sense my heart's sorcerous energies. It still weighed on me quite a bit more than my typical cotton tanks and tees did, though.

I pulled off the billowy dress and then the vest. A shudder of relief ran through my body as the weight lifted. I draped the thing over my messenger bag, not sure where else to put it at the moment, and rubbed my arms.

I felt... grubby. I hadn't had a proper shower in a regular bathroom in days, and it'd been a few since I'd even had the benefit of the cramped stall on the small yacht we'd sailed around on. I glanced around the room again and raised my chin.

Fuck it. If Rollick wanted to perv out, let him. I wasn't going to sit around stinking the place up out of probably imaginary fears for my modesty. For all I knew, those intense blue eyes could see right through my clothes even when I was wearing them.

I headed into the bathroom and found a stack of luxuriously thick towels on a shelving unit in the corner, along with a basket that contained everything from shampoo to bath oils. Why would a being who could erase all the grime from himself simply by slipping in and out of the shadows need all that?

Ah. Presumably it was for the female guests he'd hinted that he regularly hosted in his bedroom.

The thought of those guests and the proposition he'd made to me left me feeling twice as grubby as before. I hustled over to the shower stall and turned on the water.

It heated up quickly, filling the room and my lungs with a pleasant steam. I grabbed the shampoo, conditioner, and body wash and stepped under the hot deluge.

At first, I just stood there and let the liquid heat stream over me. Wouldn't it be nice if this shower alone could sweep away everything that was wrong with my life right now? But the sense of escape only lasted a few minutes. Then all my worries started creeping back in.

I lathered myself thoroughly from head to toe, breathing in the sweet lilac scent of the bath products, and rinsed myself until I was sure every particle of dirt and grease had to have gone down the drain. I'd just turned off the water and stepped out onto the plush mat to grab the towel when Rollick's languid voice carried through the door.

"I'm just letting you know that I've dropped off your backpack, sans computer. In case you wanted anything else in there."

My pulse skittered, and I tugged the towel around my body, but he didn't make any move that I could hear toward coming into the bathroom. It *would* be nice to change into a fresh set of clothes from the backpack.

"Thank you," I called tentatively.

The demon didn't respond. Maybe he'd already left while I'd hesitated.

Oh, well. Considering everything, showing him gratitude wasn't at the top of my priority list.

I peeked out into the living area and found it empty at least to my human eyes. Rollick had left the backpack just outside the bathroom door. He'd probably gone through it looking for anything else he wouldn't want me having while I was here, but I couldn't see anything missing other than my computer.

I retreated into the bathroom to pull on a clean tank top and shorts and then brought the backpack, my messenger bag, and the vest over to the bedroom. Even if it gave me the creeps thinking about what Rollick usually got up to in this bed, the covers smelled freshly laundered. It wasn't all that different from sleeping in any regular hotel room—actually, I wouldn't be surprised if the demon kept his own abode to a higher standard of cleanliness.

It'd beat sleeping on the sofa, anyway. Besides, who knew what he'd gotten up to *there*? It wasn't like he'd have changed the leather cushions every time.

Okay, now I was never sitting on the sofa ever.

I pulled the granola bar that was my last snack on hand out of my bag and gulped it down. What was I supposed to do for food after that? Rollick would remember that I needed to eat even if he didn't, right?

He'd sworn not to cause me bodily harm. That should include starvation.

I flopped down on top of the comforter and stared up at the ceiling. Fatigue rolled over me. My sleep schedule had gotten awfully messed up over the past week of monster escapes, and I'd been too keyed up to nap on the plane. I'd just close my eyes for a minute or two...

The next thing I knew, I was waking up to sunlight slanting at a much lower angle through the window. I sat up, rubbing my eyes, and checked my phone. It was almost evening.

My stomach grumbled louder than before, but I ignored it to walk to the sliding door that led onto the same terrace I'd seen from the living room.

As I stepped outside, a crisp ocean breeze swept over me. It was still hot, but not quite the same as I was used to in Florida. Even here by the ocean, the heat had a drier feel to it, not quite so sweltering with humidity.

I walked across the clay-tiled floor past the lounge chairs to the railing and peered over the edge. Jazz music was traveling faintly from somewhere nearby, but I couldn't see the source. Like Rollick had said, the terrace was totally private. I couldn't make out anything but a stretch of white wall on either side of the space, and it was high enough and close enough to the beach I had to assume was below that I couldn't make out the sand, only the expanse of turquoise water.

No one would have been able to see me except by swimming far out or sailing by in a boat, and at that distance I doubted they'd even be able to tell whether I was male or female, let alone recognize exactly who I was.

There were no boats in sight now. I gazed out over the rolling water, a sense of awe rising inside me. I typically preferred views with more architecture to admire, but I'd always had a healthy respect for oceans. So big and powerful, almost eternal.

Another pinching of my stomach sent me back inside. I looked around for an intercom or hotel phone or anything that might have let me contact my host, and just then a whirring sound emanated from the wall to the right of the fireplace.

There was a fixture there that I hadn't paid much attention to before: a square cut into the wall at about waist height, about a foot and a half wide and tall, with a notch that I realized might be a handle. I walked over to it and tugged it open like a door, just as a large tray carrying two covered plates rose into place in the compartment on the other side.

At the same moment, Rollick emerged from the

shadows next to the suite's door. "I see you discovered the dumbwaiter."

Oh. I'd heard about those but never stayed anywhere that actually had one before. I peered at the two plates with their steel dome covers, silverware and glasses set around them. "This is dinner?" A sweetly savory smell that had my stomach gurgling again reached my nose.

"Yes. I thought we could eat together." His eyebrows arched slightly. "Unless you have some objection."

"Um." I hesitated, and then decided it was better to save any arguments for subjects that mattered more. I didn't really *want* to spend more time with him than I had to, but I was going to have to find out what he wanted with me at some point. Maybe he'd enlighten me over the meal. "Well, all right."

"Such enthusiasm. I promise I'm an excellent dinner companion." He strode over, and I stepped back so he could lift the tray, seemingly effortlessly despite how much it held.

He carried it to the terrace and opened the door to the terrace with a motion of his foot that must have given off a pulse of supernatural energy. Goosebumps prickled up my arms at the overt show of power. He didn't emphasize it, though, just stepped out, set the platters on the small patio table off to the side of the terrace, and brandished a bottle of sparkling water he'd had tucked under one arm.

"I'd have brought some excellent wine, but I understand alcohol doesn't always interact well with your medications," he said as I eased out after him.

I blinked, startled that he'd even considered that factor. "Yeah. Thank you."

"It wouldn't do me much good to take you into my protection and then send you into heart failure, now would it?" His grin turned a little crooked on one side, and okay, it was kind of charming. When I wasn't reminding myself about that whole thing where he'd maybe wanted to *eat* my heart just a few days ago.

He motioned me toward the table, and I came, abruptly curious about what might lie beneath the domed covers.

"You do have everything you need in that department, don't you?" Rollick asked. He poured the sparkling water into both glasses and then pulled out my chair for me. "Torrent said he picked up your full supply of medication from your house."

I nodded, thinking of the pill bottles I'd stashed in my messenger bag. "I usually get ninety days at a time with my prescriptions, and I stocked up not long ago. So I'm good unless I'm here for more than two months or so."

I studied the demon's expression, wondering how likely he thought that was, but he didn't give away any hint of concern. "I'm glad to hear it," he said smoothly. "Of course I could easily have arranged an additional supply if you had needed it—I have sources for just about anything anyone could need." He flashed those bright teeth at me again and lifted the lids off the platters before settling into his own chair.

The rich smell filled my nose twice as strong as before, with a hint of lemon. The plate held a glazed salmon fillet and a large assortment of roasted vegetables, and I could already tell from the scent that they were going to be delicious.

It was also the perfect meal to fit within the sort of diet

my doctors preferred I kept to—the one I normally *had* kept to except for on special occasions until the shadowkind had barged into my life. I hadn't been able to be as picky about my eating habits while we were on the run.

My gaze darted up to meet Rollick's. The demon lifted his fork. "I'm very pleased with the hotel's main chef. This seemed like an ideal option that you'll enjoy without any guilt." He winked.

My throat closed up for a second. I didn't know how to handle this much thoughtfulness from a man I'd expected to hate. I forced myself to pick up my own fork and take a bite of the salmon.

It was perfectly tender, melting in my mouth with the savory, citrusy flavor, a balance so delicious I nearly swooned. "It is good," I had to say, and then I couldn't stop myself from shoveling several more bites into my achingly empty stomach.

To my relief, Rollick didn't study my reaction to the meal too closely. He dug into his own dinner with a pleased expression that suggested he really did enjoy the food too. But then, the other shadowkind men had told me mortal food was one of the pleasures that brought them to the mortal realm in the first place, so I supposed that wasn't surprising.

Curiosity bubbled up despite my initial desire to get this encounter over as quickly as possible.

"How do you know so much about... human health concerns?" I asked. "The other guys barely seemed to understand that it was possible to have a heart transplant."

Rollick waved his fork in a casual gesture. "I've been around a lot longer than any of them. And I make a point of educating myself as thoroughly as possible on any matter that's of interest to me. Like you are." The corners of his dark blue eyes crinkled with well-worn smile lines. Somehow the slight marring of his otherwise smooth face made him even more striking to look at.

His explanation prompted a whole different line of questioning. I knit my brow. "You knew there was something special about me—or about the heart transplant —or something. You sent the three of them to keep an eye on me and see whether anything happened. You knew where they'd find me—the other shadowkind looking for me were only following the energy my heart gives off." And they hadn't tracked me down until months after his three underlings had already been observing me.

The demon hummed in agreement. "I find that a large number of my brethren don't make very good use of the resources available to us mortal-side. They can't be bothered to learn new technologies or human social customs unless it's something they can pick up quickly out of necessity. Whoever exactly it is who's set their sights on you, it appears *they* didn't really understand what it meant that the sorcerers' daughter had given you her heart, let alone how to trace the journey that heart had taken."

"But you did," I filled in. "You dug into the hospital records... How did you know to look for me at all?" A chill washed over me. "Were *you* part of the attack on that house in—"

He cut me off with a brisk shake of his head and a grimace. "If the idiot sorcerers don't bother me and mine, I don't bother them. You learn pretty quick that there's no point in seeking out trouble. But I understand the beings that did orchestrate the attack found some evidence that pointed them in your general direction. Word went out through various back channels that important figures were looking for a girl in Florida named Quinn who was in possession of a sorcerer's heart."

I swallowed thickly. "So they figured I had the heart in a jar or something?"

Rollick let out a bark of delighted laughter that left his eyes sparkling. "That sounds about right. I put the pieces together and did a little digging into the family that was killed and the destination of the daughter's heart, and that led me to you." He cocked his head. "You're *lucky* most shadowkind aren't so medically or technologically aware."

"I guess I am." I looked down at my dinner plate, my appetite having vanished. But I needed the fuel. I poked my fork into a chunk of sweet potato. As I chewed, I couldn't help wondering how much this dinner was actually kindness and how much Rollick was simply trying to butter me up for... for whatever he wanted with me.

It wasn't as if he'd admit to manipulating me. But since he'd mentioned tracing medical records, I could ask about another worry that'd been on my mind.

"If you looked up the daughter who died—do you know if there were any other organs donated?"

"A very good question," the demon said with an approving tone that shouldn't have warmed me the way it did. "You're unique. The other essential organs were too damaged in the accident to be of use."

Well, at least I didn't need to fear for the lives of any other human beings who otherwise might have been facing the same danger I was. I let out a breath and considered

Rollick more closely, doing my best not to let his movie-star aura distract me.

"Are you going to tell me yet what it is you expect me to do here?" I asked after a moment.

He gazed back at me with a similarly contemplative air. Then he said the last thing I'd have expected.

"I want you to tap into your sorcerer powers."

For a second, I could only stare. Then I regained control over my tongue. "You want me to try... compelling shadowkind?"

"We might as well determine what the limits of those powers are and how they can be used. I hear you compelled one of the fiends that came after Crag this morning—that both of you might have died if you hadn't."

So Crag had noticed what I'd done—well, how could he not have? I wet my lips, my gut knotting even more than before. "I didn't even mean to. It just happened."

"Survival instincts are a wonderful thing," Rollick said conversationally. "But you'd rather know what you're doing, wouldn't you?"

I frowned at him. "Would *you* really want me to know what I'm doing? What if I started compelling you around?"

He gave another laugh, lighter than before. "I don't think you're going to reach that level of power in an instant, if you do at all."

But what would he do to me if he decided I could get there? Would he kill me after all, as soon as he could without violating his oath? Any warmth I'd gotten from his presence fled with the salt-tinged breeze.

"I—I don't know if that's a good idea," I said.

Rollick considered me. "Why wouldn't it be? Wouldn't you like a little more say over your fate?"

When he put it that way—hell, yes, I would. But the situation was more complicated than that.

"The more power that stirs up inside me, the easier it's been for the other shadowkind to track me," I pointed out.

Rollick flicked his fingers dismissively. "I assure you I have more than enough protections here."

And there was also... I hesitated and then allowed myself to admit my biggest fear—the one that should have been his biggest fear too. "What if I wake up more power, but I still don't know how to control it? I don't want to hurt anyone."

The demon gazed back at me steadily, his forehead furrowing just for a split-second. "I think that's very unlikely," he said. "I'll see that you're properly guided."

"*How?*"

"Leave that to me."

When I didn't answer right away, still tangled up but not sure how to express my resistance any more convincingly, Rollick stood up, his plate cleaned. "This isn't a request. It's a condition of our deal. You cooperate, I keep you and my three mutinists safe. I'll have everything in place for you to start practicing soon, so you should get used to the idea."

He vanished into the shadows without giving me a chance to protest.

CHAPTER FIVE

Torrent

I watched Rollick slide into the back seat of the chauffeured sedan, aiming a wave at the patrons lined up outside the hotel night club as he did. The car drove off into the L.A. night. I waited in the shadows in front of the hotel for several minutes longer to be absolutely sure he wouldn't double back for one reason or another.

Not that he typically did. But I no longer trusted my instincts when it came to my former-and-possibly-still-current boss. I wasn't even sure whether I'd misjudged him only a little or horribly to begin with.

There was definitely plenty he *wasn't* telling me, my men, or Quinn, and as long as I didn't have the full story, everything about him was suspect.

I was reasonably sure that he wouldn't be back for at least a few hours. His evening business meetings tended to involve a lot of drinking and schmoozing, something he'd playfully complained to me about more than once. He wouldn't want to show any sign to the outside world that something had changed about his habits, even around mortals. You could never be totally certain who else might be watching.

Anyway, he hadn't forbidden us from having any contact with Quinn at all. If he caught me schmoozing with *her*, he might be pissed off, but he couldn't claim I'd gone against explicit orders.

I slipped through the shadows up through the hotel. On the high level where silver and iron slats lay interlaced within the floor, there was no way for the average shadowkind to continue upward other than via Rollick's secure elevator… or through a secret entrance he'd keyed to just a few select employees' energies with his demonic magic. Thankfully his shaken trust in me had been outweighed by his desire to have as many invested parties as possible keeping his "prize" safe, or no doubt I'd have been locked out of that.

I had to be careful in his own rooms, of course. I wouldn't put it past Rollick to have surveillance in his private space, video or audio or both. If I could avoid him finding out about this visit, I'd prefer to.

The terrace outside his suite looked clear enough. I scanned the eaves and the walls and saw nowhere a camera could be hiding. It was just a matter of getting Quinn out here.

She was in the lounge room, tucked into one of the armchairs with a book open on her lap. There mustn't be much for her to do stuck in that suite. It'd be killing her being so cut off from her family and school.

My mouth twisted at the thought. I wasn't sure my visit would make things much better, but at least I could offer a little company and information about what was going on outside these rooms.

I emerged into physical form on the darkened terrace, just close enough to the sliding door that I could touch the handle with the tip of one tentacle. I gave it a slight jostle, small enough that it could pass for a gust of wind but loud enough to make Quinn glance up.

As her gaze caught on my face, I held my finger to my lips. She'd startled a bit at the noise, and thankfully that covered any additional shock from her first sight of me. Being the astute woman I'd discovered her to be, she composed her features into an expression of calm and turned back to her book as if she hadn't seen anything at all.

Satisfied, I drifted through the shadows to the side of the terrace to wait. Impatience gnawed at me, but I wouldn't want her to come too quickly and give the game away.

Moonlight rippled over the ocean. I watched it and listened to the distant chatter and music from the rooftop lounge overhead until the door from the bedroom whispered open. As I dragged myself back out of the gloom, Quinn eased outside to meet me. She walked over to the railing next to me and then raised her eyebrows in question, not even sure whether she should speak.

She'd learned a lot of caution in the past several days— or maybe she'd developed that instinct years ago thanks to the restrictions of her health.

"I think it's fine for us to talk here," I said quietly. "But I checked earlier—the hotel room around the corner of the building is empty. If you trust me to help you over, we could talk even more freely there."

Quinn nodded without hesitation, sending a pang through my chest. She'd only known me for a matter of days, and in that span she'd uncovered at least one major betrayal, but she believed in me enough to put her life in my hands. I guessed I had saved it far more times than I'd put it in danger, but her trust felt like a gift all the same.

"Stay here," I murmured, and leapt into the shadows along the building. It was a long span of wall to reach the corner, and then a few feet around the side to the railing of the other room's balcony. There, I re-emerged and unleashed two more of my tentacles than usual, leaving me with eight limbs: four from my shadowkind state and four humanesque.

My natural appendages were far stronger than my human-like ones. I hooked one tentacle firmly around the railing and then drew myself back around the building by gripping the wall with my suckers. Quinn didn't show any sign of alarm at my increased monstrousness. She waited while I got a solid grip on her railing. Fully extended, I could hold on to both, but I wouldn't want to risk stretching myself across a much farther distance.

I held out a third tentacle to her. "I'll hold on to you and carry you across," I said.

"Okay." She clambered onto the upper part of the railing with the skills I'd seen watching her tramp around abandoned buildings and high-rise rooftops back in her regular life, and I looped my tentacle around her waist. It was a little strain drawing her to my torso, but she wasn't all that heavy.

She smiled at me when we were face to face. As I passed her to my fourth tentacle, her gaze slid down the building, taking in the lights and other terraces below. Then I was hefting her around the corner to where she could scramble onto the other balcony.

I followed quickly, heaving myself over the railing after her and ducking into the shadows to unlock the balcony door from the inside. The moment I opened it, Quinn darted inside—and flung her arms around me.

"I'm so glad you're here," she murmured against the fabric of my button-up, her warmth spreading all across my body. "I'm so glad you're still *okay*. Lance and Crag—"

"Are just fine too, last time I saw them, which was this morning," I reassured her, and allowed myself the simple but nearly overwhelming pleasure of hugging her tighter to me with my arms while my tentacles braced my damaged legs.

The gargoyle liked to call her "soft," but what I felt more than anything was the strength in her. The resilience that had kept her going through so much chaos and so many setbacks.

As much as I wanted to gather her up completely for myself, I forced myself to add, "They'd be here too if they were able to. Rollick sent them on missions farther afield, and they haven't gotten back yet. He's gone out too—we should have at least a couple of hours before there's any chance he'll notice I've kidnapped you."

"Is that what you're doing?" she asked, tucking her head against my neck. "Kidnapping me? I thought we agreed that it was better to wait out the deal and see what we could find out with Rollick's input."

"That is still the plan," I admitted. "This is only a temporary kidnapping. I figured you'd want to be filled in on what we know so far—and to have the chance to talk to someone other than him, as enthralling a conversationalist as I know he is."

Quinn snorted, which told me Rollick had at least tried working his charms on her. The thought made my arms tighten around her, even though she obviously wasn't particularly impressed by him.

What Rollick wanted, he tended to get, one way or another. Which was all the more reason we had to figure out how to free her from him for good before that happened in a more permanent fashion.

An ache was starting to creep up my calves from standing like this. I adjusted my weight minutely, not wanting to disturb Quinn, but she reacted immediately. She'd always been particularly alert to my difficulties, which both irritated me and tugged at my heart.

"You should sit down," she said, glancing around the room. The only places *to* sit were a narrow armchair that I could already tell would squish my tentacles—it wasn't as if Quinn could carve that into a more monster-friendly version in the short time we had—and the bed. A pang that was both uncertainty and anticipation wavered through my chest, but Quinn drew me toward the bed without a second's hesitation.

I sat down on the edge near the foot and swept my gaze around the room in another precautionary glance. It seemed unlikely that Rollick would risk putting cameras in the guestrooms where there'd be a scandal if one were discovered, and I saw no sign of one. I relaxed just slightly, setting my hands on the covers.

Quinn switched on one of the small bedside lamps so we could see each other better and hopped up next to me, turning toward me and sitting cross-legged. She obviously wanted to have a real part in this conversation, not just to lean on me for comfort. That was part of why I'd fallen for her too.

"What have you found out so far?" she asked. "Do you have any idea who these shadowkind are that keep sending their horde of allies after me?"

Right down to business. My lips twitched with a fond smile. "We know more than we did before. From combining what Rollick's been able to tell us about what happened after the sorcerer family was attacked in Miami with our own observations over the past several days, we're completely sure that whoever's searching for you—and putting pressure on Goldie and whatever else—was also behind that attack. We also know that this is part of a longer pattern. Rollick's dug up information on a dozen or so prominent sorcerers across the continents who've been slaughtered in similar ways."

Quinn winced. "With their vital organs removed?"

"Yes," I said, because it wouldn't do her any good to shy away from the full truth. "It's starting to seem increasingly likely that the one or few higher shadowkind responsible *have* gained some sorcerer power of their own and are using it to compel some of the lesser beings to their bidding, along with more typical methods of coercion. Although I'm sure some of them are simply along for the ride to win favor or for the thrill of it."

Her shudder reflected how unnerved I felt by that revelation. A shadowkind compelling other shadowkind... It was bad enough when humans enslaved us and manipulated us to their will. To turn that perverse power against your own... There were some lines that shouldn't be crossed, no matter how much of a monster you were.

"Who *are* they?" Quinn asked. "Do you know anything about the powers they had before they started murdering sorcerers? Or about what they want to do with all the new powers they're getting?" She paused, her head drooping slightly. "Or why they seem to want to capture me now rather than tear me apart on the spot? Although maybe that's just so the underlings can bring me to their boss, and that's when I'll get torn up."

"That is possible," I admitted, as much as I hated to. "We've talked about it, and even Rollick agrees that at this point it seems unlikely. They've put a lot of energy into tracking you down, and with the number of sorcerers they've already devoured, one heart doesn't seem like it should be so important to them."

"But what else could they possibly want from me?"

I dragged in a breath. "We've determined that they have at least one higher being with persuasive abilities working with them—she can't compel shadowkind, but her powers work on mortals, and she's used that to help during their search for you. It could be that they want to have you in their grasp so they can compel *you* into compelling other shadowkind."

Quinn knit her brow. "And that would be better than eating my heart?"

I smiled thinly. "Power direct from its natural source is a lot more potent than power diluted by mixing it with other factors. Quite possibly once you get a handle on your abilities, you'd be able to command more shadowkind alone than our enemies could with a dozen sets of organs in their guts."

A shiver ran through her slim frame, and she hugged herself. Wisps of her pale hair fell across her cheeks as she glanced down at her lap. Then she squared her shoulders and met my eyes again with those stunning sky-blue eyes. "Well, we're obviously not letting that happen. What about my other questions?"

I thought back to what else she'd asked. "The mastermind—or minds—behind this whole situation have kept themselves very much in the background, letting their lackeys do all the grunt work. We're not sure what kind of beings they are or their natural powers. We do seem to have benefitted from their not being all that familiar with this country. Most of the other killings were in Europe and Asia, and they've only been 'recruiting' assistance here on the ground pretty actively in the past several months—they don't seem to have had much of a presence on this side of the ocean until recently."

Possibly that was the only reason we'd been able to stay a few steps ahead of them.

"We're still working on that," I went on. "It's only been a couple of days. Rollick sent Crag off to talk to a being who tangled with the group and might have clashed with the leader directly to see what we can find out there. Lance is following another trail. I'll try to update you again soon

—maybe all of us will be able to come together. Rollick has meetings and other events pretty frequently."

Quinn gazed past me toward the balcony, her expression pensive. Then she met my eyes again. "*He* wants me to tap into my sorcerer powers. Rollick. He told me that yesterday."

I frowned. Was that all the demon wanted—a pet sorcerer he could use to compel shadowkind to his bidding? The idea made even less sense to me than the thought that he'd wanted to devour her heart and take on that power for himself. I could maybe see him enjoying adding to his own capabilities, but he exerted plenty of authority over any shadowkind he encountered already. Getting a human to order them around in his place didn't sound like him at all.

Quinn was studying my reaction. "That's not what you'd have expected."

"No. I have no idea why he'd want to bring out your magic—but I doubt he'd tell me if I asked."

"He wouldn't tell *me*. And you're not even supposed to know, since we aren't supposed to have talked about it." She sighed. "Before this whole thing, you respected him, didn't you? You didn't think he was some horrible villain."

"I didn't think that," I agreed. "He... I mean, we're all shadowkind, not human. There's a reason we get called monsters, and it's not just because of how we look. I won't claim he follows the same moral compass someone you'd consider a "good person" would, but neither do I. I can say that in the decades I've worked for him, he's only seemed harsh when prompted, not out of pure sadistic enjoyment. And while he plays with the mortals who come to this place, it's never been in a way that leaves them scarred. He doesn't let the shadowkind patrons outright harm them either."

"So he's got *some* sense of morality," Quinn muttered. "Or at least of maintaining a balance for whatever selfish reasons."

"I don't think it's all selfish." I flexed my tentacles on either side of me. "He didn't need to take me on as a lackey and then a lieutenant. When I presented myself to him and asked for whatever work he could give me, I expected him to laugh in my face. I haven't gotten much more than sneers and ridicule from other shadowkind over my infirmities... and I can't deny that they make me less capable. But he saw something in me and decided it was worth taking the gamble. He's the only one who gave me a chance like that."

Quinn was quiet for a moment. She scooted closer to me, and I shifted my nearer tentacle so it slipped around her, letting her get close enough that she could rest her hand on my thigh.

"What did happen to you—to injure your legs and...?" Her hand rose to my bashed-in cheek. "If you don't mind telling me."

I didn't like talking about the past with anyone. Shame burned through my body at just the briefest memory of those times. The words rose in my throat to put her off— but she'd told me about the most traumatic parts of her own life. She'd bartered her freedom to save me from Rollick's anger.

She deserved to know exactly what kind of man—and monster—I was, didn't she?

I forced myself to speak. "For most of my existence, I wasn't anyone you'd have admired or probably even liked. I got a thrill out of all the indulgences of the mortal realm, and that was what I focused all my time and energy on. I grifted to make money and connections; I roamed from party to party; I delved into every recreational drug there is; I went through multiple sexual partners in a night."

Quinn hadn't tensed or shown any sign of distress yet, just waiting patiently for me to go on. I swallowed hard and continued.

"I don't even remember exactly what happened, I was so high at the time. All I know for sure is that I got it in my head to hassle some other beings in some way, a prank or something like that, and it turned out they were more powerful than I must have realized in my messed-up state or I wouldn't have targeted them. They were pissed off, and I didn't have the wherewithal to really defend myself. They battered me good... I wouldn't be surprised if they'd have killed me if we hadn't been on a beach and I managed to propel myself into the water where I was more at my element and could flee."

I paused, and then reached to untie the laces on my boots. Let her see the full extent of my deformity. This was who I was now. This was who she could decide to stand by or push away from.

As I slid the boots off, a little pained sound worked from Quinn's throat. On one side, the foot was merely broken, the ball and toes missing just as the very tip was on the matching tentacle when I was in full shadowkind form. My ankle canted inward at an odd angle too.

The other side was worse. My attackers had crushed

everything from below the anklebone so completely that my left foot had simply fallen away. There was nothing but a stump. The boots I conjured out of shadow held the necessary fixtures to keep me upright when I needed them to.

Quinn's fingers curled around my arm. I found myself unable to look at her.

"That's the story," I said, my voice roughening. "That's who I was. The beating worked as a wake-up call. I *couldn't* indulge the same way I had before, since I couldn't move among mortals on just my two feet, and I didn't want to lose even more by keeping up the same carelessness anyway. But I still love a lot about this realm. The job for Rollick gave me access to a few minor pleasures. And the rest I can at least enjoy vicariously here and there."

Now she'd seen it all. She knew just how much of a ruin I was. My muscles clenched, bracing for—I didn't even know what, but some act to extricate herself from me.

Instead, she bobbed up to press a kiss to my fractured cheek like she had in the yacht a few days ago. My heart wrenched.

Quinn stayed there with her head tipped close to mine, her breath tickling over my skin. After a moment, she spoke softly by my ear. "Thank you for telling me. It doesn't change who I know you are now. Or how I feel about you."

I finally dared to turn my gaze toward her. "And how's that?" I murmured.

She touched my jaw and brought her lips to mine.

As our mouths melded together, something hummed through my chest, as if she were pouring pure light straight into me. I wanted to soak it all in, to revel in the passion she still meant to offer me.

Here we were on this bed with no one to disturb us. I had her all to myself. And if she wanted me, then I was going to make sure she got every possible pleasure I could offer *her*.

CHAPTER SIX

Quinn

Torrent's answering kiss was only hesitant for the first split-second when our lips met. Then he leaned into it, his mouth aligning perfectly with mine, claiming me as if there was nothing in the universe he'd rather be doing. With every passing moment as his hand rose to cup my cheek and the tentacle he'd slung around my hips teased up my back, more confidence radiated off him.

Good. I hadn't liked the sense of shame I'd gotten from him while he'd given his confession about his past. If he really thought I'd judge him for the injuries he'd taken or how he'd acted ages before I'd even been born, this was the best way I could show him how wrong he was.

If anything, now I was more impressed by the calm leadership with which he'd directed our little crew, knowing how hard-won that self-control and assurance was. Knowing that he'd spent decades remaking himself into a man he *wasn't* ashamed of, even when most of his kind had seen him as a lost cause because of his disability.

And he was still remaking himself when he saw the need to. He'd recognized that I was more than a pawn to be used in a game between his boss and whoever else wanted me, and he'd abandoned his former loyalty to fully protect me because he'd felt that was the right thing to do. There weren't many humans who were willing to adjust their sense of morality that easily.

Of course, morality wasn't exactly the first thing on my mind right now. Torrent hadn't touched me anywhere all that sensitive yet, but he'd encased me in his warm embrace, and every inch of my skin was tingling for more. I kissed him again and again, wondering if this was what it felt like to be drunk.

Only one tiny practical part of me stayed alert enough to pull me just a couple of inches back from him, my breath gone ragged. "We don't have to worry— You're sure Rollick won't be back for a while?"

Torrent's eyes gleamed, no doubt understanding why I was asking. "I'd expect him to be out for at least a couple more hours, if not longer," he said. His tentacle trailed down my spine, and the tip hooked under my shirt. "And if he returns early and realizes what we've gotten up to, then let him. He can't hurt us."

A thrill quivered through my chest, unexpected and yet familiar. I'd always liked taking risks, thumbing my nose at danger when I felt I could get away with it. We both knew Rollick wouldn't be *happy* about us taking this interlude together, but he hadn't ordered us *not* to do it. Defying him added an extra spark to the giddiness already bubbling through my veins.

"Then there's no reason not to enjoy the moment to its fullest," I said with a grin, and dove in for another kiss.

I hadn't gone farther than this with Torrent before. The one time we'd gotten into a heated make-out session, Rollick's arrival had interrupted us before we'd done much of anything. I *really* hoped the demon didn't show up soon enough to stop us before I got to experience everything he had to offer.

Torrent's tentacle grazed up and down my spine beneath my shirt, the suckers pressing into my skin with a subtle pressure that felt like he was kissing me all across my back too. His hand tucked between us to fondle my breast through my bra. When he flicked his thumb right under the cup, a gasp jolted out of me.

"There's so much I want to do with you," he murmured, dropping his head to kiss the side of my neck. "So much I *can* do for you that no other mortal woman could have handled. Do you want all of it?" His second tentacle reached over to glide across my thigh.

An ache of need was already forming between my legs. Lately I'd been discovering just how stimulating monstrous features could be in bed, from Lance's dragon claws to Crag's gargoyle tongue. I'd just let this man carry me over a fatal height with his tentacles—trusting them with my body in less death-defying ways was a no-brainer.

"Yes, please," I said, my voice breaking with a whimper when he swept the curve of his tentacle right over the seam of my shorts. Just like that, my panties were drenched.

Torrent captured my mouth again with an approving

hum that reverberated through me and set off all kinds of other tingles. The tentacle at my back deftly unhooked my bra, giving him access to caress my breasts without that barrier in the way. I gripped the front of his shirt, at first simply holding on through the waves of heady sensation and then fumbling with the buttons.

My other monstrous men had removed their clothes simply by stepping into the shadows and leaving everything that wasn't their innate physical form behind. Torrent let me peel his button-up off him, tracing my fingers over the leanly sculpted muscles of his shoulders and arms as I did. A sound carried from his throat that was closer to a growl than a hum.

My hands encountered the ripples of other scars, low ridges that marred his equally sculpted torso. Superficial but still unshakeable remainders of the long-ago assault. At first brush, I jerked my fingers back instinctively, afraid of pressing a tender spot. But when Torrent's muscles tensed at my hesitation, I stroked them carefully and then more confidently, hearing the hitch of his breath that was nothing but eager.

"You don't have to worry about hurting me," he said, nipping the lobe of my ear. "It's only my lower legs where there's any residual pain, and it comes from putting my weight on them, not simply being touched."

"Okay," I whispered. "Good." I ran my hands down his chest again, all the way to the waist of his slacks.

When I skimmed the bulge behind his fly, Torrent groaned. He shifted his weight, tugging me with him to tumble over on the bed, and yanked off my tee with hands and tentacle as we sank down. He caught my jaw in his fingers and kissed me again as two tentacles tucked around the hem of my shorts and pulled them off as well.

He'd brought out more of them, I realized through the haze of pleasure. Along with his hands and mouth, there were four sinewy, suckered limbs teasing over me now. Two of them coiled over my breasts, setting a sucker over each nipple and squeezing as if plucking them.

The rush of bliss was so intense I jerked into his hold, kissing him even harder. He delved his tongue between my lips like a smaller echo of those lithe appendages. As it tangled with mine, he squeezed my nipples again and again. The pleasure shot me higher each time until I was writhing against him, desperate for more.

Torrent didn't leave me hanging. His tongue kept exploring my mouth and his tentacles continued working over my nipples, but another eased under my panties to curve across my sex.

He let out another rough sound at the wetness he found there. The tip of his tentacle glided back and forth over my opening while a lower sucker settled against my clit. When it squeezed on the little nub like the others were plucking my nipples, I nearly arched right off the bed.

The giddying bolt of sensation left me quivering. When he did it again, I couldn't help crying out against his mouth. Torrent swallowed that sound even as he coaxed more out of me, sliding his tentacle farther so it could curl right up inside me.

I'd been fingered before, but this—this was something totally different. Something totally heaven. No human fingers could have filled me like his lithe extra limb did, or reached so easily to the sensitive spot inside that produced the most pleasure. No fingers could have pulsed into it so perfectly while flexing against the walls of my pussy and massaging my clit at the same time.

I clung to Torrent and bucked with the sinuous thrusts, all kinds of gasps and whimpers spilling from my mouth now. Between his grip on my pussy and his continued suckered caresses to my breasts, bliss flooded every thought from my mind. All I could do was soar higher and higher on it, until so much was swelling through my body that I thought I might literally explode.

"That's right," Torrent murmured. "You take to it so well. I always wondered what I could do if—" He hesitated and kissed the crook of my jaw. "I'm glad I got to find out with you. It'll only be you from now on."

I couldn't find my voice to answer him despite the pang of affection his words sent through me. Somehow the wave of sensation was propelling me even higher still. My fingernails dug into Torrent's shoulders. He plucked at my clit a little more firmly than before in perfect synchronicity with the pulsing against my G-spot, and I careened right over the edge like I'd leapt off a cliff.

The blaze of ecstasy was like the whipping of the wind, hurling me higher instead of letting me fall. My throat choked up. I all but sobbed, my head jerking back against the pillow, sparks dancing behind my eyes.

Torrent wasn't done with me even then. He eased on the pressure while I floated hazily down and then ramped it up again, stroke by stroke. I'd have thought I'd be wrung out after that epic orgasm, but somehow more pleasure was building in me already, propelling me toward another peak.

As I rocked with his strokes, that final tentacle slipped

around my hip to draw my panties right down to my knees. It rose again and traced the line between the cheeks of my ass. The contact woke up an even headier shiver.

"Have you taken anyone here before?" Torrent asked in an unusually husky voice, swiveling the tip of his tentacle around my back opening. In combination with the bliss he was summoning all through the rest of my body, his touch there made me buck even more wildly.

"No," I mumbled, struggling to speak at all. "I—I've been curious, but—it's risky, for infection and things—"

I wasn't sure how coherent that answer was, but Torrent seemed to understand. His lips moved against my cheek with his reply. "We'll wait until I can prepare you better for the full experience, then. I'm looking forward to filling you in every possible way."

If it somehow felt even better than the way he was simply rimming me now, I was looking forward to it just as much. I writhed between his tentacles, moaning as he sped up his thrusts in my pussy and his plucks of my clit and nipples. I probably looked crazed, but every particle of my body was singing with the pleasure he'd brought me. It seared hotter and brighter, fresh jolts crackling through me and stealing my breath.

"Oh, God," I mumbled. "Oh, Torrent. Fuck." And then I shattered all over again, even more epically than before. For a few seconds, I couldn't even feel my body, only a roar of bliss that swept me away.

I sagged bonelessly into the bed, and Torrent kissed me on the mouth, his lips curved with a smile. Then his tentacles started to work me over yet again.

I gasped, shivering with delight, but I'd come back to

earth enough to know that this wasn't all I wanted out of our encounter. I slid my hand back down to the fly of his slacks again and cupped his erection through the fabric.

"Your tentacles feel fucking *fantastic*," I said, feeling the need to make that clear after his earlier uncertainty, "but I want you to come with me this time."

Torrent's eyelids dipped, lust darkening his eyes as I rubbed his cock. Without a word, he helped me peel off his slacks and drew his probing tentacle out of my sex. As he poised himself over me, he paused and gazed down into my face as if searching for something there.

I raised my hand to caress his caved-in cheek while curling my other fingers around his rigid erection. "It isn't hard on your legs, holding yourself like this? We could—"

"I'll be fine," he said in a strained voice. "I want you under me. I just—it's been a very long time. I might have had plenty of practice in the distant past, but I don't know how long I'll last after all this time. And when it's you."

The adoration of those last words brought a poignant ache into my chest. I beamed up at him. "You've already made me come—*twice*—so hard it'll be a wonder if I can walk for the next day. Believe me, I couldn't be more satisfied. I just want to feel you totally with me now."

Something shifted in his expression, tender and almost peaceful. He dipped his head down to kiss me, softly and then more passionately. As his mouth moved against mine, he plunged inside me.

It wasn't the same sensation of having my centers of pleasure perfectly stimulated, but it felt so good all the same. I rocked with his thrusts, absorbing the tremors of delight that ran through his body, reveling in the way our bodies aligned in harmony, seeking our release together.

Sweat had started to form on his skin. I stroked my fingers over his chest and then along his sides, following the base of his tentacles where they protruded near the base of his rib cage and then lower down his waist. He groaned and wrapped one across my chest again to suck at my nipples while he used his arms to brace himself over me.

I was so wrung out from the first two orgasms that I wasn't sure I could have gotten there again anyway. But when Torrent's breath started to stutter and his hips jerked faster as he neared his own climax, the sense of him giving himself over to this moment with me renewed the spark inside me. I arched into him, and he tucked another tentacle between us to flick just the tip against my clit.

I gasped and clenched around him, coming more like a gentle wave than a tsunami this time but enjoying it no less.

Torrent swore under his breath. He bucked even faster and tucked his head next to mine as he came inside me.

He sank down onto his side and immediately pulled me into his arms, his tentacles wrapping around me for good measure. I rested my head against his sweat-damp shoulder.

"Anyone who can't handle the tentacles has no idea what they're missing," I muttered.

Torrent let out a startled guffaw and kissed my temple. "They're all for you, so everyone else will have to keep missing them."

I glanced up at him, the joy of the moment dampening at the thought of how brief our interlude was likely to be. How long it might take before we could spend any time together even talking again.

"Do you really think we can find a way out of this?" I found myself asking.

I didn't need to explain what I meant. Torrent's arms tightened around me.

"I don't know," he said a little hoarsely. "But I'm going to do everything in my power to see that we do."

CHAPTER SEVEN

Rollick

"The nymph said the one she was around briefly never showed his shadowkind form, but he had a sort of earthy vibe to him," Crag reported, standing stiffly by the door to my office. "And a strong vibe in general, very large and powerful. The ground shook with his steps. She never saw any other being that was clearly in charge, but the earthy one referred to 'we' a few times in a way that made her think he wasn't making his plans alone."

I strolled through the room, turning over everything he'd told me in my mind. "Earthy and very powerful... Could be a particularly established giant or troll, or an earthen elemental... Dwarf seems unlikely given the size. I can't think of any specific being I've crossed paths with who'd be a definite candidate. But then, I haven't traveled much overseas in recent decades."

I'd been focused on the hotel and establishing my business ties here in L.A. Putting down roots as well as one ever could in the mortal realm. I didn't expect *this* location to stand the test of time across centuries, but if I continued solidifying my network as I'd always done, it'd take no time at all to rebuild wherever I liked. I'd been through that cycle more times than I could count as human society shifted, rolling with the punches and coming out back on top.

But these new fiends... they were a problem I'd never encountered before.

"At least we have more information?" Crag said, giving me a hopeful look.

I'd have appreciated the gargoyle's dedication to this quest more if I hadn't known it was mostly for the mortal woman's benefit and not my own. I stopped by my desk and leaned against it, folding my arms over my chest and holding his gaze. There were other plans I needed to set in motion. I could never have kept my spot at the top of my game if I wasn't juggling a dozen balls at once.

"It's a start," I said. "Too early to tell how much of one when we don't know how long a trail we'll need to follow. You're impatient to tackle these fiends."

I definitely didn't like the firmness with which Crag gazed back at me, totally at ease with the admission he was about to make. "I want to know they won't get near Quinn ever again. They've hurt her enough as it is."

I raised my eyebrows. "And do you think that playing her protector is going to stop her from getting bored with you? You expect that her gratitude will make her feel obliged to continue that dalliance even after the initial thrill has cooled off?"

Crag's mouth twitched into a frown. "That wasn't something I'd worried about to begin with."

"Oh, my poor fellow. You've never associated with mortal lovers before, have you?"

His hand rose to rub his rocky jaw. "I haven't had the opportunity. But Quinn doesn't mind—she accepts the—"

I waved off his protest before he could even finish it. "Of course she doesn't *mind*. You've found one of the curiosity-seekers. Rare but predictable. She gets off on how unusual you are, but they're just like the shadowkind tourists in reverse, you know. Dabbling with the fun of the other side but never committing to anything. It's just a way to get her kicks until she's tired of that and on to something new."

I expected the gargoyle to look concerned or embarrassed, but instead he only drew up his ample frame straighter with an air of undeniable and irritating defiance. "You don't really know her. She didn't seek us out as lovers. Lance was the one who pushed for that sort of intimacy. She trusts us—she cares for us. And I *will* be worthy of that trust."

"I'm only trying to look out for you in your inexperience, friend," I said with a tsk of my tongue. "How long have *you* known her, really interacting with her rather than watching from the shadows—a little more than a week? Humans don't typically form long-lasting bonds even with each other in that short a time. How could you fit into her regular life if you can win it back for her?"

"We would figure it out," Crag said gruffly but without hesitation.

I didn't want to harp on the subject and risk building more animosity toward *me*. The best thing was to have planted the seed so it'd have time to sprout and grow. Not that the soil appeared at all fertile. I supposed it wasn't surprising that the gargoyle could be stubborn as stone.

Well, that too had been only a start. I made a dismissive motion, and he wavered into the shadows without another word.

Time to work on yet another angle of my plans. I gave my humanesque body a little shake to dispel any tension from the unsatisfying conversation, flashed my brightest smile just to warm up my expression, and headed downstairs to my private rooms.

I didn't bother knocking. It was a careful balance between showing consideration for the woman's preferences and keeping her just a little off-balance. She should never forget whose generosity she was relying on right now—who these rooms belonged to.

Quinn didn't notice my arrival at first anyway. I spotted her sitting in a patch of shade on the terrace, her sketchbook propped on her lap. Her head bowed with concentration as she moved a pencil over the page. She didn't react to my presence until I eased open the sliding door to step outside.

Her head jerked up, her pencil stilling. I ambled over to peer at the picture she'd sketched: a tower that curved like a narrowing helix up to a magnificent spire. I couldn't say I'd seen a mortal building quite like it before, but that might mean it wasn't especially practical. She did have a taste for grandeur.

"I expected you to relax and recover after your ordeal," I teased. "And yet it seems you can't help putting yourself to work."

Quinn shrugged and closed the sketchbook. "It isn't really work. I love imagining what I might be able to see built from my designs—it's *fun*. Anyway, it makes me feel a little better about the fact that I can't do my *actual* work since you've confiscated my laptop." She narrowed her eyes at me.

I had to grin. Her obstinacy did make my life a little harder, but her boldness was enough of a delight that I wasn't sure I minded. Most humans—most shadowkind, even—automatically cowered at least a little before me, sensing instinctively that in the universal hierarchy they were prey and I was predator.

This woman had definitely acclimatized to the idea of monsters very quickly during her time with my mutinous underlings. She was wary of me, absolutely. But she didn't see me as enough of a threat that she felt the need to kowtow—or at least, she didn't give enough of a shit about the consequences to rein in her snark.

It was very refreshing.

"Give you that laptop and I might as well throw you straight to the wolves," I said. "You wouldn't want that. Not only would it be very painful, you'd also lose out on more of my delectable company."

Quinn tried to control her reaction, but I caught the flicker of a smile before she schooled her expression into blandness. She did enjoy the banter whether she wanted to or not.

"You think very highly of yourself," she said dryly.

I grinned and leaned against the doorframe. "I'm simply drawing the most obvious conclusions from the available evidence. Are you deprived of anything—other than disastrous contact with the outside world? Let's see if I can't provide it."

Quinn raised an eyebrow. I had the sense that she was debating trying me—seeing what she might get away with. The thought invigorated me more than it probably should. I did love a challenge, and so little challenged me these days.

She looked as if she were about to say something, her lips parting in a way that sent a twinge to my groin, but then she shut her mouth again and shook her head. "Okay, I'll admit you've been catering to my needs very well."

I stepped closer, letting her absorb the heft of my presence without actually touching her. It'd be so much better if she crossed that final distance first if we were going to mesh that particular way. And if we didn't, well, I'd survived worse disappointments. There was no denying she'd be *fun*, though.

"What about your wants?" I said, letting my voice turn silky. "Your desires? There was something you almost asked for. Don't hold out on me now."

If I'd turned that voice on another woman—or man, as the mood took me—I'd have expected them to melt into a puddle of compliance in a matter of seconds. I thought I saw a little quiver run through Quinn's body, but then she simply shrugged. Fascinating. Maybe that sorcerer heart of hers gave her extra resilience against my innate demonic magnetism.

"I guess I'd just like to know when you're going to get on with this plan of yours that I factor into somehow," she said finally, studying me with the distrust I knew to expect.

I kept my stance casual and chuckled. "I was under the impression you needed time to get accustomed to the idea of taking on your natural role. But if you've had enough time, I have the necessary pieces ready to begin our experiments into human sorcery."

Her posture stiffened automatically at the word, a most unusual response. She should have been *glad* to have access to that kind of power—the opportunity to potentially work it against her enemies.

Instead she was mulishly worried about how it might affect my three traitors.

I didn't actually believe what I'd said to Crag. I'd watched many bouts of human affection come and go, and Quinn clearly cared about a lot more than what my mutinous men had in their pants. It wasn't the thrill of being with a monstrous being that made her so reluctant to experiment with a magic that might hurt them.

No, she was genuinely concerned about their well-being. I didn't know how it had happened or how long it would last, but the devotion was there on her side as well as theirs.

And it was highly inconvenient.

"I've been thinking about that," she said, drawing out the words.

"Yes? And what conclusions have you drawn?"

"I still think it's a bad idea."

I resisted the urge to roll my eyes and instead tilted my body forward, resting my hand on the back of the lounge chair just an inch from the cascade of her light blond hair. Tipped that close, I caught her scent: a tang of sunscreen mixed with something fresher, like spring wildflowers just coming into bloom.

"Maybe you've forgotten," I said. "Our deal—the

whole part where I keep you and the men who defied my orders safe—is dependent on *your* cooperation with me. You wouldn't want to violate that over some vague fear of the unknown, now would you?"

Quinn gazed up at me, a hint of sharper warmth flowing from her skin just for an instant. She wet her lips, drawing my attention to that lovely mouth again. Her eyes darted away from me momentarily before returning to meet mine.

"I was thinking about that too," she said. "And I wondered... since you did swear not to cause us any harm, and *you* can't know for sure that my powers won't harm them—or me... if *I* honestly believe that the sorcery could harm us, then wouldn't it violate our deal for you to insist that I try anyway?"

I blinked at her, my mind abruptly whirling. She couldn't really have found a loophole—surely that logic couldn't hold—

But I was abruptly certain that it did. She'd found a weak spot in our agreement, one that gave her a free pass to ignore me without consequences over her own worries. Frustration prickled through me, my teeth itching to shed the veneers that hid the vicious points.

This was a little *more* of a challenge than I'd have preferred.

I kept my composure, because I hadn't lived millennia by losing my cool every time events didn't go exactly my way, and let my grin widen instead. "I suppose I'll just have to soothe those fears to the best of my ability, then."

"Not sure how you're going to do that," Quinn said steadily, but her pupils had dilated. Oh, I did have some effect on her. No being mortal or shadowkind was totally impervious to the impact of my presence.

"Hmm." I straightened up and took a couple of steps away, rubbing my chin as if debating my options. But I'd already known one move I wanted to make, and this gave me a reasonable opening.

I turned to face her, flexing my shoulders in the fitted suit that would have been sweltering in the summer heat if I hadn't been built for climates even hotter than this. "Maybe you need a little help wrapping your head around the idea that using those powers could *protect* whoever you want to save more than they're likely to hurt them. Because the beings we're up against could very well be even more imposing than me."

"I don't think you're—" Quinn started, and then her mouth snapped shut as I shifted into my shadowkind form.

I loomed even taller and broader, my shadow stretching across the terrace to her feet even under the midday sun. I swiped my hand past my mouth to remove the veneers, revealing the rows of razor-sharp teeth. My clothes vanished, leaving behind only a landscape of ruddy skin over bulging muscles. It was marred here and there by paler scars, including a slash of one just above the side of my waist where this particular mortal had stabbed me a few days ago, but those added character to the terrain. A reminder of how much I'd survived without faltering.

My horns shot up from just above my ears. Claws jutted from my fingertips. My tufted tail lashed beside my hip, and my feet condensed into cloven hooves most mortals associated with pure evil. I flexed my shoulders and grinned.

It was always a relief, letting my demonic self loose. Filling all the space I was meant to.

Quinn's eyes had widened. She couldn't disguise her reaction now—both the horror and the spark of interest that danced alongside her animalistic panic. Especially when her gaze dipped to particular endowments.

"You have two," she blurted out, and flushed flame-red, jerking her eyes upward again. "I mean—I've never seen— it's no big deal."

I smirked wider, letting my pointed teeth gleam in the sunlight. Oh, let her just imagine how big a deal two substantial cocks could possibly be. She liked her men monstrous—she might as well know what she was missing out on if she passed on the most monstrous of those on hand.

"My apologies," I said in the more resonant voice that came with my true form. "We monsters tend not to go around clothed while we're being monsters." I flicked my tongue over my teeth. "Lucky for you, I'm on your side. But imagine facing off against a being like me—or even more savage—and knowing you could have defended yourself and everyone with you... if only you'd figured out how to purposefully draw on your accidental powers."

Her throat bobbed as she swallowed. She tucked her legs closer to her chest, but her pupils were still huge. A little frightened? I should hope so. But also so very, very curious.

"That's a lot to think about," she said, keeping her voice steady and even a bit tart.

I had to suppress a startled guffaw. She'd pulled most of her composure together with incredible speed.

This one was going to be hard to crack. But I'd get there. I was more than familiar with playing a long game.

"I'll leave you to that thinking, then," I said in a low rumble, and gave her a wink before ducking to step back into the lounge.

As I reached the far door, I shifted back into my human-like body, conjuring my clothes around me again. The full demon presence would lose a little of its impact if I went around flashing it everywhere.

Besides, I kept my phone in my trousers, and I couldn't hear it ringing if I dismissed it to the shadows. It did start ringing now when I was halfway up the stairs to my office. I checked the number and raised it to my ear.

"Yes, Aspen?"

The lackey on the other end drew in a hasty breath. "I'm sorry to bother you, Rollick, but there've—there've been some new developments in Florida that I figured you'd want to hear about sooner rather than later."

CHAPTER EIGHT

Quinn

When dinner arrived, a single covered plate humming to the top of the dumbwaiter, I was still having trouble shaking the image of Rollick in his full demonic beastliness from my mind. I carried the plate over to the coffee table in the sitting area on autopilot, not able to summon much hunger.

My men had told me he was a demon—a powerful one. But I'd never seen him in anything other than his human guise, which was compelling and sometimes even electrifying but hardly monstrous. Now, there was no denying just how immense a foe he'd be if I defied him.

In physical heft, he wasn't that much larger or more beastly-looking than Crag's gargoyle body, which I actually kind of liked now that I was used to it. I wasn't used to Rollick's demonic form, though, and I sure as hell didn't trust him never to tear into me with those jagged teeth and claws or pummel me with those bulging limbs. And the aura of power that emanated off him even when he looked like a man, full of equal parts promise and menace, had amplified to the point that *my* whole body had shivered with it.

If he was right and the other foes I was up against were as formidable as him—or worse—I couldn't help thinking that I was totally screwed.

Annoyingly, I wasn't even totally unnerved by Rollick's display. I might not trust him, but I was now well aware of how... enjoyable certain monstrous features could be. A small part of my mind couldn't help speculating about what it'd be like to have a monstrous lover I *could* trust who came endowed with not just one but two cocks. That image kept swimming up from my memory too, the one jutting out over the other above a single set of balls, both sized to match the rest of his massive frame even when flaccid.

God, how big must they be when *erect*?

I slapped my hand to my forehead as if I could jostle those unwanted thoughts out of my brain and forced myself to focus on my dinner. I needed to eat and keep my strength up, because who knew if I'd need to go on the run again with no more access to hotel-quality food.

I'd say this for the demon—he had been very conscientious with my meals. Every spread that'd appeared in the dumbwaiter, three times a day, had offered up something mouth-watering but within the realm my doctors would have approved of. Yesterday a delicately flavorful mango sorbet had arrived at just the right timing for me to indulge right after I'd finished my dinner without it being at all melted.

So, the whole being held under captivity experience was ten out of ten for sustenance, which was about all I could recommend about it.

Tonight's spread included a chicken breast drizzled with nuts and a fruity sauce, with a fresh-baked whole-grain roll and a pear and spinach salad on the side. Plus another bottle of sparkling water, since Rollick seemed to feel I shouldn't be reduced to drinking from the tap with my meals even if I couldn't partake of his preferred beverages.

There was also, poised on the edge of the plate as if it didn't totally belong there, what it took me a moment to realize was an apple carved with deft precision into an ornately petaled rose.

My chest hitched with a pang of sudden affection. I recognized Lance's work immediately. He mustn't have had a chance to come right up to see me, but he'd stolen a moment to show he was thinking of me and to sneak this little present in with my meal.

I picked up the carved apple, cupping it between my hands. I wasn't sure I could bring myself to eat it—but then, I probably shouldn't leave it lying around, because I doubted Rollick would approve.

For a second, tears pricked at my eyes. God, how I missed the dragon shifter's sly warmth and playful energy. I could just imagine spending hours in here telling him about all my adventures around Florida and explaining the parts of human life he didn't totally understand, finding out more about his life before he'd crashed into mine, challenging him to an impromptu sparring session... and of course all the other fun we could have been having together, alone or with the other two men.

He didn't seem to take much very seriously—other than my protection. It'd have been so much easier not to let my worries consume me with him around.

I swallowed thickly and made myself bite into the apple. Mouthful by mouthful, I swallowed it down. Closing my eyes, I savored the sweetness and the texture of the carved petals and imagined telling him how much I'd appreciated the little gift when I did get to see him again.

However long that took.

When I set the core aside, I considered the rest of my dinner. My gaze caught on the knife at the right side of the plate. With past dishes, I'd only ever received a dinner knife. This one was a steak knife—for greater ease of cutting the chicken breast, I assumed. The serrated edges gleamed under the room's artificial lights.

I picked it up and cut into the chicken. The meat parted with only a light pressure, as if I were slicing through butter. Of course, the hotel restaurant wouldn't want to give its guests ineffectual cutlery.

How convenient that it could also be a weapon.

I ate the rest of the food mechanically, only paying enough attention to note that it was as delicious as always but not taking much enjoyment out of the fact. A different memory was replaying in my mind now—the moment when I'd first fled from Rollick after he'd come to collect me from the other men. When I'd stabbed him in the side with the silver-and-iron blade I'd grabbed from the sorcerers' house, buying me a chance to escape despite his strength and supernatural prowess. I'd seen the small mark of a scar I assumed was from that wound on his side today.

This knife would be stainless steel, of course. No way

would a shadowkind keep literal silverware around. The men had said that the iron in steel didn't affect them the same way as the pure metal because of the different composition.

But shadowkind *could* still take regular physical injuries. It'd been the beast's claws, not any kind of magic, that'd torn up Crag's wing. A blade like this could make the difference between freedom and imprisonment, or even life and death if push came to shove.

The kitchen staff wouldn't bother the hotel owner about it if a knife didn't happen to return from his rooms, right? They'd assume it'd been misplaced and would be sent back when it was discovered. Not worth hassling the man in charge when they'd have plenty of other knives to work with.

The decision to hang on to it sent my mind spinning off in other related directions. After I'd finished eating, I got up, keeping the knife in my hand, and prowled around the room examining every object and fixture in it with fresh eyes.

I stopped by the empty fireplace, eyeing the ornate mantle clock perched there. The arched case looked like mahogany, and the numbers on the face were printed with aged ink, but the needle-like hands glinted with a silver sheen.

It looked old and fancy. The makers wouldn't have used steel for a display piece like that, would they? I could just see Rollick taking a perverse delight in having a tiny bit of the noxious metal in his rooms, like showing off to any other shadowkind he allowed to come up here that he was impervious to it.

And probably it didn't bother him at all with such small pieces tucked away behind the glass face. But if someone stabbed one of those pointy bits into, say, his eye or his throat, he wouldn't be laughing about that.

With a rush of resolve, I grabbed the clock and went to retrieve my multi-tool from the pocket it'd been relegated to in my messenger bag, since I hadn't had much use for it here. I stuffed the steak knife into the same pocket and got down to work.

Sitting cross-legged on the bed, I found the glass face popped open on a hinge. All I needed to do was unscrew the pin that held the hands in place and then tug the minute hand right off. Since it was longer, I figured it'd be a bit more useful.

Of course, Rollick might very well notice that his clock no longer had a minute hand. Then again, how much did a demon care about the time? The clock was just a decoration, one he'd seen thousands of times. There was a decent chance that one small change wouldn't actually catch his attention, at least not for a little while.

And if he did realize it was missing, well, he hadn't ordered me not to take steps to protect myself. I could claim that I'd repurposed it as a weapon against powerful shadowkind other than him. I mean, I'd happily stab any of the other monsters that wanted to capture me too, so that wouldn't even be a lie.

This two-inch long sliver of silver wasn't going to do me much good on its own, though. I pondered my options and after some experimentation determined that I could actually fit the hand into the lead end of one of my mechanical pencils. I adjusted it so it was half in, half out, figuring that was the most stable position that still allowed for a fair bit of stabbing length.

I stood up and was contemplating how best to keep my makeshift weapon on me where I'd be able to grab it quickly and effectively when a sudden warmth wafted over my skin with the materializing of a body right behind me.

"What an impressive contraption," Rollick said, peering over my shoulder, his chin nearly grazing my hair. "Were you planning on jabbing it into me?"

He arrived so suddenly and with such horrible timing that I couldn't restrain a yelp. I practically jumped right out of my skin. My fingers twitched, and I had to fumble to avoid dropping the pencil-turned-dagger on the floor.

I whirled around, my heart hammering at my ribs, holding the weapon down by my thigh even though a significant part of me wanted to jab it into the demon right now. When I'd already lost the element of surprise, I wasn't going to get anything out of the attempt other than wrecking our deal surprise.

"How long have you been spying on me?" I demanded, my entire body rigid. Had he seen me tuck the steak knife away in my bag when I'd first come into the bedroom?

Rollick gave me an amused look. It was deeply disconcerting seeing his movie-star handsome face with my recollection of his demonic form overlaid on it. "I don't think it's 'spying' simply to walk into a room in my own suite. The door was even open."

Damn it. I'd assumed the fact that he hadn't joined me for dinner meant that he wasn't going to show up anytime soon. It sounded like he'd presented himself pretty much as soon as he'd arrived, though, which at least meant he shouldn't have realized about the knife. And I still had my excuse for the weapon he had noticed.

"I'm sorry about your clock," I said. "I didn't figure you needed it as much as I needed a weapon against potential shadowkind attackers." I allowed myself to raise the makeshift blade, eyeing it with a trickle of embarrassed anticipation. "It *is* silver, isn't it?"

Rollick chuckled. "Of course you would find the one bit of the stuff in the entire suite. Are you that uncertain of my protective abilities? I promise, none of the idiots searching for you will find you *here*—as long as you don't tell anyone where you are. Which I've made sure you can't."

He didn't sound as if he was particularly worried that I had intended to use the silver against him, which didn't relieve me as much as it should have. Maybe he simply knew it wouldn't have done much anyway.

"Torrent and the others thought we were safe lots of other times when it turned out we weren't," I said quickly, shoving the weapon into my shorts pocket. "It seems smarter to be prepared for the worst. I don't suppose you've found out anything more about the shadowkind that are after me?"

"That's not for you to worry about," Rollick said breezily. "If you can contribute to our investigative efforts in any way, I'll let you know. *You* need to focus on getting control of your sorcery."

I grimaced at him. "We already talked about that."

"And I was hoping you'd reconsidered." He sighed and pulled his phone out of his pocket. "But maybe you need additional motivation—thinking of *all* the people you might want to protect. I got word this morning about some activity in your home city that made me concerned your stalkers may be identifying your usual haunts."

I stiffened all over again. "In Jacksonville? You mean like my house?"

"I've averted potential catastrophe." The demon flicked at his screen and then held it toward me. "Your parents will be perfectly safe for the next several days under my roof."

It took me a few seconds to process what I was seeing. The photo Rollick was showing me was of my parents: Mom with her fancy camera hanging around her neck in full tourist mode, Dad with the dorky headgear he called his "safari hat." They were standing at a gleaming black reception counter, a logo showing on the wall behind them in vibrant red: *Sunshine Sin Hotel*.

"You brought them *here*?" I said, my insides recoiling from the idea.

"It was safer than leaving them in Jacksonville," Rollick said without the least sign that it'd occurred to him I might object. "I arranged for them to 'win' an all-expenses-paid trip here. They'll have a wonderful time."

He grinned at me, but the shiny white teeth only brought back the visual of the jagged tips I'd seen this morning. I swallowed thickly.

The demon was acting like he'd invited my parents here out of the goodness of his heart to keep them safe for my benefit. But I wasn't an idiot. The implicit threat was clear.

I hadn't made him promise to do no harm to my family. It hadn't occurred to me in the moment we'd made the deal that my parents would factor into the situation. Now they were under his roof, under his control...

If I continued resisting, even if I technically met the

terms of our deal, there was nothing to stop him from exerting pressure to get what he wanted in other ways.

Like seeing that my parents met some unfortunate accidents.

"Thank you," I said roughly, since it seemed wiser to play along rather than to make the threat that much more concrete. "I'm glad they'll be okay. I guess I can't see them while they're here."

"Not in person. As far as they know, you're still in Florida."

"Right." I inhaled slowly and raised my chin. "Okay. Fine. Tell me how you want me to try out this sorcerer stuff, and we'll see how it goes."

CHAPTER NINE

Quinn

"We'll ease into it," Rollick had assured me last night, but it didn't feel like all that relaxed an approach when he turned up right after breakfast the next morning to make sure I was ready to get started. He waited until I'd put the empty dishes back in the dumbwaiter and washed up before pointing to one of the armchairs. "Sit down, gather your focus, and I'll be back in a few minutes."

It was the chair I'd normally been sitting in, I couldn't help noticing. Was that just a coincidence, or had he been paying that much attention to my behavior?

As I sank down onto the soft leather surface, the demon vanished, a stark reminder of just how easily he *could* pay attention to me without me having any clue. But he hadn't mentioned the steak knife yesterday. That one time he hadn't been peering at me from the shadows for very long before he'd announced his presence.

Other times... who knew?

Rollick had told me to gather my focus, but that was awfully difficult when my thoughts were being pulled in so many different directions. Would he really keep my parents safe here? What would he do to them if he wasn't happy with my progress? Was giving in to his demands that I try out my powers a mistake?

What if I *could* get strong enough to compel him a little, despite his confidence that I'd never get that strong? It was worth a little risk to give myself an advantage over both him and my other enemies, wasn't it?

I just wasn't sure whether it was only a little risk or a huge one. I felt like I was balancing on the edge of a rooftop with only clouded darkness below, no way of knowing whether I was walking next to a drop of five feet or five hundred.

And at least when I was navigating a rooftop, I knew what I needed to do to avoid a fall. I had no clue what was the safest way of testing the strange energies inside me and what might speed us toward disaster.

Selfishly, I wished the three men were here. My men. Torrent would have assessed the situation for me in his pensive way, giving me a more accurate sense of just how much shit I might be throwing myself into. Crag would have loomed menacingly as if he could intimidate my powers into behaving. Lance would have cracked jokes and flirted with me like nothing could possibly go all that wrong.

But it was better that they were far away when we

conducted this experiment. Less chance that anything I woke up inside me would hurt them. Especially Lance. The thought of how unnervingly wild he'd gone after we'd visited the sorcerers' house where my donor had lived, almost frantic in his rampage through the forest, made my stomach twist up.

Other sorcerers had already hurt him—hurt him badly enough that it'd surprised him that I'd hate the thought of doing the same. I never wanted his joyful demeanor to shatter because of something I'd done.

My mind was just meandering in yet another direction, wondering what the three of them were up to now and whether Rollick's orders were putting them in other kinds of danger, when the door swung open. I straightened up in my seat, a little surprised that Rollick hadn't just slipped through the shadows, but then I saw the man he was ushering in ahead of him.

The guy was human—it seemed I'd spent enough time around the shadowkind that I could sense his mortal status at a glance. He didn't look much older than me, maybe his mid-twenties, skinny enough that his elbows stuck out in points where he had his arms folded over his narrow chest and his dark eyes seemed to protrude a bit from his sallow face. He glanced at Rollick nervously, and the demon prodded him forward.

"There she is. Go have a chat. Be cooperative, and you can go back to your awful but insignificant existence soon enough." Rollick lifted his gaze to meet my eyes. "I've brought in a minor sorcerer to talk you through the basics. It seemed like a good idea for you to get a grounding in the theory before you actually try to boss any more shadowkind around. In the magical way, at least."

He flashed one of his charming grins at me and then wavered away into the shadows again, though I had trouble believing he was actually *gone*. He wouldn't let me talk with a sorcerer without listening in on our conversation, would he?

The man crept forward with tentative steps and lowered himself into the chair opposite me. He looked at his hands, at the now-empty coffee table, and finally at me. "He—he said you want to learn sorcery," he mumbled.

Geez, how badly had Rollick traumatized the guy "bringing" him in?

"Want" was way too strong a word for my actual feelings on the subject, but I didn't think it'd help the situation to get into the complexities with my unexpected guest.

"Yeah," I said. "Sort of. I mean..." It occurred to me that I didn't even know where to start this conversation. There was so much about sorcery I didn't know and so little I did. "How did *you* start learning?"

He wet his lips. "It was my mother. My mother taught me. It's mostly in families, you know. We aren't a very strong one, though. There's no reason to kill us. We'd never even try to work our skills on a higher shadowkind." His gaze darted toward the rest of the room as if he was talking more to Rollick, wherever the demon was lurking, than to me.

My gut twisted. "*I* don't want to kill you. And I think he only wants you to teach me." Rollick had sounded like he meant it when he'd told me he didn't bother sorcerers as long as they didn't hassle him.

The man's shoulders twitched. "There've been—we heard—just in the past few days, a couple of other families were slaughtered. More powerful than us, but not *that* prominent."

Oh, shit. So the shadowkind after me were ramping up their efforts to devour all the sorcerer organs they could from other sources too. My stomach turned.

"That wasn't Rol—that wasn't the shadowkind who brought you here," I said, remembering at the last second that Rollick probably wouldn't want his name tossed around freely. "We're trying to stop the monsters that are killing people. If I can learn how to use sorcery, that might help."

At those words, the man seemed to calm down a little. He peered at me. "Are you from a family? I realize every now and then someone totally new gets brought in as an apprentice, but I don't know how to check whether they'll be capable, or how to awaken the right energies..."

As if on cue, an emphatic flutter of the energy that'd already awakened in me beat at my chest. I restrained a flinch. "Actually, I've already got some power. I—I had a connection to a sorcerer family that I didn't know about until recently, and they can't teach me now. I just need to figure out how to use it."

"Okay." The man let out a shaky laugh. "That's the most important part right there. Tapping into it. Once you're aware of it, you just need to use it, and with practice you get better at knowing how. It comes more and more easily."

I frowned. "But I don't know how to use it in the first place. There was—I compelled one shadowkind, but it was totally by accident. I just said some words I didn't even realize I knew, that I can't remember now, and it worked."

The sorcerer nodded eagerly. "That's how it is. The power and the language to wield it are written into our own beings. We just have to open ourselves up to it and let it emerge, and you'll simply *know* how to conduct it."

This all sounded way too woo-woo and not at all concrete enough. I thought back to what I'd seen at the sorcerers' home near Miami. "I thought you used drawings and symbols, like with chalk and things—summoning circles or—"

I cut myself off when the man shrugged. "Those are tools that can help ground your intentions. But you still need to open yourself up to work them right. The symbols and shapes come from inside you, and you use your energy to make them real and potent."

I tipped my head to the side, still having trouble wrapping my head around how ephemeral his explanation was. "You're really saying that it's all inside me—everything I need to become a sorcerer? To become a major one, even? There aren't any, like, guidebooks or special rituals or whatever that I'd need to learn? Where does the energy even *come* from? How can it work like that?"

He splayed his hands. "I don't know. Honestly, it's kind of a fantastic mystery. I used to ask my mother a lot of questions when I was first getting the hang of it, but after a while, you just accept that as the way things are."

Just accepting and letting things happen as they felt like it wasn't my usual approach. I believed in figuring out what

I needed to do and then doing it step by step—that was how I'd approached my architecture studies and my urban exploring as well, delving into abandoned and off-limits buildings. But as far as I could tell, this guy really didn't know anything more than what he'd said.

"How do you open yourself up?" I asked finally. "Is there anything special you do to tap into the energy and let the understanding or whatever come to the surface?"

"I wouldn't call it special," he said. "It's like meditation. You focus on the energy and... sort of listen to it. It's almost like it whispers into your head if you pay enough attention to it. And you hear it more and more clearly the more often you welcome it. You can picture what you'd like to accomplish and it'll answer that. But once you get good at using however much power you've got, it'll become more automatic. You think what you want to do and it comes to you without having to pause and really concentrate."

More color had come into his face as he'd talked about sorcery, as if even thinking about using it invigorated him. I guessed there was something pretty exhilarating about being able to command monstrous creatures to do your bidding even if you only had enough power to do it with the animal-like ones. If you didn't think they deserved free will anyway.

I rubbed my mouth, straining my brain for anything else I should ask and coming up empty. "I think that covers everything then," I said. "Thank you."

Rollick appeared next to us an instant later, abruptly enough that the sorcerer startled in his chair. It appeared he didn't have any questions of his own, because he simply motioned the man to his feet. "You've served your purpose. Good man. Let's get you out of here."

I stood up too with a hitch of my pulse. The guy hadn't been especially helpful, and I had pretty iffy feelings about sorcerers in general, but he had tried to help. And it didn't sound as if he was personally doing anything all that horrendous.

"What's going to happen to him now?" I asked Rollick pointedly. I didn't think the demon would want a sorcerer running around able to say that a demon had brought him to this specific hotel so he could talk to a woman with my description.

Rollick chuckled. "No need to worry about this pipsqueak." He patted the slight man in the head with a patronizing air. "I have a succubus on staff who can compel him into not even thinking about, let alone speaking of, what went on here. As far as he'll know, he went on a little day trip to the next town over."

Okay, so the guy definitely wasn't getting murdered. He looked relieved even as he tensed up at the demon's words. "You're going to mess with my—"

Rollick shot him a firm look. "Would you rather I messed up the rest of you? How many shadowkind minds have you addled over the years, hmm?"

The man's mouth snapped shut. Apparently he couldn't come up with a very good counterargument to that point.

I shifted my weight, resisting the urge to hug myself. "What about the other sorcerers out there? He said they're being targeted—murdered. Wouldn't we want to stop that?

I mean, I know you don't like them, but it does mean the murderers are getting more power."

Rollick waved off my concerns dismissively. "Not much, from what I've gathered. I'm not extending my resources guarding all of those pricks. They knew the risks they were taking when they decided to start enslaving our kind."

"It could be a chance to find out more about the beings we're up against," I pointed out.

Rollick gave me an amused look. "Why do I think that's hardly the real reason you're concerned? Such a bleeding heart, mortal. I can add keeping an eye on the more powerful sorcerer families I'm aware of to your favorite trio's duties, though only because it serves *my* purposes."

He nudged the sorcerer toward the door and called one last remark over his shoulder. "You've got the rest of the day to work on listening to those whispers, sweet sorcerer. We're going to begin target practice tomorrow."

CHAPTER TEN

Crag

"He might not be gone for very long," I felt the need to point out as the three of us raced up through the shadows toward the hotel's upper levels.

"We have enough time for a brief talk," Torrent said. "When Rollick breaks out one of those crystal bottles of cognac, he plans to savor it. We just won't let ourselves get sidetracked by unnecessary diversions."

I suspected that last comment was directed mainly at Lance. The dragon shifter was by far the most likely among us to get distracted, and the woman we were hurrying to see had become his favorite diversion. Every time we'd been able to talk amongst ourselves since arriving in L.A., there'd been an irritated edge to his jokes, along with some grumbling about certain demons restricting our access to "our mortal."

"Gotta take the time we have, or he'll steal even more from us," he said now in a jaunty but urgent tone, rushing ahead of the two of us.

"Hold on." Torrent's tone was firm enough that Lance slowed. Our squad leader took the lead as we moved through the small opening in the layer of silver and iron. "We need to handle this so that Rollick doesn't realize we snuck in. He probably has surveillance in his rooms, but I've checked over the terrace, and it seems clear. But we'll need Quinn to come to us."

"Yes, yes, invite her out to the party." Lance leapt forward again. "I can be careful."

He could, or he wouldn't have been part of the squad to begin with. We were the ones Rollick sent on the secret missions he didn't want anyone knowing he was invested in. No other shadowkind was even aware that we worked for him.

Which was a good thing now that half of the beings that'd been rampaging around Florida had seen one or all of us, or even this hotel wouldn't have been safe for Quinn.

When we reached the terrace outside Rollick's private suite, Torrent emerged by the railing overlooking the ocean. Lance and I followed suit. Our leader was the only one who'd managed to speak to Quinn since Rollick had sent us off a few days ago; he knew how to best handle the situation.

Or, I thought that, anyway. Lance started toward the glass sliding door, and Torrent caught his arm. The dragon shifter let out a soft growl of annoyance, but hung back next to Torrent as the other man extended one of his tentacles to lightly jostle the glass.

I hadn't spotted Quinn at first. But as I stepped forward to stand beside my companions, I noted a hint of her pale blond hair peeking over the top of the armchair that faced away from us. It didn't stir.

"You need to smack it harder," Lance said to Torrent.

Torrent gave the dragon shifter an amicable nudge to the shoulder. "She heard. She'll know. She's just being smart and waiting a few minutes so that it won't be obvious she thinks there was something significant about the noise. Come on, we should stay as far back from the windows as we can."

He darted through the darkness and reformed in the most shadowy corner of the terrace. Lance and I came after him on foot. It was getting late into the night, stars glinting in the vast sweep of the sky overhead, the ocean not much more than a vague expanse and a rhythmic hiss of waves. I couldn't make out the thumping bass of the nightclub on the lower floors anymore, but the less aggressive melodies from the rooftop patio filtered down. If it was still open, we weren't calling on Quinn at an unreasonable hour.

Lance stirred restlessly on his feet, and I tamped down similar impulses inside myself. It'd been too long since I'd been in our woman's presence. I'd sworn to myself and to her that I'd protect her, I'd done everything in my power... and it hadn't been enough. She'd had to make this deal to protect *me* as well as herself. My jaw clenched at the thought of the scars that still ached a bit when I extended my reformed wing, which would never quite be the same.

Quinn didn't leave us waiting too long. She came out through the bedroom door, closer to our current post. The smile that sprang to her lips at the sight of all three of us was so brilliant it nearly erased all my agony at being apart from her.

She dashed forward, and naturally Lance caught her first, snatching her into an embrace so swift and emphatic it was a miracle he didn't skewer her with those fatal claws. He spun her around and nuzzled the side of her face with a long inhalation as if drinking in the scent of her hair. "I've missed you, baby girl." Then he kissed her so deeply an approving sound hummed from Quinn's throat.

"I missed you too," she said in a choked-sounding voice. "Thank you for the apple."

Delight sparked in his eyes. "I'll toss more in whenever I get the chance."

I wasn't sure what they were talking about, but he didn't get to soak up *all* her affection. As soon as she'd eased back from him, I tugged her into an embrace of my own, reveling in the softness of her body against my solid frame —and the strength I could feel emanating from within that softness. "He's not the only one who missed you," I said gruffly.

Quinn squeezed me back tightly and bobbed up on her toes to press a kiss to my mouth that brought my more heated desires roaring to life. "And I missed you too. All of you." She glanced around at us, her gaze settling on Torrent, and smiled at him. Then she turned back to me with a flicker of concern in her eyes. "How's your wing? Has it healed up all right?"

I hadn't known I could feel fonder of this woman, but a renewed surge of affection rushed through me. I let my wings extend from my back without transforming all the way into my gargoyle body, letting her see the sealed tears with their mottling of scars in the thin flesh. "Almost good as new. If we need to fly, I'm ready."

"Hopefully that won't be necessary." She stepped closer, running her fingers tentatively over the marks, and a shiver of my own delight shot straight to my groin. The flesh there was sensitive both to damage and to a more tender touch. I swept the wing forward, tucking her into an embrace next to me, and she leaned against my arm with a sigh of contentment.

Her gaze slid back to Torrent. "Are we hopping over to the other room again?"

Something about the slight arch of her eyebrows and the unusual warmth to Torrent's answering smile made me wonder exactly what the two of them had gotten up to when he'd visited alone two nights ago. But then, it wasn't as if I should resent Torrent for getting to embrace Quinn as intimately as I already had. The three of us were in this together, watching over her together... Showing our adoration in every possible way together.

"I don't think there's any point," Torrent said. "Rollick's downstairs in the club—I wouldn't want to risk staying more than half an hour as it is. We can talk just as easily out here."

Quinn tensed against me. "Are you sure it's safe for you to have come at all?"

And that was exactly why I knew Rollick had been wrong when he'd suggested Quinn was only using us for a thrill. Her first thought wasn't to be upset that we couldn't stay longer and engage in the more thrilling pursuits we'd discovered together—it was to be worried about how our visit might have negative consequences for us. She might be rare among mortals, but there was no denying her commitment to us.

I would have fought to the bitter end to ensure her freedom, but she'd given it up so that I could keep my life. Rollick had no idea what he was talking about.

I *was* going to prove myself worthy of her devotion. She needed to believe that her imprisonment here was only temporary, that we were making progress toward destroying all her enemies and clearing the path back to her former existence. If I couldn't accomplish that for her, then she was the one who should have been scorning me, not the other way around.

"I'll sense if he's approaching," I said. The one useful feature of the demon's immense power from my perspective was that I could sense the vibrations of his presence through my rocky nature at a much farther distance than the average being. I wasn't aware of him right now through the layer of silver and iron, which was exactly why Rollick had added it to the building—though mainly so he couldn't be sensed when he was up here, not the other way around. But as soon as he traveled past it, I'd know.

Torrent nodded. "If he comes while we're still here, we can make ourselves scarce."

"I still say we slice and dice him," Lance announced, clicking his claws together. "Too tricksy—so annoying. Keeping us apart from you, giving us all the work."

Torrent made a dismissive noise. "It's more than just his 'tricksy'-ness that's the problem, as you know. If we don't have to fight him at all, we're a lot more likely to come out of this situation still standing. And the work we've been doing should eventually help us come up with a feasible plan."

Quinn hugged herself within the shelter of my wing. "It's going to be even harder going against him now. He brought my parents here to the hotel—he says it's for their protection, but our deal doesn't cover them. Even if I'm technically sticking to the terms, if he isn't happy with me, he could take it out on them."

My muscles flexed automatically, my fangs itching at my gums, eager to emerge. "We won't let him harm them either."

Torrent frowned. "That does complicate the situation... but really, we need to neutralize the threat of the other shadowkind after you, who don't seem inclined to make any deals at all, before we worry about Rollick anyway."

He was right, even if the difficulties with accomplishing that task loomed as large as a mountain in the back of my mind, more daunting than an actual mountain would have been. But we had to find a way. They couldn't have Quinn. That was all there was to it.

"Have you found out anything else about the beings who are searching for me?" Quinn asked.

Lance raked his claws through the air and then slung his arm around her waist to pull her away from me to nuzzle her again. "*They* like to slice and dice. No deals. No negotiations. Anything in their way, they pulverize it."

Like the crumpled garage at the sorcerers' home, an image that made me wince inwardly. I prided myself on my strength, but strength might not be enough against these brutes.

Torrent was nodding. "They seem to be pretty... old-school in their approach. All overt violence, turning to aggression to handle any problem—earning the 'monster' label very thoroughly. The two or more beings in charge have stayed in the background letting their followers handle most of the work, so we're not sure of their exact powers yet, but they're clearly not afraid of other shadowkind noticing their activities."

"Like Rollick is," Quinn said. "I mean, he's been very careful to make sure no one finds out he's at all interested in me and my powers, right? He sent you out in secret. Does that mean these beings are even more powerful than he is?" Her mouth twisted.

"Not necessarily," Torrent said. "Rollick's mostly concerned with running his businesses and enjoying the fruits of his labors. He wouldn't get anything out of all-out war. So it suits him to avoid it, whereas these other shadowkind seem to welcome that kind of conflict. Maybe they're out to prove themselves the top dogs around. Maybe they've got a specific agenda." He let out a frustrated huff. "We're still not sure what their end goal is."

"They've been killing other sorcerers." Quinn motioned vaguely to the world beyond the hotel. "At least a couple of other families since we arrived here."

"Good riddance," I said automatically, and regretted the words at the tensing of Quinn's stance. I wasn't going to wish for the safety of the malicious humans who enslaved shadowkind, but I had to remember they were closer to her own kind than we were. And she didn't seem to like to see any sort of being suffer.

"Serves them right, but it's no good for shadowkind to

grab those powers," Lance said with a snarl for emphasis. "They should be better than that."

"I might not be safe even *with* Rollick protecting me then," Quinn said. "If these monsters are close to as powerful as he is and more willing to fight..."

Torrent extended a tentacle to give her forearm a reassuring squeeze. "Oh, he'll fight if he needs to. He just prefers to choose his battles wisely. He obviously thinks defying these fiends is important, or he wouldn't have involved himself to begin with."

"What does *he* want with Quinn?" the dragon shifter murmured, pressing a kiss to the back of her head. "Other than her loveliness. That's enough for me, but I don't think so for him."

"No," Quinn agreed, her expression clouding.

I pictured what a battle like that might look like, shadowkind assaulting the hotel, Rollick hitting back with his demonic powers and the allies he could call on. The whole place might end up rubble by the time both sides had finished battering each other...

The thought brought a spark of inspiration into my mind, a sensation I wasn't all that familiar with. It took me a moment before I felt confident enough to voice it.

"What if... what if we let them deal with each other?"

Torrent cocked his head, studying me but with interest rather than the skepticism I'd been afraid of. "What do you mean?"

"If we made it so the other shadowkind found out that Rollick was keeping Quinn here," I said, "they'd attack, and he'd *have* to fight back. They'd take out a bunch of each other's forces, maybe even take *each other* out and leave no one in any shape to continue chasing after her. We'd have to make sure she was safely away before the fighting started, of course, but..." I glanced between the others' faces, hoping my explanation hadn't sounded completely absurd.

Quinn nodded slowly. "That makes sense. Let them exhaust themselves against each other... Even if neither side is totally destroyed, they should both end up a lot weaker than they are now."

Lance grinned. "Very tricksy. We can play that game too."

Torrent rubbed his chin. "There could be something to that. We'd need to set it up very carefully—if Rollick got wind that our enemies were coming much in advance, he'd take off with Quinn and leave them nothing to find. And even if they take him by surprise, if she turns out not to be here, that could diffuse the conflict and simply leave him *very* pissed off at us."

"We have time to think through the possibilities," Quinn pointed out. "The deal holds for at least another six days. The more we know about who we're up against and why they're doing this—on both sides—the better. At least now we have the start of an approach that could work." She aimed one of her bright smiles at me. "It's a really smart plan, Crag. Better than anything I've been able to think of."

I couldn't help beaming back, as strange as the expression felt on my face. She was impressed by an idea *I'd* come up with. And if we needed to, we'd see it through, whether Rollick liked it or not.

CHAPTER ELEVEN

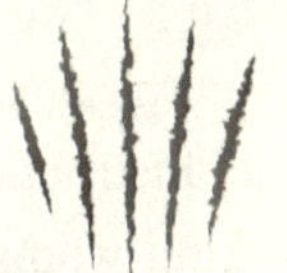

Quinn

I had no clue what to expect from the "target practice" Rollick had mentioned. With every passing minute after I woke up, I dreaded it more. Not even the joy of seeing my three men last night could stand against my anxiety.

I forced down my breakfast of spinach omelet and fruit salad, took my morning pills, and finished the rest of my typical routine on autopilot. Then I paced around the living room, unable to sit down for more than a minute or two without a restless urge driving me to my feet again.

Somewhere on one of the floors beneath me—or out in the city, if they were getting in some sight-seeing—my parents were roaming around, unaware of the dangers circulating around them. Unaware that I was possibly just minutes away.

But how could I have told them even if I'd had a way to reach them? If I'd warned them about monstrous attackers now or when I'd had the chance before, they'd have thought I was crazy.

They probably *were* safer here than back in Jacksonville... as long as I didn't defy Rollick. As long as I kept him happy.

I'd tried to meditate with my apparent sorcerer powers like the guy yesterday had instructed. Before, following the suggestions of a shadowkind woman named Sorsha who'd been trying to help me suppress those energies, I'd only concentrated on suppressing and disguising them. But that hadn't worked so well.

When I focused on them and encouraged the wavering sensations in my chest, I did get a reaction. The wobbly flutters had been coming more frequently since my first attempts. I'd gotten to the point where I could provoke one if I tried to, not that I really wanted to. And with them came little murmurs of sensation, as if some innate instinct I didn't understand really was whispering in my ear, directing me in how to use it.

I'd had nothing to aim those instincts at, though. All I'd been left with was even more jitters inside me and a knot in my gut.

I didn't know whether to be relieved or upset that Rollick arrived fairly promptly, just a half hour after I'd started my pacing. How well did he know my morning routine? He entered without a knock, as usual, carrying a black box about the size of a cat carrier.

"Ready to go?" he asked me with a dimpled smile. He really shouldn't be allowed to look that gorgeous while acting as my jailor.

"What are we doing?" I asked, eyeing the box. "What's in there?"

He motioned for me to follow him out onto the terrace. There, he set the box on the patio table where we'd eaten dinner just a few days ago. "This is a contraption developed by the human 'hunters' who catch shadowkind beasts either because they want to exterminate them or to sell them to collectors," he said. "You mortals do come up with some interesting inventions. I don't care for the practice in general, but it worked for my purposes for today. I believe in making use of all the tools available to me."

It took me a few moments to piece together that rambling explanation enough to draw a clear conclusion. "There's a shadowkind creature in there?"

He nodded. "Just a weak little thing, not much more than a lost kitten. One shaped like a lizard with little spikes instead of scales, but given the chance, it'd wisp away rather than confront you. You have nothing to fear."

I swallowed thickly. Did *it* have anything to fear? "What do you want me to do with it?"

"I want to see if those sorcerer powers of yours have woken up enough that you can put them to some small use on demand. I'll open up the box, you compel the beastie to, oh, let's say hop on top of it and stay there. That's simple enough, but not what it'd do given the choice."

I raised an eyebrow at him. "And if I fail and it disappears into the shadows? Do you have a whole menagerie ready to stock these experiments?"

The demon shot me an amused glance. "As little faith as you apparently have in me, I can manage to wrangle one minor shadowkind. It can't get very far from this level of the building anyway. If it runs, I'll bring it back. We have all day. I'm sure you'll tap into your inner sorcerer eventually."

"Maybe you could tell me why *you* want me to tap into these powers so much," I suggested, partly procrastinating and partly because I really did want to know. "It'll help me to focus my attention properly."

Rollick guffawed. "Nice try." He offered a languid smirk. "How about you give it a shot, and we'll see how conversational I'm feeling if you pull off a little compulsion?"

I managed not to grit my teeth in frustration and yanked my gaze to the box rather than his face. Apparently satisfied that I was cooperating, Rollick slid out the two latches that secured the container's door and eased it open.

A light was beaming inside, brightly enough to highlight a patch of shadow that was quivering within the box, even though it barely appeared to have any physical presence. That was the creature he wanted me to compel. I opened my mouth and closed it again, an ache forming behind my sternum.

The shadowkind *hated* mortals who used this power. It was stealing their free will as much as Rollick had stolen mine—more even.

"I'm pretty sure nothing will come of simply staring at it, though you're welcome to prove me wrong," the demon put in.

I darted a hasty glower at him and focused on the little shadowy beast again. I wouldn't be like other sorcerers because I didn't *want* to be. The very fact that I was so uneasy about using this power meant I wouldn't use it badly, right?

Asking this little creature to sit on top of a box was hardly terrible. And what Rollick might do to my parents if I didn't make the attempt could very well be.

I inhaled deeply and let part of my mind detach from the outside world, concentrating on the rhythm of my pulse and the flow of energy around that most vital of organs inside me. Strange sensations rippled through me with each beat of my heart. When I acknowledged that energy, it seemed to twitch to attention in awareness of the shadowkind nearby—both the little thing in the box and the much more powerful presence standing next to it.

It recoiled from Rollick, obviously aware that I was in no position to compel *him* into doing anything just yet. But it seemed to reach through me toward the lesser being eagerly, with a tug on my nerves.

On top of the box. I wanted the creature to step out and hop up there, that was all.

Sweat broke out on the back of my neck, though I couldn't have said whether it was from effort expended or just my trepidation. I opened my mouth again, a quiver raced up my throat, and a few unfamiliar syllables fell off my tongue like when I'd sent the flying beast away.

The shadowy patch shuddered and then leapt forward. As it burst from the box, I caught a glint of the spikes Rollick had mentioned and a gleam of eerie green eyes. A conflicted jolt of triumph hit me in the second before the creature spun around—and dashed toward the edge of the terrace rather than taking the seat I'd intended.

Rollick leapt forward twice as quickly, faster than any human even with that muscular body could have moved. He snatched the moving shape of what was mostly still shadow—and it solidified into a hissing, writhing creature in his hands, his fingers clamped around its neck.

He tsked his tongue at it and brought it back to the table, where he set it next to the box and looked expectantly at me. "The world didn't end, did it? See if you can persuade this beastie a little better the second time."

"What, you weren't looking for a workout?" I said glibly, but the joke landed flat. My heart was beating too fast, and I was too aware of the fact that the power I had exerted was flowing from that organ. The organ that'd been stitched into my chest from another girl, that I only managed to keep in my body because my twice-daily meds convinced the rest of me that it was a welcome friend rather than a foreign invader.

Over the years, I'd come to think of the medications as reflecting a reality my body simply had trouble accepting. Right now, it was hard not to think that my body might have been right after all.

Rollick glowered at me, his lips still curled in amusement. "I know you can master this, Quinn. We just need to work on *you* knowing that."

His confident words sent a weird buzz of exhilaration through me—to have a millennia-old, immensely powerful demon praising *my* capabilities. Of course, it was probably just a pep talk to get me to do what he wanted.

Which I needed to do anyway. I dragged in a breath and scowled at the spiky creature.

It'd remained in physical form, maybe nervous of what Rollick would do to it if it tried to escape again. That made it easier for me to concentrate. I pictured it leaping on top of the box, the *need* for it to do that condensing within my ribcage.

I had to prove to Rollick that I was cooperating. That I didn't need any further motivation, especially not of the cruel kind.

It was just a short hop. No reason for the creature to not want to do it. Just give it a little nudge...

One of those unsettling wobbles ran through my chest, forceful enough to make my pulse stutter. Another burst of meaningless sound spilled from my mouth. I hurled it at the creature, my skin tingling with the energy my voice carried—and the beast stiffened for just an instant before springing on top of the box as if its life depended on it.

Rollick gave me a languid round of applause and a pleased smile. "There we go. Now let's see if you can compel it back into the box. It won't want to go in there, so you'll have to be firm about it."

Wonderful. But maybe once it was in the box, the demon would be satisfied for the day and we could stop this charade of me being a sorcerer.

That flimsy hope girded me. I tensed my arms at my sides and stared the lesser shadowkind down.

Into that glowing space. In between those walls. It *would* go there, because I demanded that it did.

A jolt of power surged up my throat. My heart hitched. I spat out the unfamiliar words rushing up from my chest. They didn't mean anything to me, and yet at the same time, I understood that I was saying, *Go inside there, NOW.*

This time, the creature didn't even pause. It darted right into the box. My shoulders sagged as a mix of relief and revulsion rolled over me.

I'd done it. I'd forced the little beast to go against its instincts, to do something it'd hated. Hurray for me.

My heart was thumping hard but not so quickly now. My chest felt tight. I had a very strong urge to lie down and close my eyes and hope I didn't wake up until this whole horrible situation was over. Except I didn't think it could be over if I tried to simply sleep through it.

"Very nice." Rollick strolled over to stand next to me, his body so close that the bare skin of my arm woke up with giddy awareness. "What should we have it do next? A tap dance? I wonder if you could convince it to leap right onto that silver spear you made."

My spine went rigid. "I'm not telling it to do that."

The demon continued in a nonchalant tone. "It would be a fantastic test of your powers. But if you don't like practicing on innocent beasties, we do have other trial subjects around. I could call the dragon shifter or the gargoyle in to see how well you can play with a higher shadowkind. I'm sure they'd be willing to offer themselves up just for your sake."

I tensed even more than I had already. My arms jerked up to fold over my chest defensively. "I'm not using any powers on them. It isn't *playing*. This isn't a game."

Rollick smiled down at me, the intensity of his presence making my pulse wobble in a totally different way. "Oh, but it is in all the ways that matter. Everything is a game, really, to the ones who make the decisions that affect the outcomes. You'll learn that soon enough, reluctant sorcerer."

"I don't think I'm getting to make any decisions here at all," I shot back. "You're the one calling the shots."

He arched his eyebrows. "I've given you plenty of leeway. But if you'd like me to act more the part of a dictator, I believe I can call Lance up here right—"

I couldn't have said what came over me. I knew it was useless; I knew I shouldn't provoke him. But the thought of inflicting my emerging power on Lance after the torments sorcerers had already put the dragon shifter through hit me with a smack of horror, and my body simply reacted.

"No!" I said, and shoved Rollick away from me.

I barely budged him. The guy had a foot on me and probably a hundred pounds more muscle, and, y'know, the whole immensely powerful demon thing on top of that. But he reacted the second my hand smacked into his arm.

One instant, I was standing next to him. The next, he'd slammed me down on the tiles of the terrace floor. He cushioned my head and back with one arm just enough that the impact rang through my nerves but wasn't more than a brief shock of pain, but his other hand pinned my shoulder to the ground. His claws had emerged. He lowered my head all the way to the tiles and jerked his first hand around to tease them along my throat, braced over me with less than a foot between our bodies.

I trembled. Most of it was fear, but a tiny flare of heat lit between my legs. Fucking hell.

And Rollick noticed it. He smiled at me, still bright but fierce, transforming his movie-star good looks into something hauntingly gorgeous.

"You don't want to get into a fist fight with me, mortal," he crooned. "But I'm not sure that's what you're really looking for, even now. I think I could take you right here on the tiles, and you'd be gasping for more."

My jaw clenched. If I denied the attraction coursing through me, he'd just laugh. "I'd hate you afterward," I said. "I can't help how my body reacts, but none of it means I trust or respect or even like you."

The demon laughed anyway, a low chuckle that reverberated into me and woke up even more heat even as I stiffened against it. He lowered his head so that his breath ghosted across my lips, not quite touching them with a kiss.

"I'm not going for 'like,' sweet sorcerer. But it's much more fun to win more than just the body. One day I will fuck you with both of my dicks, and it'll be because you've welcomed me. And you'll be ever so glad you did."

Before I could formulate a response, he leapt off me with typical languid grace. He picked up the box with the shadowkind creature and sauntered off the terrace before I'd even willed myself to sit up.

The trial was over—for now. Maybe that was some kind of victory? But my muscles were still trembling, and I was starkly aware of the dampening of my panties. Not even the floor beneath me felt stable enough to hold me steady.

He wasn't right. I wouldn't let him be. I would *never* welcome a fiend who'd treated me the way he had.

But I had no idea what happened now.

CHAPTER TWELVE

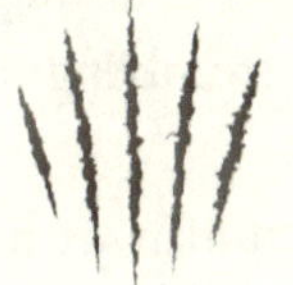

Lance

I knew Rollick had arrived from the shifting of the energies in the shadows. His tricksy presence always loomed large even when you couldn't see it.

"What is it that you had to call me all the way out here about?" he drawled, but I could tell he wasn't happy about the request despite his casual tone. I might not be the most sensitive being around, but even I could pick up on the tremor of tension that emanated off him.

"You didn't want us consulting with anyone else," I reminded him. "And you also didn't want us stirring up trouble with shadowkind who aren't any part of this. How could you decide whether I should pursue this without seeing what I'd found?"

The demon made a dismissive sound, but he came closer. "What exactly *did* you find that's made you so nervous, dragon?"

I motioned to the mountain range we were positioned

at the base of in the shadow of a spiky-leafed tree. Rollick had sent me roaming out to the area mortals called Utah because a few sorcerers had been slaughtered and devoured here a few days ago. I'd only been meant to check the murder scene for clues that might identify the beings involved. I'd ended up stumbling on what felt like a much more momentous trail.

"There are a few human paths farther along," I said, "but they don't really come out this way. *Something's* been active around there, though. Lots of rocks looking bashed up with claw marks on them. Shuddery energy left behind. The whole place gives me the impression that I should want to be anywhere but here, which isn't because of anything *I've* actually seen. It's shadowkind power, isn't it?"

Rollick let out a more thoughtful hum and motioned for me to take him closer. I leapt from shadow to shadow where they formed at the base of rocks and shrubs and dips in the earth across the uneven terrain. Where the slope really started to angle upward, I pointed to a mess of chunks that looked like a shattered boulder.

The sense that I should be going someplace else hit me stronger here. It made me want to dig my claws into the rocks and snarl at whoever was trying to boss me around with their magic. But whoever that was probably had pretty big claws too. Or some other sharp appendages. There were broad scratch marks here and there on the broken chunks of stone.

Rollick examined them, prowling around through the shadows, and then peered up the side of the mountain. "You haven't followed the trail much farther?"

I shook my head, knowing he'd sense the movement

through the gloom. "There's another smashed rock like this a little ways up. After that I stopped. I can spy on whatever might be up there without being noticed, I think. But I don't know for sure what other magic they might have. Or maybe you can tell what being it is and that we shouldn't get involved."

I kind of hoped the latter was true. I'd much rather head back to California—to the hotel, where I might get to drop in on Quinn again.

And I didn't like the idea of a fiend with this kind of power being after her.

"I don't recognize it," Rollick said, and moved closer to one of the chunks of stone. "These aren't claw marks, though. Those are horns, or curved spikes of some sort." His frown came through in his voice. "How did you get here from the murder site?"

"There was a beastie hanging around the spot," I said. "It ran off when it saw me. I was thinking maybe it was keeping watch to see who came around. I followed it quietly so it wouldn't realize I'd seen it, but when we were close to here, there wasn't as much cover. So I smashed it. But if it was going to report to someone about me, I figured they'd be around here, so I explored some more."

Rollick nodded. "Or it could simply be that it was randomly passing by."

I shrugged. "I didn't say that wasn't possible. You asked how I got here."

"I did." Rollick paused again, with a pensiveness I didn't totally like. I was used to this solemn consideration from Torrent—it felt right from him. Rollick was all easygoing confidence except when he was really mad. If something about this situation outright worried him, there couldn't be anything good about it at all.

"Go up the mountain," he said finally. "See what you can see—but don't let anything or anyone see *you*. That's the most important part. If you don't think you can stay hidden, retreat and report back whatever you were able to discover."

I would have saluted him the way I'd seen humans do sometimes to people giving commands, but there wasn't much point in the shadows. "I can do that. I'll be sneaky. Twice as careful as with the beastie."

"If anything urgent comes up that can't wait until you can make it back in person, you know how to reach me by phone," Rollick reminded me. "Although I'm sure you're in a huge hurry to be back to that mortal woman."

I bristled instinctively at his reference to Quinn. "I'm here to make sure no bigger beasties get their claws—or horns, or whatever—into her. I won't let her down."

Rollick clucked his tongue. "I suppose you'd better hope she doesn't let *you* down then, hadn't you? I know this is all new and exciting to you, Lance, but humans don't settle down with dragons. And the more fiends try to stick their claws into her, the less thrilling she's going to find yours."

I thought of Quinn's eager shivers when I traced the tips of my talons over her skin and had to smile. "I don't think that will be a problem."

"Well, you know better than most what horrors humans are capable of. Just because she's shown you her softer side doesn't mean there isn't a vicious edge to her too."

I couldn't help snorting, as disrespectful as that might be to the man who'd somehow become my boss again. "She can be vicious against the beasts that deserve it. I'll cheer her on." I didn't have the slightest doubt that she'd never lash out at *me*. He hadn't seen how worried she'd been over a light smack to my eye.

"Fine," Rollick said. "Don't listen to the demon who's seen more human relationships begin and end than breaths you've taken. Go find out what we're dealing with here."

It didn't matter how many other humans he'd known. He didn't really know Quinn.

I set off up the slope, slinking from shadow to shadow, stopping in each one to test the energies around me and ahead of me. The vibe warning me off got stronger, but I didn't pick up on any other supernatural forces. I simply ignored it. No one was bullying me into changing my course.

At least, that was what I intended. I reached a point in the rough path that wound up the increasingly steep mountainside where I simply couldn't push myself onward. I looked at the shadow I wanted to leap to, I braced myself to jump—and my body refused to go on. A blaring *No!* echoed through my essence.

That was cheating. More tricks to keep me from finding out their secrets. I'd just have to figure out another way.

I slipped along the edge of that boundary, the point where my nerves couldn't withstand the push away. The energy woke up some sort of prey alarm in my brain that felt totally foreign.

I was a dragon. Nothing preyed on me. I was the one who slashed and slaughtered. But somehow I couldn't convince myself of that when I challenged the supernatural barrier.

After a while, I roamed right around the side of the mountain. There was a sharp peak ahead of me, topped with a layer of snow even in the summer. The growing chill itched at me through the shadows, but this part of the mountain range didn't appear to be quite as protected. I darted up it, moving faster but still pausing now and then to check my surroundings.

Whoever was lurking up here would be trusting their warning vibe to keep spies away. They wouldn't need many other protections if they were strong enough to propel even a being like me in the opposite direction.

The chill might have affected me, but traveling through the patches of darkness without any physical form didn't tire me particularly. Especially once evening fell and the whole landscape was dark. I raced to the edge of the peak and peered down over the terrain I'd circumnavigated.

Enough of a pale glow shone down from the mostly full moon that my already sharp eyes could make out many details even with the dwindling sunlight. In the distance, between this peak and a couple of others, a large lake shimmered. There were a few buildings near the edge of the lake, rough huts that I suspected only held one room each. The rocky terrain showed a few gouges large enough for me to make out even from the distance, as if some huge creature had dug right into the mountain.

I watched the water and the land around it. For a while, nothing moved. Then I made out a creature here and another there, one slipping into one of the huts, another heading down the mountain by the way I hadn't been able to come up.

There were probably more in the shadows, too far away for me to make them out, let alone tell what sort of beings there were. There could be just a few or dozens, even hundreds. No way for me to know.

I gritted my teeth in frustration. But then I caught a sense of motion from much closer by. Another being, a higher shadowkind but not all that powerful, passing through the gloom no more than fifty feet away.

Because I'd been crouched motionless and she'd been in motion, she hadn't picked up on my presence as far as I could tell. Nothing about her passage betrayed any nervousness.

I couldn't think of any reason for a shadowkind to be up here who wasn't connected to the bunch hanging out around the lake. That meant she might be able to tell me more, even if I couldn't get down there myself.

I waited until she'd come a little closer, moving on a diagonal past me, and then I flung myself across the short distance to tackle her.

Her sinewy form jerked and flailed as it snapped into physical form beneath my emerged dragon body. I hauled the being—not a type I'd encountered before, but with a scent that reminded me of the dryads I'd once met—around the slope out of view of the apparent mountain den. Then I pinned her down firmly and let enough of me transform that I could speak.

"You've come from the lake," I said with a growl in my voice.

The being just stared at me, her thin face bluish-gray,

although maybe it was naturally that color and not just turned it out of horror. Her lips wobbled.

I leaned closer, showing my fangs. "You will tell me about it. Who's there? What are you doing? Are you the ones who killed the sorcerers near here?"

When she stayed silent, I dug a claw into each of her wrists. She let out a little squeal. Then she said, "I can't—I can't talk about it. It isn't allowed. There's nothing I can say."

I recognized the desperation in her words with a cold smack of revulsion. She'd been compelled—compelled like sorcerers did. Except there weren't any mortals hiding out up here in the mountains.

This was an enclave of the beasts we were fighting against—the beasts who'd been gulping down sorcerers' innards to take on their powers for themselves. And they'd used those powers on this being along with so many others.

A swell of regret washed through me. She might not want to be helping them. It might not be her fault at all. Not any more than it'd been the fault of any of the other shadowkind enslaved alongside me all those years ago.

"Can you come with me?" I asked. "The power will fade given enough time away from the ones who cast it. Or I might know someone who can help shatter it." Surely a demon like Rollick could manage to clear her mind from that influence?

But the shadowkind woman shook her head with a miserable expression. "I have my tasks," she said, her voice a croak now. "I must stick to my duties."

It was sickening, hearing her. A snarl hissed through my fangs. Well, I just wouldn't give her a choice then.

I shifted back into my full dragon form and clamped her to my scaled chest with one leg. My other limbs scrabbled down the mountainside as fast as they could carry me. Who knew what she might be able to tell us if Rollick could break through the magic on her? She could be the key—

She twisted in my hold abruptly. I whirled around, ready to snatch a firmer hold of her if she tried to escape—but she hadn't been trying to flee after all. At least, not that way.

She whipped her hand with its own much finer claws to her neck and tore it open all the way through to the spine.

Her filmy blood gushed up in a cloud. Her body went limp in my grasp. I growled in frustration, laying her down on the slope, but there was nothing I could do for her. She'd practically gouged her head right off her shoulders.

Had her masters ordered her to do *that* too? I grimaced with another surge of disgust.

I took only a moment to mourn the loss of my possible victory. I couldn't afford to stick around here in physical form very long. There was only one thing left I could do.

I sucked in the cool mountain air and then breathed my dragon fire over the body, just hot enough to incinerate the rest of her in a final gust of smoke without charring the ground beneath her.

She blew away in a quickly fading haze. There was no trace of her left—no evidence that anyone had caught her, that she'd been forced to take that desperate step. I glanced back toward the higher reaches of the mountain again, but a tug in my chest brought me leaping into the darkness down toward the base again.

There were powers here I couldn't challenge. But we'd discovered one of our enemies' bases of operations. That was some kind of victory still, wasn't it?

I just hoped I'd scrounged it up quickly enough for it to help Quinn survive these villains and their horrible intentions.

CHAPTER THIRTEEN

Quinn

By the end of my third session of sorcery, I'd compelled the little spiky creature to walk all along the railing from one end of the terrace to the other, jump into Rollick's arms—which it definitely did *not* want to do—and in an impromptu moment of inspiration for the demon, pounce on a gull that very unwisely decided to land on one of the lounge chairs.

The last command made me balk the most. I'd dawdled, hoping the gull would realize its impending doom and get the hell away. But Rollick had arched his eyebrows at me, and I'd thought about my parents somewhere below me. That'd been enough motivation to propel the strange words from my throat.

The creature had slammed the bird right off the chair onto the tiles as it tore open its throat. I didn't think I'd ordered it to *kill* the gull, but maybe the sorcery words for "pounce" and "slaughter" were the same... or maybe the mini monster simply couldn't imagine doing the former without also doing the latter.

Blood smeared across the tiles, and my stomach lurched. I jerked around, nausea continuing to roil in my gut.

Rollick seemed to realize he'd pushed me to my limit. He snatched up the beast by the scruff of its neck like it was an errant kitten, stuffed it back in the box, and did something with his supernatural powers that I couldn't follow but that resulted in both the bird and most of the blood vanishing within a matter of seconds. All that remained was a faintly pinkish smudge on the pale gray tiles. He cocked his head at it. "The next rain should take care of that."

The demon turned to me then, his dark blue eyes glinting slyly despite his haste to end the session. "You're doing very well, sorcerer. Maybe I'll bring a bigger beastie next time and see how well you can exert your will on it."

Maybe we should see what happens if I exert my will on you, I thought, but I kept the snarky words to myself this time. I hadn't forgotten how he'd threatened to make me practice on Lance. And over the past few days, I'd become increasingly conscious of the time ticking away before our deal was dissolved.

It'd been almost exactly seven days since the moment we'd made that deal. Rollick had snuck me into his suite a week ago. What was going to happen after three more days had passed? Was I impressing him enough, or would he decide my heart was more useful to him as dinner?

If I had impressed him... what was he going to want me to do next?

After he'd left, I roamed around the terrace and the living room, even more restless than usual. At least I might be able to negotiate safety for my parents if we set new terms. But on the other hand, I'd lost a lot of my bargaining power. Before, Crag could have fought for me on turf that wasn't any more familiar to Rollick than it was to the gargoyle. We could have made a run for it. Now, Rollick controlled almost everything about my situation.

What leverage did I really have?

Out on the terrace again, I squinted against the bright sun, peering at the terrace above mine. The one that jutted from Rollick's office, ending at the edge of his personal apartment's roof.

I'd made a lot of tricky scrambles over the past several years. Climbing up maintenance ladders, scaling fences designed to keep out the curious, hefting myself to a higher floor of an abandoned building through nothing but a hole in the floor. I should be able to manage that climb if I planned it carefully.

There was more on the uppermost levels of the hotel than just Rollick's office. I doubted the office itself was significantly bigger than his entire personal apartment, and the sub-penthouse floor had other regular hotel rooms like the one Torrent and I had made use of. I'd heard distant music and laughter from above before—one of the men had said something about a rooftop bar.

It still wouldn't be wise for me to let anyone else *see* me, but I'd like to know what I was working with here. Get a better sense of the layout of the hotel. Figure out what my potential escape routes might be if I felt I needed to make a run for it later.

Anything that might add one small advantage to my side.

I studied the patio chairs and dragged the sturdiest one over to the inner corner of the terrace. If I started to lose my balance, I could hop down on its padding, and it wouldn't be too bad a landing. I clambered from it onto the railing— first the stucco edge, then the steel bar that ran half a foot above the more solid wall.

From there, I could just reach the base of the office terrace. Rollick had opted for maximum visibility rather than privacy there, which served my purposes just fine. The whole barrier along the edge was made of steel posts with decent gaps in between them.

I grasped them and swung my legs up. I'd been keeping up my regular exercise routine during the long hours of boredom in the hotel room, and I hefted my weight without much trouble. In a moment, I was hooking my feet around two of the bars. With my legs holding the rest of me more stable, I pulled myself upright hand over hand until I could unhook one foot and then the other and swing right over the railing onto the terrace proper.

When my sneakers hit the tiles, which matched those on my own terrace below, I froze. For all I knew, the demon had come up to his office after he'd left me.

There wasn't much of anywhere to hide on this smaller outdoor space, which appeared to be intended mainly for schmoozing with potential business prospects rather than private relaxation. There were no chairs or loungers at all, only a couple of small, bar-height tables that looked designed to hold drinks while the people around them stood.

I waited for the space of several heartbeats, but no one emerged from behind the glass door that led into Rollick's office. Straightening up, I slunk over to it. Who knew what leverage I might be able to find in there?

I wasn't really surprised to discover that the door was locked, though. I peered through the glass into the shadowy interior, but I couldn't make out much beyond the thin wash of light that spilled through the windows, which revealed a thick carpet like the one downstairs and the shape of a desk with a bulky leather chair. Nothing particularly useful.

Better not to hang around on Rollick's immediate turf too long anyway. I went back to the railing, walking the length of it to get the full view from this slightly higher vantage point. I couldn't make out much more than the sprawl of ocean water I could see from my own terrace.

Jazzy notes were already lilting through the air from somewhere less distant now. I moved to the inner corner of the terrace and studied the wall.

The building protruded on either side of the terrace to hug its sides with solid, windowless stucco all the way up, no railing to clamber onto. But there was a rectangular bulge just above my reach, some kind of maintenance fixture, and a decorative slat above it that I thought would be wide enough to get my fingers around.

I eyeballed them for a minute, picturing the movements I'd need to make, and then dragged over one of the little tables. It wasn't as steady as the chair I'd used before, but when I braced it in the corner, I could heave myself onto it and balance with only a little wobbling.

From that height, I could hook my elbow over the

rectangular box. I leapt up, bracing my feet against the wall, and caught hold of the slat by the fingertips of my other hand.

For one dizzy moment, I thought I was going to skid back down to fall on my ass. Then I managed to shove my legs farther up and push off the box. Once I had one foot planted on it, hauling myself upright wasn't too much trouble.

I could see onto the roof over Rollick's office now—and it was just roof. The music and faint chatter I could now hear from the bar seemed to be coming from beyond a tall white wall that ran along the roof about twenty feet away, making sure no patrons wandered too close to Rollick's private domain. The area I could see was a plain, smooth white surface, dappled with rain-streaked grit here and there.

It obviously wasn't meant for visitors. There was no railing at all other than a simple bar that stood less than a foot high along the lip. But I was familiar with rooftops. I yanked myself up and over, crawled a few feet from the edge for safety's sake, and then walked the rest of the way over to the wall.

I didn't want anyone on the other side to get a glimpse of me, but I had to figure out whether the patio bar was accessible to me at all. If the hotel patrons used it, there must be a way to get down through the hotel from there. A potential escape route for desperate times.

But I'd only just reached the slanted shadow that fell along the looming wall when an unfamiliar lithe figure leapt into being a few feet away from me.

He jumped into my frame of view at an angle as if he'd

hopped over the wall. If I hadn't known shadowkind existed, I'd probably have believed that was what he'd done. But I knew he hadn't been there a moment ago—he'd flickered into being right out of the shadow above.

I backed up a step, tensing as he grinned at me. The stranger didn't look particularly monstrous at the moment, pale eyes gleaming amid peachy skin under a fall of rumpled chestnut hair, but I had no idea who he was either. And Rollick had been *very* clear that he didn't want any shadowkind at all finding out I was here.

Shit. Just how much had I potentially fucked up the security of my hideout by exploring like this?

And what the hell did I do now?

As my heart pounded, the shadowkind man cocked his head in a casual motion, looking me up and down. "You must be one of the owner's toys," he said in an amused tone. "Decided to do a little wandering? Has he kept you all caged up?"

"No," I blurted out. "I—I'm fine. I just wanted to get the best possible view." I motioned vaguely toward the seascape beyond the roof.

I had my silver pen-dagger in my pocket, but suddenly it felt woefully inadequate. I had trouble imagining where I could stab it that I could manage to land and that would slow this guy down even slightly. Attacking him might make the situation ten times worse. My hand dropped to my pocket just in case.

He stepped closer, and I automatically retreated, starkly aware of how much roof I had left before I couldn't back up at all. But the shadowkind man didn't pursue me any farther.

A slow smile stretched across his lips. When he spoke next, there was a strange melodic quality to his voice that shivered through my thoughts and into my bones.

"You'd like to play with me now. It's awfully hot up here, though. Better take that shirt off."

I wanted to sputter a laugh in his face. No way was I getting undressed because some random dude asked me to. But before my mouth could even open, my arms were rising, my hands grasping the hem of my tank top.

My pulse hitched. What the fuck? I tried to stiffen my muscles against the movement, but I couldn't stop them. It was like my common sense had been locked away by whatever magic he'd cast on me, and I couldn't regain control no matter how I wrenched at myself inside. Some deep part of my mind thought there was nothing odd at all about lifting the fabric up over my bra and—

With the cloth pulled up partly over my face, I only saw a blur of motion. There was a thump and a hiss and the start of a shout, cut off with a gurgle. The vice-like grip on my free will shattered. I whipped my hands and my shirt down, my skin damp with a chilly sweat.

In full demon form, Rollick had the other man, whatever kind of monster he was, pinned to the rooftop. He'd already slashed right through the guy's throat with his claws, sending smoky blood billowing up. He snarled down at the intruder, his demonic face twisted with vicious fury.

"This is what you get when you mess with me and mine," he spat out, and snuffed out whatever life had been left in the man by crushing the remains of his neck.

I hugged myself, my pulse still racing, as Rollick straightened up. Gripping the body, he dove into the shadows and returned an instant later empty-handed. Only a small smudge of smoke remained, wisping away into the air as I watched.

The demon turned toward me, wiping his hands together as he contracted into his less monstrous form. His normally cheerful face was darkened by a savage frown.

"Was that—was that one of the shadowkind that've been killing the sorcerers?" I asked. "He compelled me—he made me—"

Rollick was already shaking his head. His frown relaxed a little. "There are many shadowkind who can manipulate *mortals* to their will," he said. "We just generally can't control each other by that sort of means." He glowered at the spot where he'd caught the other man. "Too many cajoling merfolk around when you're near the ocean. Never trust a siren."

"Oh." My gaze slid to the water, mythic tales swimming up through my mind.

Was that how it felt for the shadowkind when sorcerers compelled them? I'd gotten one brief taste of supernatural persuasion, and even that had been horrifying.

I looked back at Rollick. "How did you know I was here?"

His expression turned to pure amusement. "I don't imagine you can blame me for being curious when I see the mortal who's *supposed* to be staying in her very nice rooms clambering around the hotel. But as you can see, I wasn't going to let you get into any actual danger. You're welcome, by the way."

"Thank you," I said automatically, but then a prickle of anger rose up inside me. The way he'd tackled the siren hadn't been so different from how he'd pinned *me* down just a couple of days ago, making promises that'd only been a shade distant from threats. I raised my chin. "Let's not pretend you're such a hero, though. You only protected me because you don't want anyone messing with your plans or inconveniencing *you*."

If he'd had the sort of persuasive power that other shadowkind had, maybe he'd have simply brainwashed my compliance just as quickly without a twinge of conscience. The only reason he hadn't let his succubus do it was because he didn't want her knowing I was here.

Rollick let out a huff that sounded more teasing than actually offended. "Whatever you think of my motivations, you're much better off now than you were five minutes ago. Did you discover all you hoped to, little adventurer?"

I gritted my teeth. "I just wanted a better sense of where I actually *am*. I wasn't going to let anyone see me—I didn't think anyone would be able to get over to this part of the roof."

"You came too close to the wall," Rollick informed me. "He wouldn't have been able to approach or affect you if you'd been over by the edge. But it's done now." He motioned to me. "Come on, let's get you back where you belong and see if we can't keep you in one piece for at least a few days longer."

CHAPTER FOURTEEN

Quinn

Any lingering anger I'd felt faded away into apprehension over the rest of the day. Rollick's growled words to the siren echoed through my head: *This is what you get when you mess with me and mine.*

He thought I belonged to him, even though I'd made it clear in every way I possibly could that I wasn't happy about being in his grasp. That I was only cooperating with him to protect myself and the people I cared about.

I was grateful for the deal he'd extended to me and the protection he'd offered, but the debt I sensed myself racking up was starting to weigh on me. Just how much was he going to end up asking for in return beyond what he'd already demanded?

I didn't know how to answer that question, and my attempts at getting more control over my situation had only made me more indebted to him. I checked my makeshift silver dagger in my pocket, not that it'd done me much good with the shadowkind stranger, and ran through my workout routine again, but no amount of exertion could burn off the uneasiness gripping me.

So, when a now-familiar soft tap sounded on the sliding door, relief rushed through my body. Maybe they couldn't fix everything that was wrong, but there was nothing I'd have welcomed more than the chance to spend more time with any of the three men I didn't mind calling me *theirs*.

I forced myself to hold off on going over to the terrace for a few minutes, puttering around sticking my dinner dishes in the dumbwaiter and finishing the current chapter of the book I'd been reading, even though the words barely sank in. Then I ambled over to my bedroom. There, I stretched my arms leisurely and drifted to the terrace door as if the mood had just happened to strike me to take in the fresh air.

My spirits lifted even higher when I saw that not just one but all three of my monstrous men had joined me again. I hadn't seen any of them in three days, and that past meet-up had been wrenchingly brief.

"It's so good to see you," I said as I hurried over to them. "How long can you stay this time?"

Torrent gave me the quiet but warm smile that he rarely brought out and that never failed to send a pleased shiver over my skin. "A few hours should be safe." He nudged the gargoyle's shoulder. "Rollick actually specifically asked Crag to keep watch down below while he had to zip out of town for the night. I don't think he expected Lance and I to make it back as quickly as we did."

"He didn't specifically say I *couldn't* watch over you from right beside you," Crag rumbled with an uncharacteristic hint of slyness in his dark eyes. I decided I liked it.

"I can't think of a better vantage point," I said with a laugh.

I grabbed them each in a hug—and naturally Lance swept me into a kiss as well, tracing his claws lightly down my spine until I was quivering against him as he claimed my mouth. Torrent cleared his throat, and the dragon shifter lifted his head with a grin. "We've left her alone too long. Need to make up for it."

"I'm sure there'll be plenty of time for that," Torrent said in a tone that managed to be both dry and laced with heat. He tipped his head toward the side of the hotel. "And since we've got the time, we can have a more relaxed conversation if we hop over to that other room. It's empty again."

Crag shifted without any further prompting, unfurling his leathery gray wings from his stony gargoyle form. My gaze lingered on the scars that gripped through the taut skin there, but he didn't show any sign of discomfort.

The first couple of times he'd flown me anywhere, I hadn't known whether I could trust him, whether he might be whisking me off to my doom. Now I stepped into his arms without hesitation. I couldn't imagine anywhere I'd feel safer.

The other two men vanished into the night to travel through the darkness to the balcony around the corner of the building. Crag leapt over the railing and crossed the distance with a few brisk flaps, staying close to the wall where it was darkest. It was only a little past dinner time, the sun completely set but lights still beaming in many windows and along the perimeter of the property I could now see below me.

The second he'd landed on the balcony, Crag transformed back into his still impressive but not quite so gigantic human appearance. He'd always seemed a bit reluctant to let me take a good look at him in his monstrous form, even though I didn't find anything about him horrifying.

Lance wavered into being next to us at the same moment as Torrent blinked into being on the other side of the balcony door. The tentacled man unlocked it and slid it open to admit us.

Torrent had told me last time that he would arrange fresh linens for the bed after he'd brought me back to Rollick's rooms. We didn't want any of the staff realizing someone had been using the suite without permission. I couldn't tell if it'd had any guests since then. The air smelled crisp and clean but a little stale. I left the sliding door open so the fresh ocean breeze could wash through the room and sat on the edge of the bed.

"How have your investigations been going?" I asked. "Have you figured anything more out about the shadowkind who're hunting for me?"

"We're hunting them right back," Lance announced, slicing his claws through the air, and shot me a brilliant grin that turned his always ferally gorgeous face even more stunning. "I found their den. Or one of their dens, anyway. We know one place they like to hang out with the poor beasties they've turned into slaves."

The triumph in his tone darkened with those last few words. He bared his teeth, his dragon fangs out in his otherwise human face. A pang of sympathy filled my chest, sharper with my guilt over the way *I'd* been bending one beast to my will over the past few days. I hadn't liked doing it, but I'd bowed to Rollick's will anyway.

I tried to push those thoughts aside. "Is it nearby? Do they seem to suspect that I'm in L.A.?"

Lance shook his head and dropped onto the bed beside me, tucking his arm around my waist. "Not even in the same state. I still don't know *what* exactly they are. They like mountains, and they play with rocks."

"One of them, anyway," Crag rumbled. "I did talk to a being that'd been around them briefly who said one of the apparent leaders gave an earthy impression."

"It's probably not their only base of operations," Torrent said. "Most likely they've got at least a few camps spread around in this country and others abroad, just like Rollick has all his properties—as much as he likes focusing on this one for the moment." He paused. "It is useful information, though, for making our own plans. We know where to find them."

If we wanted to pass on a message about my current location, he meant. "Well, that's something." I tried to sound optimistic, but I suspected I'd failed.

"We'll put all the pieces together and then shred *them* to pieces," Lance said with typical vicious confidence. I wished I could be that optimistic.

Crag gazed down at me, his broad brow furrowing. "Are you all right, Quinn? You seem more... dispirited than before."

It was true that my initial joy at seeing them had faded with the realization of how far we still were from a solution.

I hadn't meant to disturb him with my worries, even if it brought a pang of affection into my chest to know he'd noticed despite my efforts.

I wasn't going to lie to him now that he had picked up on my feelings. I rubbed my hand over my face. "It's just—there are only three more days in the deal. I don't know how Rollick will want to change it then, or whether he'll even agree to making another one."

"If he won't guarantee your safety, we'll figure out something else," Torrent said. "You know we can get to you and take you away from here if we absolutely have to."

"But there's still so much we don't know about who we're up against or what they want."

"We have three more days to figure that out," Lance declared. "We've made a lot of progress already. Have faith, baby girl." He nuzzled the side of my face playfully and then trailed his claws along my arm, his voice dipping lower. "Maybe what you need is a distraction from all the worries wiggling through that pretty head."

I swallowed thickly, but a flare of heat had washed over my body at his skillful touch. "What kind of distraction did you have in mind?"

He snorted in amusement and leaned in to nip the crook of my jaw. "I think you know. I haven't gotten to enjoy my lovely explorer in a *week*. We can do all the things you like, and maybe discover new things you do too."

The vibe in the room had shifted, the air seeming to warm despite the cool current from the air conditioning system, all three of my men's focus narrowing down to me with an intense alertness. Another quiver ran through me, but it seemed to provoke a jolt of energy through my heart

—a jolt of that sorcerer power that made my pulse shudder. I sucked in a breath.

"I've been compelling a shadowkind creature," I said abruptly. "A little lesser beast that Rollick's keeping caged. He's getting me to tap into the magic more and more."

I expected Lance to recoil at my statement, even braced myself for it, but the dragon shifter's lips kept nibbling down the side of my neck. "When we get you away from him, you won't need to do that either."

Something in me unwound just a little. If even Lance, who'd been tormented by sorcerers for I had no idea how long, didn't blame me for going along with the demon's demands, then maybe I shouldn't blame myself either. Maybe I shouldn't hold myself back from what I wanted out of some sense that I didn't deserve it.

I did want this—I wanted the shadowkind men who'd stood with me through all the chaos so far. Not just to stoke the heat kindling low in my belly, but to reconfirm with kisses and caresses as we already had with words that nothing could tear us apart from each other. Rollick hadn't been able to stop us from having this interlude, and we wouldn't let him stop us from winning our freedom either.

For a moment, it seemed that simple. I raised one hand to stroke my fingers into Lance's silky curls and over his scalp. He let out an encouraging hum and grazed his fangs across my shoulder. At a much more enjoyable skip of my pulse, I glanced up at my other two men.

Crag had shared me with the dragon shifter before in an encounter on the yacht, the memory of which made the heat inside me flare twice as hot. But Torrent... that time, Lance had invited both of them to join in, and the tentacled man had turned his back on us before I'd even been able to agree.

But that was before we'd understood each other better. Before I'd been able to show him that I saw him as more than a curiosity, and he'd shown me that he'd defy his own boss to protect me. We were in a very different place now, and not just geographically.

As if he sensed my uncertainty and wanted to reassure me, Torrent met my gaze and sank down onto the bed at my other side. He let one tentacle trail across my shoulder in a tender caress. "I look forward to seeing how much you can enjoy yourself with all three of us on the task."

So did I, especially when that hungry note crept into his voice. I reached toward Crag to make sure he knew he was fully included, and the gargoyle gave me a smile that was almost shy as he knelt at my feet. "We'll take very good care of you, Softness."

He slipped off one of my sneakers and then the other, the undressing oddly seductive even though it was only my feet. Lance tugged at my shirt. "You don't want me slicing this up."

It could be thrilling having him undress me in his... uniquely savage way, but— "I think Rollick might notice if one of my few outfits ends up in shreds. And my current wardrobe is small enough as it is."

"I'm sure we can manage to take care of your clothes too," Torrent said wryly, tucking his tentacle under the hem of the top. With a deft tug and the lift of my arms, he pulled it right off me.

Lance had watched that motion with an avidness I didn't totally understand until he caught my arms before I lowered them again. He glanced across at Torrent with a sly grin. "Hold her wrists." Before I could worry that he was still nervous of me after all, he licked his tongue along my jaw and murmured, "It shows her how much she's ours."

Well, if that was the only reason he wanted me restrained, I wouldn't argue about it. Especially because a giddy shiver ran through me as Torrent carefully coiled his tentacle around both my wrists, pinning them together above my head. The suction cups seemed to mouth my skin like a dozen simultaneous kisses, and the slight stretch made my breasts rise within my bra.

Lance managed to flick open the clasp with his nimble claws without severing the fabric. He tugged the bra aside with his teeth and flicked his now-ridged dragon tongue over the peak.

I gasped at the shock of headier pleasure, and there was something erotic about the way my hands caught in Torrent's grasp. Holding me on display, baring me for my men's attentions—making this moment all about what they could do for me without any expectation or even possibility of me returning the favor.

I did want to return the bliss as much as I could before the interlude was over, but for now, this was a different sort of fun for all of us.

As Lance worked over my breast and Crag stroked his large hands along my legs, Torrent leaned in to capture my mouth. His kiss had the passion of a stormy sea, the yearning in it leaving me breathless. When he released my lips, he eased behind me on the bed to leave more room for the other men, never loosening his grasp on my wrists.

He slipped another tentacle around my torso to pluck

at my other nipple with the suckers until I leaned back into his lean frame with a whimper. The need building between my legs made me squirm. Torrent let out a heated chuckle and tucked the tentacle under my breast as if to offer it up to the man in front of me.

Crag didn't hesitate to accept the invitation. He pushed up on his knees and leaned in to taste my breast, his tongue stretching from regular human shape to its extended, sinuous gargoyle anatomy before my eyes. He wrapped the tip right around my nipple and tugged, and I jerked with a desperate mewling sound.

Lance was still conjuring all kinds of sparks in my other breast with his own special tongue. He wasn't diverted from finding even more ways to bring me pleasure, though. He delved his hand between us to deftly undo the fly of my jean shorts. Crag rumbled and tugged the shorts off me without pausing his administrations.

The dragon shifter stroked his claws lightly over my sex, and I spread my legs wider with an eager trembling at the delight his wicked touch provoked. Then a tentacle was slipping down my belly to pluck my clit the way it had my nipple. A full-out moan reverberated from my lungs, and Lance raised his head in time to catch the end of it with his mouth against mine.

I swayed and writhed between the three men, bliss rushing through me from so many directions that the room around me blurred. But I heard Crag's deep thrum of a voice clear as anything when he said, "I haven't tasted her yet."

"Mmm," Lance murmured. "You shouldn't miss out

on that. Better than any food I've ever eaten." He laughed and began charting a new scorching path along my neck.

Crag gazed up at me as he tugged my panties down. Without the use of my arms, I couldn't reach out and pull him to me to show him how much I wanted this experience too, but I shifted my hips toward him. "If you want to..."

"Oh, very much," he said with an odd formality that somehow made the moment even hotter. Torrent raised his tentacle to tease across my breasts again, clearing the way for the gargoyle to lower his head between my legs.

His tongue slid over my clit, encompassing it so thoroughly another moan burst from my lips. "Even softer here," he said with a sound like a sigh, and then he was pressing his whole mouth against my pussy.

His upper lip massaged my clit while his extended tongue delved right inside me. It had the same wonderful flexibility as Torrent's tentacles, but the combination of his hot breath and the rocky texture of his jaw against my thighs made it a totally different sensation. A fucking amazing sensation.

I rocked against his mouth, unable to do more than that and whimper as Torrent tweaked my nipples and Lance trailed his claws over my belly and down my back. God, when had I ever felt as *alive* as right now, with these three fearsome men focusing all their attention on bringing me to the greatest heights of pleasure they could supply?

Whatever happened in the future, I was definitely never going back to mortal guys. None of them had ever really understood me anyway. With these three men, as inhuman as they were, I felt strangely understood. Seen in ways I'd never felt comfortable letting any person get a glimpse of.

Crag growled and lapped his tongue deeper inside me. I was shuddering with the unfurling bliss now, rushing higher and faster with every movement of his mouth and the other men's touches. "Oh, fuck," I mumbled as he clamped his lips even more firmly on my pussy, and arched to meet him. Then my release crashed over me, leaving me shaking and slack between the three men.

Lance nuzzled my hair. "And she does enjoy the meal so much," he said with fond amusement.

Crag pressed one last kiss to my folds and beamed up at me, his normally hardened face radiant with his satisfaction. "Then that makes two of us."

The dragon shifter vanished and reappeared in the blink of an eye, leaving his clothes behind in the shadows. He swiveled me toward him, his violet eyes gleaming. "My turn. It's been too long since I got to feel her all around me. My favorite place to be."

He grinned at me, and an urge came over me to make this my own claiming as well as theirs. If I belonged to them, then they belonged to me just as much.

I yanked at my wrists, and Torrent must have sensed there was a different quality to the motion than my earlier instinctive resistance. His tentacle uncoiled, and I swiveled around to land right on Lance's lap, straddling him.

Surprise flickered across the dragon shifter's face, but it came with a flare of hunger. "Our mortal wants to take charge," he teased. "What are you going to do with me now, baby girl?"

I rocked my slick cunt against his already rigid erection, making him hiss as his eyelids drooped with pleasure. His total trust that whatever I had in mind would be just as enjoyable for him too set off a surge of twined affection and exhilaration inside me. "I'm going to let you feel me all around you," I said with a smirk, echoing his earlier words, and sank right down onto him.

His cock filled me so well, even more so when I felt the head swell larger inside me into its dragon shape. My breath caught, and Lance smirked right back at me, knowing the effect his monstrous features had on me. He glided his claws up and down my thighs as he gazed at me.

There were other benefits to sitting up instead of being pinned under him, I realized. As I found the best position over Lance's lap, swaying up and down over his cock experimentally, the other two men drew closer on either side of me. They'd only meant to keep up their assault of pleasure, Torrent trailing his tentacle over my body, Crag capturing my mouth, but it occurred to me that in this position, I could bring them all with me and Lance on this ecstatic journey.

"Both of you, clothes off too," I mumbled around a groan as Lance pushed his hips up to meet me, filling me deeper than before. They performed the same trick the dragon shifter had, shedding their clothes in an instant and revealing their own sculpted bodies to my eager gaze.

I kissed Crag again, stroking my hand over his bulging arm, and then turned to where Torrent was kneeling beside me. With my other hand, I traced the rows of suckers that protruded from the back of his upper arm—the one shadowkind feature he couldn't leave behind completely, although his tentacles were almost essential now to support his legs. He brushed one of those beneath my chin to giddying effect, and it occurred to me that I hadn't tasted *him* yet. His cock was standing at rigid attention within my sights.

I twisted at the waist and lowered myself carefully, stretching my arm to trace my hand down Crag's body at the same time as I dipped toward Torrent. Catching my intent, Lance leaned back on his hands and both of the other men shifted even closer. Torrent's chest hitched as I flicked my tongue over the head of his erection.

"Quinn," he muttered, nothing but longing in the way he said my name. It made me twice as eager to take him.

I wrapped my mouth around his cock and my fingers around Crag's thick shaft at the same time. Lance had held still, watching my progress with apparent delight. As I found a rhythm with the other two men, he started to roll his hips against me again.

"That's right, baby girl," he said, his voice becoming strained with need. "You were meant for all of us. Look at you."

His last words cut off with a growl. He thrust into me more forcefully, and I gasped around Torrent's cock. Rocking with the dragon shifter, I slicked my tongue around Torrent's length to lap up the salty flavor that tasted so much like the ocean and gripped Crag's shaft tighter with the pump of my hand.

The gargoyle groaned and pressed kisses over my back. Torrent looped a tentacle all the way around my waist, the tip dropping to stroke my clit just above where Lance and I were joined. I moaned and sucked him down as deep as I could without choking. His hips jerked toward me with a growl of his own.

It was a maelstrom of desire and bliss, and it wrapped

around me so thoroughly that everything faded away except the joint motion of our bodies and the pleasure blazing through me. Crag's fingers dug into my hair with a grasp that was just shy of painful. I squeezed him harder, and he came with a grunt and clamp of his mouth against my shoulder blade.

Lance hummed encouragingly and rocked with me faster. Torrent's tentacle tightened around my waist, the tip strumming my clit into a chorus of ecstasy, and I swayed with them both, driving us all toward release.

Despite my intention of getting the men there before me, I broke first. Lance surged up inside me at just the right moment with the flick of Torrent's tentacle, and pleasure exploded through my body.

My pussy clenched around Lance, and he came with me in a spurt of heat. My mouth closed more firmly around Torrent too, and he grasped the back of my head. "I'm going to—"

Good. I sucked him down, and he emptied himself into my mouth with a ragged cry that nearly tipped me over the edge all over again. *I'd* brought him that much pleasure.

I'd taken all of them, my monstrous lovers, and shown I could handle it. Shown just how good we were together in every possible way. They understood me, and I understood them. Maybe we'd all become something more by finding each other.

Lance yanked me down next to him on the bed, and the other men tucked themselves close. Surrounded by their heat, I let myself doze for just a moment, adrift on the satisfaction of knowing this one thing Rollick couldn't steal from us.

CHAPTER FIFTEEN

Quinn

I woke up in Rollick's bedroom to the beeping of my alarm. As I sat up and grabbed my pill case, the memory of last night's encounter with the three shadowkind men—whose bedrooms I'd rather have been staying in—rushed through my body with a pleasant achiness of muscles well-worked. Then I thought of the hour we'd spent afterward, dozing companionably and then talking about all the things we'd want to do together when I wasn't being pursued by any kind of villains, and the heat turned into an ache of affection.

Maybe I really could someday swim in the ocean with Torrent, and fly over Crag's favorite landscapes with him, and sample every flavor of ice cream in the supermarket with Lance. People had overcome worse obstacles than this, hadn't they? I'd like to think so, anyway.

I missed them already, but something about the sensation gave me a fresh burst of confidence. I still had cards to play. I wasn't a total victim. By the time Rollick showed up after I'd showered and eaten, I was ready for him, bolstered by my growing resolve.

He stepped into the room carrying a black carrier that looked a little larger than before. I remembered his suggestion that he'd bring a creature that was more of a challenge this time. My chest clenched up momentarily, but I stood firm, bracing my feet against the floor and squaring my shoulders.

Rollick took in my stance and paused rather than walking straight across to the terrace. He raised his eyebrows. "You look like a woman with a mission," he said with a smile as if he enjoyed seeing it. "Still plenty of energy to spare, I see."

I wasn't sure what he meant by that comment when it was first thing in the morning. What would I have been expending my energy on before now? But the demon could shove his charm up his ass regardless.

"Before we do any more training, I want to see my parents," I said.

Rollick's eyebrows arched a tad higher. "I thought we'd already covered *very* thoroughly why any interaction with people from your regular life is a bad—"

"I'm not asking to talk to them," I interrupted. "I know I can't do that without making a big mess. But they've been right here in this hotel for days. You're a super powerful demon. There's got to be some way you can let me get a look at them in person, even if they can't see me. I just want to confirm with my own eyes that they're totally okay."

And it was an excuse to take a look at more of the hotel itself as well. What surreptitious ways would Rollick bring me through the building that I might be able to make use of on my own later?

Rollick set the carrier down on the sofa and leaned against the arm in a casual stance. "Unfortunately, that's impossible."

I resisted the urge to roll my eyes at him. "Impossible, or you just don't want to?"

"Your parents aren't here anymore," he said. "I arranged for their trip home yesterday, which to the best of my knowledge went perfectly smoothly. The activity happening back in Florida that concerned me petered out, and there was no sign that they'd be in any further danger there. Frankly, if the idiots after you aren't looking for you over there any longer, your parents are safer outside your current orbit."

"Oh." I didn't know what to say to that. I didn't know what to even think about it. He'd given up a major point of leverage over me... Probably because he'd decided I was cooperating enough that he didn't need the immediate threat to propel me along. It wasn't as if we didn't both know that if he wanted to hurt my parents, he could have them in his clutches again in a matter of minutes.

But the information had taken the wind out of my sails. I couldn't stand firm and make demands when fulfilling those demands actually *was* pretty much impossible. I sucked my lower lip under my teeth but caught myself before I'd worried at it more than a few seconds. Then I narrowed my eyes at Rollick. "How can I be sure that you really did send them home and you're not just saying that so I won't insist on seeing them?"

"I don't know," he said, sounding not at all bothered by

the possibility that I might consider him a liar. "It's very difficult to prove the *non*-existence of something—in this case, the non-existing of your parents within this city. I could take you on a tour of the entire hotel and no doubt you'd accuse me of tucking them away someplace else. We have more important matters to focus on." He tapped the top of the box he'd brought.

My hackles rose. "Important to *you*. I didn't want to be throwing my sorcerer powers around in the first place."

"But look at how much progress you've made already! It really is impressive. If you have another horde come at you like I'm told has happened a few times already, you'll at least be able to deflect a few of the lesser creatures without any trouble. Maybe even send them after their own allies." He motioned toward the terrace. "Let's get on with it. I'd rather not conduct this experiment inside. I like my furniture enough not to want to see it clawed up."

My frustration at yet another failed strategy boiled over. My back went rigid. "No. I don't want to participate in any more 'experiments' until you tell me what it is you're hoping to gain out of all this. I know you're not just looking to help me protect myself. You wanted me. You think I'm going to be useful to you in some way. I think it's about time you properly explained."

Rollick cocked his head, still smiling. My hands clenched against the urge to smack the grin right off his face. I could practically hear him thinking how ridiculous it was that I thought I could demand anything from *him*.

I wasn't sure what I would do if he refused. At what point would he claim I was reneging on our deal and bring out more concrete threats to my own safety? But I was so tired of him assuming he could call all the shots here.

To my surprise, he didn't threaten or argue. He pushed off the sofa and strolled closer to me, his grin turning sly.

I backed up a step, but I was already just a couple of feet from the bookcase. I stopped before my shoulders hit it, my pulse thumping faster. And, damn it, when he loomed over me close enough for the warmth of his body to touch me even though no part of him had actually brushed my skin, the adrenaline rushing through me wasn't only apprehension.

"Is my sorcerer so restless that she needs other kinds of stimulation?" the demon asked in a crooning voice. He traced his fingers through the air following the line of my arm but not quite grazing my flesh, and a shiver ran through my nerves. "Have I not been giving you enough attention after all? You only need to ask for what you're craving."

"I'm not craving *you*," I spat out. Some stupid part of my body was curious about what he could do for it, sure, but I had no problem ignoring that part when it came to how I actually acted.

"Maybe I just haven't found the right approach yet," Rollick suggested. "Would you like me better if I took the decision away from you? Tied your arms over your head so you had nothing to do but respond to me? Hmm, from the look that just came into your eyes, I think that might be just the thing."

"Don't you dare—" I started, and then froze with a rush of cold that washed away even the flickers of attraction

I'd been suppressing. The image he'd presented sounded way too specific. Way too familiar.

He'd never said anything about restraining me before, and now, the morning after Torrent had "tied" my arms over my head on Lance's instructions, the demon was bringing it up out of the blue? And bringing it up so confidently too, as if he'd been sure I'd react well.

I jerked away from him, moving around him into the more open area of the room where I had space to maneuver. My heart was suddenly thumping twice as fast, but it was only horror reverberating through my veins now. "Were you *watching*?" The men had said that Rollick had left town for the night, but it could have been a set-up—had he suspected and wanted to catch us?

But he hadn't confronted us then or even now... What was he playing at?

"What was there to watch?" he asked, but I thought his gaze had gotten more intent as he studied my reaction. "Have you been naughty, my little mortal?"

My teeth set on edge. Every nerve in my body was screaming to run from here, but there was nowhere to run. No way of getting away from him. And what if I was just imagining the connection?

My mind tripped back through our entire conversation and stuck on that odd remark he'd made about how much energy I still had. As if he knew I'd been occupied in a rather intense physical encounter last night.

No, it couldn't be just a coincidence. Maybe *we'd* been idiots to think he wouldn't find out.

"So you're a pervert and a liar," I shot at him. "You can't even own up to... to..." To violating my privacy. To leering at us from the shadows. Just thinking about it made my skin crawl.

Something shifted in Rollick's expression. A hint of a fiercer light glinted in his eyes, a glimpse of the monster lurking behind them showing through. "I know everything that goes on in this building, no matter how clever the beings within it think they are. A prime sub-penthouse room doesn't stay empty just by happenstance. And I have every right to record what goes on within my property."

To record... Then he hadn't been there in person. He really had left last night, but he'd had some kind of cameras running. I didn't know if that made the situation better or worse.

It occurred to me in another icy splash of revulsion that the first time he'd been particularly provocative with me, when he'd shown off his demonic form not just as a threat but a sort of promise of sexual gratification, it'd been the morning after my first interlude with Torrent. My stomach churned.

"So you treated me like pornography and then decided to use what you saw to advance your own agenda, whatever the hell that is?" I snapped.

The demon blinked slowly, that fucking smile still in place if cooler now. "I've never hidden the fact that I believe in drawing on every advantage at my disposal. You're a difficult one. But if I understand you better, then it's to your benefit as well as my own."

Because he still thought I was going to let him put his hands on me. I suppressed a shudder, backing away one step and another. Rollick prowled after me with languid steps, his grin turning wry again. Like he figured he could charm away my horror.

I had my silver sort-of dagger in my pocket, but I couldn't imagine stabbing him with it doing any real good. I tried to picture jabbing it into his eye—but then what? Even if I pulled off that move without him stopping me, I'd have a furious demon on my hands and nowhere to go.

I wavered, definitely not at all predator now no matter how I'd taken charge with my men last night. In Rollick's presence, I felt all prey—and it wasn't a comfortable feeling.

The demon advanced again, and instinct took over. I darted into the bedroom and slammed the door. It was a useless gesture against a being who could slip right through the tiny gap beneath it—or smash the whole door down—if he wanted to, but the gesture gave me a fragment of a sense of control.

"Leave me alone," I shouted through the door. "I'm not doing *anything* for you or with you, so just—just go away."

And then I braced myself for the retribution to come.

CHAPTER SIXTEEN

Quinn

I stood in silence for one minute and then another. No sound carried from the living room. A gust of ocean wind warbled past the windows across from me. Then I thought I heard the click of the suite door closing.

Could Rollick really have *left*, just like that? I was still shaking, both keyed up and afraid, and the thought of opening the bedroom door to check made every muscle in my body lock up even though it was hardly a significant barrier to the demon anyway.

I gulped in breath after breath, struggling to settle my nerves. But my mind kept leaping from thought to thought, each jolting me with fresh spikes of panic.

Had my men and I said anything incriminating during our guestroom interludes? Did Rollick have audio recording in the room or only video? We'd been out on the terrace when we'd first discussed turning our enemies against each other, but was it possible Torrent had missed a recording device out there?

Would Rollick have focused on my sexual proclivities if he thought we were plotting against him? I had no idea. He obviously played a long game, by standards incomprehensible to my human morality. I had no idea what he'd consider acceptable, what he'd be willing to let slide for now so he could turn it against us later.

I stalked over to the sliding door and then back to the bed, my hands opening and closing at my sides. My thoughts slipped back to last night, to the tenderness and passion I'd enjoyed with my three men, and queasiness bubbled up inside me. I couldn't take any comfort in the memories now that I had to imagine Rollick watching the whole scene, taking in every gasp and moan I made, scheming about how he could manipulate me by knowing what turned me on.

He'd watched every single intimate moment I'd shared with my lovers since I'd gotten here. Ogled my naked body. Watched me writhe and shudder with abandon...

My stomach outright heaved. I shoved open the bedroom door and only just made it to the bathroom in time to puke my breakfast into the toilet.

I crouched there on the cool tiles for several minutes until I was sure I wasn't going to vomit again. The shakes gradually subsided, but I still felt off-balance, both in my head and my stomach. Gradually, it occurred to me that if Rollick *had* still been lurking in the suite, after that display he'd probably have come to make sure I was all right.

Gathering myself, I crept out into the living room. By all appearances, the demon was gone, as was the carrier he'd brought. I guessed he'd figured I needed some space to process what I'd learned. No doubt he'd be back again in a few hours, acting like nothing had changed, expecting us to go on with my training session after all.

My body went rigid at the idea. Resistance clanged through every part of me. To go along with his demands, to keep bowing to his whims, when he'd shown just how monstrous he could be... I'd rather throw myself off the damn terrace.

The second that thought passed through my mind, everything in me went still. I paused and then walked over to the sliding door.

The breeze was light today, wafting over me with a faint saltiness and tickling my hair across my shoulders as I stepped out onto the tiles. A grayish haze muted the summer sunlight, making the ocean look darker and deeper. I glanced at the spot where I'd met up with my three men last night, but of course they weren't there.

Rollick would have sent them off on some new mission, of course. Who knew if he'd even let them come see me again at all? He'd known they were sneaking in all along, so he probably had ways to keep them out if he really wanted to. Now he'd gotten all the information he needed, and he knew his tactics had been uncovered. He wasn't learning anything else from me in this hotel.

I couldn't wait for them. I couldn't count on them getting to me before the deal ended and Rollick could set new terms—or simply have me for lunch, if he decided that was the best option. I still had my phone. He'd taken the SIM card, but it had Torrent's phone number programmed into it. If I could get out of here now, while the demon thought I was too shell-shocked to do much of anything, I'd be able to find another phone and get in touch with them again.

I wavered over the decision for a few minutes, knowing how risky it was. But every time I considered sticking this situation out, waiting until Rollick came with more demands, my gut twisted tighter and my skin started crawling.

I *couldn't* stay. I couldn't stand to spend one more minute in that monster's presence. My parents were back home—and he couldn't threaten them if he couldn't talk to me about what he might do. I just had to get away, as far away from him as I could.

My pulse thrumming faster, I pushed into the bedroom and dug the silver-and-iron vest out of the bottom of my backpack where I'd stuffed it. Running away wouldn't get me very far if the demon and my other enemies could track me the second I moved past the protective barrier a few floors down.

I pulled the vest on over my tank top. Then I filled my water bottle to the brim, grabbed the remaining snacks from a basket that'd been sent up a few days earlier in between meals, and stuffed everything into my backpack, including my messenger bag. It'd be easier to carry one bag rather than both. I slung the straps over my shoulders, secured them tight, and headed back out onto the terrace.

I already knew I could handle the climb to the roof. I also knew that there were guestrooms with balconies around the corner of the building beyond Rollick's suite. I couldn't reach them directly from the terrace without the help of tentacles or wings, but I could go up and over. At least in theory.

There was no telling when Rollick might return. For all I knew, he was already watching me from the shadows. Another shiver of horror rippled over my skin, and I hurried over to the corner.

I went through the same motions as yesterday briskly and efficiently, knowing exactly what I needed to do now. The backpack threw off my weight a little, but by the time I'd clambered onto Rollick's office terrace above, I'd adjusted to it. I normally carried a bag with me during my urban explorations, so the sense of bulk on my back was more familiar than going without.

With another quick scramble, I made it onto the roof. I hurried over to the side where I knew the guestroom balconies were, staying within a few feet of the edge rather than venturing closer to the barrier wall where the siren had used his persuasive influence on me. Rollick had said there were protections here.

But none of them were strong enough to stop *him* from moving all over the hotel. How had I ever thought I could stand a chance going head-to-head with him?

My deal had bought myself and my men some time. Maybe that time had ended up exposing me to the demon in ways I'd never have wanted, but I wasn't going to let myself regret that choice. Now I just had to make some new ones.

At the northern side of the building, I peered down over the edge of the roof toward the balconies below. To my relief, I discovered that there were rooms on the same level as Rollick's office as well as the floor below. I didn't have to attempt a twenty-foot descent to find solid ground. All the way below was the side alley where Rollick had dropped me off. No one was walking around in there. The building across from the hotel had only a few windows on that wall. I should be able to go unnoticed.

Even a ten-foot descent was going to be a little unpleasant. Now I appreciated the tiny railing along the roof. I gripped it with both hands and eased my body over the edge, walking my feet down until the soles of my sneakers hit the edge of the room's window frame. My metal-beaded vest rustled against my torso. I pushed a little farther, my toes skidding against the glass and my body stretching, and then let myself drop the last few feet.

The impact jarred my legs, but I'd felt worse. I shook them out and peered through the balcony's sliding door into the guestroom above the one my men and I had occupied for a short while just yesterday.

No one stirred inside. I jiggled the door handle and confirmed it was locked. Too bad I wasn't a shadowkind who could just slip through the shadows—although then I'd have been trapped by the silver and iron Rollick had built into the hotel anyway.

It was easier to take a lay of the land by daylight. Glancing along this side of the building, I saw there were two more balconies, each spaced just a few feet apart. I should be able to manage that jump. At least one of them was occupied, a towel draped over the railing to dry and a book left on a table next to a lounge chair. That didn't mean the door would be unlocked, but if the inhabitants were around, I could hope they'd let me through their room. Or at least give me an opening to make a run for it through the space to the door.

If none of them opened... I supposed I could find a way to descend to the next level of balconies. I didn't want to think about that yet.

The nervous adrenaline coursing through my veins pushed me onward. I scrambled onto the bars of the far side of the balcony railing, wishing that these ones had the same stucco wall as Rollick's private terrace for a broader base, and studied the gap I had to cross.

No looking down. Looking down would only eat away at my courage.

I needed to be as light as possible for this leap. I took off my backpack and tossed it across ahead of me. The ease of the throw and the soft thump of it hitting the floor on the next balcony soothed my nerves a little.

With my hand against the hotel wall for balance, I braced my feet on the top bar, crouched with leg muscles coiled, and sprang.

I knew better than to try to hurl myself right onto the balcony. Instead, I only aimed to catch the opposite railing. I flung my arms over it as my chest smacked into it and simply clung there for a few seconds, catching my breath and recovering from the impact. That probably hadn't been great for my heart.

But Rollick was a hell of a lot worse for it.

Gritting my teeth, I hefted myself over the railing and checked the next room. No sign of the guests staying there; no response when I tapped on the glass. That door was locked too. Shit.

One more to try on this level before I had to worry

about my journey getting even more complicated. If the next door was locked too, I could always smash the glass and get in that way, right? If I could manage to hit the pane hard enough—they'd be made of tough stuff. And that might set off an alarm...

I pushed those worries aside to focus on simply getting over to the last balcony. First, toss the backpack over. Then, clamber up on the railing. Prepare and leap—

It should have worked as easily as the first time. But I hadn't realized that whoever was staying in the last suite had gotten the railing wet, maybe with a hanging bathing suit they'd since taken inside. My arms slammed over the top of the railing—and slid on the layer of water before I could get a proper hold.

I groped out at the railing as I started to plummet. My fingers snagged around a vertical bar, but they were pulled down by the weight of my falling body, and an instant later they smacked into the base of the railing. The impact broke my hold.

My heart lurching to my throat, I clawed at the wall beside me—and grasped a decorative hook where maybe hanging flowerpots were sometimes displayed. I managed to scrape my feet against the wall enough to slow my fall, clinging on to the hook as tightly as I could. The thing was only as wide as my hand. My palm was already aching, the metal edges digging into my skin.

I slapped one hand on top of the other, leaning against the hotel wall as well as I could while dangling and fighting through my panic. I was maybe three feet below the balcony I'd been aiming for—there was no way I'd be able to reach my arm high enough to pull myself back up there.

Back to where I'd left my bag. My phone, my pills, all my things—

I squeezed my eyes shut, doing my best to tune out those frantic thoughts and the pain spreading through my arms and shoulders. None of that mattered if I ended up flat as a pancake on the ground below.

I cast my gaze downward for the first time, my gut flipping with dizziness at the sight of the several floors below. Then I realized something even more horrifying.

The suite I was dangling next to didn't have an outdoor area at all, only a row of tall glossy windows. The one at my other side had a small balcony, but it was farther off to my right, the top of it level with my knees right now. If I tried to swing in that direction, I was afraid the remaining strength in my hands might give out.

And even if I could land my feet on the railing, that wouldn't do me much good. I needed to hook a limb right over it to be sure of catching myself when I let go. I wasn't sure I was tall enough to manage that.

Tears started to burn behind my eyes, as much from fear as the pain creeping steadily deeper into my hands and arms. I swallowed thickly, scrambling for a solution.

And then the sound of screeching metal brought my head jerking up.

Rollick was crouched on the balcony I'd tried to jump to. He was in human form, but he'd exerted his demon strength to wrench the bars aside so he could lean down toward me. Somehow he was still fucking smiling.

"Looks like you got yourself into a bit of a jam, my stubborn sorcerer," he said, extending his arm. His hand reached to just a few inches above my own where they were locked around the hook. "It's a good thing I noticed you were missing and came looking. Grab hold, and I'll pull you up."

I stared up into his smiling movie-star-handsome face, and something in me recoiled. A chill washed through my whole body, sharper than my panic over the fall beneath me.

No. I couldn't put myself back under his power. Couldn't let him cage me up again with even less hope of escape now that he knew how far I'd go.

I might as well be dead if I let him control my life. I might be *worse* than dead.

Maybe it would be better to just let go. A few seconds of horror, and then it'd all be over, painful but immediate. No more monsters chasing me down or trying to use me. No more worrying about how the strange power in me might lead to the people I cared about being hurt—might even force *me* to hurt them.

I could leave it all behind me, just like that. How many years had I really had left anyway?

Rollick's smile faltered when I didn't immediately take his hand. His forehead furrowed, and he pushed himself closer. His fingertips brushed my knuckles.

I almost let go right then. My fingers started to loosen. But an answering surge of emotion, even more defiant than my initial revulsion, rushed through me.

I wanted to live. That was all I'd ever wanted—to squeeze all the time out of this world that it would give me. As long as I was alive, there was a chance to get out of this mess, no matter how small it was.

I couldn't quite convince myself to give up that hope completely, no matter how miniscule it was.

A sob caught in my throat. I glanced over at the balcony that was just a little too far away again, not that I could have escaped Rollick by that route now that he'd found me regardless. Then, with a tearing sensation searing through my abdomen, I thrust one hand upward to clasp Rollick's arm.

CHAPTER SEVENTEEN

Rollick

Quinn hadn't spoken since I'd brought her back to my suite. She'd barely *moved*. She'd sunk into what appeared to be her favorite armchair and had been simply sitting there for the past half an hour, her arms wrapped loosely around her knees, which she'd folded up to her chest. Her gaze stared aimlessly across the room.

I'd brought her a glass of water in case she needed hydration after the shock of her near-death, but she hadn't touched it. She'd taken no notice of the backpack I'd retrieved and set near the base of the chair.

I'd lounged on the sofa near her for a little while in case she decided to talk and then wandered around the suite, hoping her tongue might loosen if I gave her some space. I couldn't quite convince myself to leave. It'd been when I'd left last time that she'd set off on her desperate scramble around the hotel.

She *had* nearly died. If I'd tracked her down a minute later... I couldn't remember the last time I'd felt alarm like the icy jolt of fear that'd stabbed through me the moment her grasp on the railing had slipped—or the wave of relief that had flooded me when I'd determined I could get to her in time.

But it hadn't been enough. There'd been a moment when she'd seriously contemplated letting go rather than taking my helping hand. I'd seen it written in her expression, reverberating through her hesitation when I'd reached out to her. I wouldn't have been able to catch her then. For all my demonic powers, I had no ability to fly.

Some part of her, a large enough part to override all mortals' instinctive drive toward self-preservation, believed death might be a better option than returning with me.

It didn't make sense, and my uncertainty gnawed at me. I'd thought I'd known what we were playing at between us. She'd taken on the role of defiant but tempted captive, and I'd been the seductive jailor, and we'd been cruising along toward our inevitable collision.

We'd bantered. I'd seen desire light in her eyes. She hadn't *seemed* scared. I knew what scared looked like.

At least, I'd thought I did. There was something painfully broken in the slump of her shoulders now, something I'd had no idea she was hiding underneath that tartly rebellious exterior.

After another few minutes passed without her stirring, I returned to the sofa. Her gaze didn't move to me as I settled onto the cushions. I gave her a moment to begin the conversation and decided I'd better take the first step if I wanted any to happen at all.

"It's become clear to me that my understanding of the situation we've found ourselves in is flawed," I said, keeping my voice smooth but serious. I was reasonably sure that she wasn't in the mood to be cajoled with jokes or charm. "It wouldn't have occurred to me that you'd go to the lengths you just did to escape what I thought I'd made clear was a safe haven. Has your time in my home been that awful? What do you need that I'm not offering?"

Quinn's attention shifted to me slowly, but the disbelief etched on her features sent an uncomfortable twist through my gut. I wasn't used to feeling this off-balance with any other being, let alone a mortal, and I didn't enjoy it at all.

"Do you really think this is about whether the suite is properly luxurious or the meals tasty enough?" she said, her voice raw but steady. "You've made it clear that you've got some purpose in mind for me that you won't tell me about. The only things I know for sure are that you're determined to make me use a power that I hate even having, and there was a point when you wanted to murder me and eat my heart, if you're not *still* considering that. That's not even getting into…"

She trailed off with a shiver, but I was stuck on her initial point anyway. I knit my brow. "When have I ever indicated that I was interested in seeing you dead? Let alone snacking on your innards? I know the fiends after you have been devouring sorcerers, but—"

Quinn's eyes narrowed as she interrupted. "You told Torrent that *you* wanted to devour me, didn't you? He and the others—all three of them are sure that's what you originally meant to do. And you seemed awfully hesitant to explain what you *did* want with me when you first came to take me off their hands."

The twisting sensation inside me pulled tighter. Ah. I hadn't quite thought—but yes, I could see how I could have made a miscalculation there. Mainly in that I'd failed to consider how much information my associates would have shared with her. It was hard to think of their connection being more than carnal even after the evidence I'd seen, but I knew there was more going on there. I should have taken their closeness properly into account, as strange as it was.

I hesitated, debating my options. She might not believe me no matter what I said. But all my wry remarks and shows of power before hadn't swayed her, so a different tactic was in order. What did it matter if I was a little more honest with this mortal than I generally was with anyone? She could hardly ruin my reputation.

I leaned forward, clasping my hands in front of me. "Quinn, I never had any intention of killing you. I've always very specifically wanted you *alive*. I sent those three mutinists out to Florida specifically to make sure you stayed that way. What I said to Torrent— The less anyone knows about my exact plans before I've carried them out, the better. It was the simplest explanation, and not one I expected him to have any concerns about."

"You didn't have any problem even with pretending you were going to 'snack' on me?"

I grimaced. "I'm a brutal, incredibly powerful demon who rules over my empire with an iron fist. Haven't you heard? If I want to make sure that people fall in line with a minimum of additional brutality, which honestly is pretty tiresome most of the time, it's best if I play into that perception rather than away from it."

Quinn lowered her legs so she could fold her arms over her chest instead, but I could tell she was paying attention, evaluating what I'd said. "Why would a brutal, incredibly powerful demon with an iron fist care so much about keeping a random human alive?"

I shot her a baleful glance. "You know you're not just a random human. You're something more valuable even than the sorcerers who brought your donor into this world, and you're worth much more than whatever minor power could be transferred by consuming your heart. As I suspect our opponents have figured out as well."

Her forehead furrowed. "Torrent mentioned that an actual sorcerer would have more power than they get from consuming the organs. Is that what you mean?"

"It's not just that. You have access to a sorcerer's powers," I said, motioning toward her. "A sorcerer with a long heritage of that power, compounded across generations. But *you* weren't raised as a sorcerer. You weren't taught techniques for shutting out shadowkind influence. You haven't learned to despise us or to see us as nothing but tools. Which makes you the perfect combination of powerful and vulnerable. You could become a tool for shadowkind, if you could be convinced to use those powers on our behalf."

Quinn studied me for a long moment. "That's what *you* want me for too. So I can be your tool. So I can enslave shadowkind for you?"

"No." I laughed, even though she wasn't totally wrong about the tool part. "I have no interest in collecting slaves. I *do* have an interest in ensuring that no idiotic ancient shadowkind go off on some crusade that'll ultimately serve only to their benefit and screw over the rest of us. There's clearly something brewing. And you're the only being I know who might be able to stop them if it gets to that point. We're definitely screwed if they get their hands on you."

Her jaw tightened. "I wouldn't do anything for those beasts."

"You probably wouldn't have a choice," I said gently. "They'll have beings on their side like that siren who took all of two seconds to cajole you into taking off your shirt. They'd enslave you into being their slaver."

As I might have done, if I hadn't wanted to keep my interest in her secret. If I hadn't had faith in my own ability to win her over by other means. I'd thought I could simply flatter and seduce her until she wanted to appease me—yes, that task had been made harder by her entanglement with my associates, but in a way her affections had also made things easier, since I could use them as motivation too.

But it wasn't going to be enough. I could see that now. Maybe the suspicion had been creeping over me for days, and I hadn't wanted to accept it.

I wasn't going to delude her into going along with my goals. Wasn't going to cloud her mind with passion to the point that she'd do whatever I wanted as long as I took care of those needs. She didn't have an ingrained revulsion toward shadowkind, but she was sharp enough to stay wary no matter what desires stirred in her body. Stubborn enough to stand firm no matter what was at stake.

To see even losing her life as a viable option if it gave her the freedom she craved.

It was becoming increasingly clear to me how three of my most trusted and reliable men might have become so enraptured with her when they'd never strayed before. There was definitely something to her that most mortals didn't possess.

Quinn swiped at her eyes. She hesitated for a stretch before meeting my eyes again. "I don't want to be a tool—for them or for you. I don't want to be in this war, if that's what it's turning into, at all. I just want to go back to my life, however much of it I still have."

My mouth tightened with genuine sympathy. I could hear in her voice how exhausted she was from the unexpected trials she'd been put through, but I couldn't give her a more reassuring answer.

"I don't think you have a choice," I said. "And I'm not only saying that because I'm concerned about what will happen to me and my domain if you don't stand against these pricks. I suspect you won't like where they're going with their schemes either."

"How so?"

I shrugged. "Maybe they'll amass some more power and simply go back and mess around in the shadow realm... but I think that's unlikely. Whatever they have planned, it's probably going to affect the mortal realm too. Even if I could figure out a way for you to keep up your old life without them discovering you, which I can't see doing regardless, this is going to affect you whether you like it or not. It's better if we deal with them sooner rather than later."

Or we might not be able to deal with them at all, even if she was fully committed.

I straightened my stance and decided I could offer a smile now without it rubbing her the wrong way. "I can promise you this much: I'm not going to force you to use your magic against your will. And not out of the kindness of my heart, but because I doubt you'd be able to reach your full potential without your will being totally behind the cause anyway. I *will* keep reminding you of why it's important, and I'm not going to let you go running off to your doom. If that's irritating, well..." I spread my hands. "I'll attempt to be entertaining enough that you don't mind too much."

Quinn wrinkled her nose at me, but I thought her posture had relaxed a little. She seemed to believe me.

The fresh relief that spread through me at that thought was unnerving. As if it didn't only matter to me that she believed me for my own objectives but because having her distrust me *bothered* me in some ridiculous way.

Why should she trust me? I was a demon, a monster. I'd played the villain enough times.

I needed to get a handle on this game again. Put myself firmly in control, ensure she was devoted to me or at least dependent on me. That was the only way I could ensure I protected everything that really mattered.

"Truce?" I said, adding a seductive lilt to my voice.

Quinn exhaled slowly. Then she tipped her head in a hesitant nod that opened all the doors I needed.

"For now," she said.

Not a problem. I could take that and spin it into forever now that I'd gotten this potential disaster back on course.

CHAPTER EIGHTEEN

Quinn

My ninth morning at the Sunshine Sin Hotel, I choked down my breakfast with nerves on edge, braced for Rollick's arrival. He'd given me the rest of yesterday to recover from my escape attempt, but he'd taken precautions. When I'd tried to step onto the terrace just to get some fresh air in the afternoon, I'd found that both of the sliding doors were locked in some way I couldn't open.

I guessed I couldn't totally blame him for that when my last venture outside had nearly ended not only in my getting free of him but in my death as well.

I couldn't really rest easy in the suite, though. He'd said he had no interest in killing me, and he'd sounded like he meant it. But the expectations he did have for me weren't much better. I didn't want to be the key figure in some supernatural war. And no matter how he phrased it, he clearly did see me as a tool... or he'd have cared more about my feelings on the subject.

Whatever he'd said, I was a prisoner here. I was trapped both by what my unwelcome powers meant to the shadowkind and by Rollick's determination to use me to stand against them.

At least I had a better idea of the full situation and his intentions now. My escape attempt had gotten me that much, somehow or other.

When the demon finally did stroll into the suite—without knocking, like usual—I found his lack of concern for my privacy weirdly comforting. If he'd waited outside politely, I wasn't sure I'd have trusted that to be real concern anyway rather than a gambit to try to convince me that he was reformed from his previous habits. He still saw me and these rooms as totally his.

I didn't like it, but I knew where I stood.

He was carrying the same larger black box as yesterday, the one that presumably held a somewhat stronger shadowkind creature. I eyed it and then him as I got up from the chair where I'd been attempting to concentrate enough to work on a sketch. Rollick stopped on the other side of the sofa from me and arched an eyebrow as if inviting a comment.

Yeah, he was still the same arrogant jerk as he'd been before, even if he'd opened up a little more. Also still way too stunning to look at, but I could keep ignoring that. All I had to do was remember how he'd remarked on my supposedly private interlude with my men, and any heat that'd formed over my skin crawled away in disgust.

"Are you going to risk your upholstery or will I be

allowed terrace access again?" I asked, keeping my voice dry even though my heart was thumping at an uneasy rhythm.

The corner of Rollick's mouth quirked up in a crooked smile. Maybe he was relieved that I had enough spirit left to hassle him about his security precautions.

"I thought, just for the one night, it was better to give you time to totally gather your thoughts," he said. "I don't want to restrict your movement any more than necessary to keep you safe, even if it's from yourself. But we do need to work together, which means a certain level of mutual trust is required. Are you willing to fully cooperate for the time being?"

"I won't run off like that again," I said, and meant it. I didn't for a second believe he was really going to give me the leeway to try. He'd probably set up additional security to prevent me from getting anywhere near that far across the building even once I could go out onto the terrace again.

It was better if he thought I trusted him, though. The more freedom he allowed me, the more space I had to figure out other plans.

"Then we have no problems," Rollick said with a wider smile. "Come on, I think you'll like this beastie. We won't do anything bloody today."

Not today, but maybe tomorrow, that remark implied. I sighed and followed him out.

Once I'd stepped into the bright sunlight, I couldn't help glancing around at the walls, checking for concealed devices. "Have you been recording me out here too? All over your suite?" In the bedroom? In the bathroom? I restrained a shudder.

Rollick paused, cocking his head as he studied me.

"You're still very bothered about that one point, aren't you?"

I glowered at him. "You violated my privacy in a huge way. I didn't want to star in a porno for your enjoyment. And you were trying to use it against me, to manipulate me —of course that 'bothers' me."

The demon set down the carrier on the usual table and then walked over to lean back against the railing. The breeze ruffled his light brown hair. He looked unusually serious while he pondered his answer.

"I can see that," he said finally. "I thought we were playing a different game from what it turned out to be. And really, I shouldn't need to resort to deception to convince you of my charms. It was an ill-advised shortcut that I will not attempt again. I'm sorry."

My eyebrows rose with automatic skepticism. "Are you really?"

His smile came back, sly around the edges. "I'm not going to get down on my knees and beg for your forgiveness. That's not really my style. But yes, I'm sorry that I intruded where I wasn't welcome and upset you."

"Because now it's going to be harder to charm me."

He laughed and gave a brief shrug. "Sure, that's part of it. But I also don't like that it drove you to the point that you risked hurting yourself yesterday. And I'm not a sadist —I only enjoy tormenting beings that deserve it, which as far as I can tell you don't. I regret doing so inadvertently."

"For a millennia-old demon, you sure aren't well-versed on what things upset humans," I said with a grimace.

"Oh, you might be surprised by how many mortals get off on voyeurism. But like I said, I thought we were engaged in a different sort of game. Absolutely my fault." He glanced toward the suite. "As for the rooms here, there are plenty of things I don't want there to be any concrete record of *me* doing. And I have better things to do than spy on your every movement or peep at your body. If I want to see a naked woman, there are plenty who are happy to show off right in front of me downstairs."

"So reassuring," I muttered. I didn't know if he was telling the truth about all that, but he still hadn't shown any sign that he was aware of my scheming against him with the other men on the terrace, so maybe we were safe at least out here.

I paused and decided I might as well find out if I could push whatever leverage I'd gained yesterday a little farther.

"I want to see Torrent and Crag and Lance again," I said, fixing him with my steadiest stare. "Without them having to sneak up here or worry about how you'll react. If you want me cooperating, it'll help a lot if I can actually spend time on a regular basis with the shadowkind I *do* totally trust."

I thought Rollick's jaw tightened just slightly, though he didn't let his smile falter. "You won't have the opportunity to make use of the guestroom next door again."

"I don't care about that. I don't only enjoy their company for hooking up, you know. It'd give me someone to at least *talk* to now that you've cut me off from all the rest of society."

"My conversational skills are so lacking?"

I rolled my eyes. "Other than the fact that you're not even here for most of the day—not that I'm suggesting you should stop by more often—I'd *rather* talk to them. Sorry if your ego is so fragile that you're offended by that fact."

Rollick blinked at me and then tipped his head back with a laugh of pure amusement. "Well, when you put it that way, I really can't deny you, can I? They *are* quite busy with discovering all we can about your real enemies, a mission I'd imagine you wouldn't want to interrupt— they'd have been sneaking in more often if they'd had the chance, no doubt. But the next time they have a break, I'll let them know there'll be no punishment for coming up here for a visit." He tsked his tongue teasingly at me. "Just don't do anything I wouldn't do."

I couldn't help snorting. "Somehow I have a feeling that doesn't cover very much."

"You wouldn't be wrong." The demon was outright grinning now, so I guessed the request hadn't bothered him too much. He motioned to the carrier. "Can we begin, or do you have more demands to make, my stubborn sorcerer?"

Stop calling me yours, I thought, but I kept my mouth shut on that one. I could choose my battles for now, and somehow I suspected he'd laugh harder at that request. "Bring it out."

When he opened the door to the carrier, this creature emerged of its own accord, slinking from the brightly lit space and cringing at the sunlight outside. It was an oddly spindly thing, nearly skeletal in the vague shape of a wiener dog, with wings protruding from its back that were covered in flesh so gauzy it might have been made out of spun spider webs. It glanced at me and bared a mouth full of piranha-like teeth.

Okay, I definitely didn't want to get too close to that one.

"What do you want me to do with it?" I asked doubtfully.

Rollick tapped a finger against his lips. "Let's start with a sprint around the terrace. Give it a good warm-up."

I dragged in a breath and focused on the small beast the way I'd been learning to do. Part of my concentration roused the wavering energy in my chest. My pulse beat faster, one of those unnerving wobbles rippling through it.

I pictured the creature darting around the edge of the terrace, focusing on the idea of it staying clear of me while it did, which I definitely wanted. And in that way I still didn't understand, a surge of energy pushed a burst of sound from my lips.

The creature leapt forward. It jumped off the table and dashed past me toward the far end of the terrace. I spun to follow its course, and weirdly... *felt* as much as saw when my control started to slip.

As it reached the far wall, its muscles coiled to spring right over the railing into the shadows farther along the building. But I knew that less because of observing its odd anatomy and more because a hint of the impulse flickered through me: to flee, to get away.

Or maybe I was only imagining that from my observations because it matched my own urges so well. I opened my mouth, knowing I needed to rein it in and having no idea how—but my sorcerer instincts kicked in again of their own accord.

The magic crackled up from my chest and over my tongue. I barked a command, and the thing swiveled in mid-spring. It darted around the side of the terrace by the suite windows without missing another beat. Then it stopped and huddled under the table where it'd started. The edges of its body hazed, but when Rollick crouched next to it with what must have been an implicit threat, it flinched and resolidified.

He looked up at me from that vantage point, grinning. "That was a nice catch. You're adapting well on the spot."

Only I had no clue how or why... I didn't understand *any* of this still. Cool nausea clamped around my gut again. How was I supposed to be the deciding force in a battle when I couldn't really control my own powers or predict how they'd present themselves? I *would* be just a tool if all I did was follow Rollick's commands by rote.

Not to mention...

"It wouldn't have worked if I couldn't see it to know I needed to adapt," I said. "My magic wasn't controlling it completely. And it's just a little lesser creature, not the powerful higher shadowkind you think we're up against."

"Patience," Rollick said. "You've made major strides in just a few days. Usually with these sorts of things, once you've grasped the basics, the rest comes much more quickly."

He couldn't know that for sure, though. He'd just been telling me yesterday how rare I was.

I paused and met his gaze. "Why are you relying on *me*? You're a super powerful demon, as you like to remind everyone around you as often as possible. If you're so worried about these assholes, why don't you just crush them before they can carry out their plans?"

"We don't know who we're up against yet," Rollick

reminded me. "It is possible they could prove a real challenge to me on my own, although I'm flattered by your faith in me." When I wrinkled my nose at the assumed compliment, he laughed and went on. "I think I might have mentioned before that I like to be thorough in my preparations. It's better if you're ready if we need you, don't you think?"

"Sure," I said, but I doubted that was the main reason. He'd also mentioned more than once that he didn't like to draw attention to himself by interfering with other shadowkind or even sorcerers. He probably just wanted to hang back in the shadows and not take any of the heat, even if tackling these villains directly would have been much simpler and easier for the rest of us.

As I turned my attention back to the creature under the table, anticipating the demon's next instructions, a renewed sense of resolve eased my earlier edginess. Rollick might not *want* to deal with the other shadowkind head on, but if I got my way, he wasn't going to have a choice. This was his fight, his game, and so he ought to be the one playing it.

CHAPTER NINETEEN

Torrent

I'd have been happier about Rollick's declaration that I could use my free time to drop in on Quinn if he hadn't made it with a slyly suggestive gleam in his eyes.

"She did seem *very* eager to have your company," he said as he ambled around his office, in a tone that somehow conjured all kinds of illicit imagery without him saying a single actually provocative word.

I didn't show any outward reaction to his teasing from where I was standing near the door. "I'm sure it puts her more at ease when she can spend time with us, since we're the only shadowkind who've completely had her back."

Rollick paused and arched his eyebrows at me. "Implying I don't. I've made my peace with her. In case you weren't clear on this either, I never had any intention of literally devouring her."

"I'm glad to hear that," I said dryly. He had his own motivations, though—motivations we both knew were to further his interests, not Quinn's. In the back of my head, I could still hear the way he'd talked about her when he'd come to retrieve her from us in Florida, like she was an inanimate trinket we'd stolen for him. The memory made me tense up inside along with a jab of guilt that I'd let *myself* think of her as nothing but a possession for so long.

Was I that much better than the demon in front of me? Well, I *had* adjusted my mindset eventually. I'd made up my failings to Quinn in every way I could since then. It seemed to be enough for her.

"You've always been so focused on the work," Rollick went on in a casual tone. "I'm surprised to see you getting so caught up in a bit of... leisure, should we call it? If you were craving more time to indulge with the mortals, you only needed to ask. I've got a hotel full of them."

My gut twisted for a second. I *had* craved it, and I'd stuffed down those cravings because I'd known as well as Rollick must that there'd been no way I could "indulge" in the same way I'd used to in my current physical state. I couldn't appear in the middle of the club with my impossibly collapsed cheek and tentacles showing and sweep some woman off her feet.

But what I'd found with Quinn wasn't like that at all. It didn't feel like an indulgence. It felt... like a calling, like a mission I'd been meant for far more than any of the jobs I'd carried out for Rollick, as much as I'd appreciated his faith in my abilities.

"I know," I said simply. "You've always provided

whatever I needed. I'm sorry our goals ended up putting us at odds." And I meant that.

Rollick nodded. "I am too. I never doubted that I could count on you before, and I thought our partnership was important to you. I'm aware that you had troubles because of your recreational activities in the past... I hope you know what you're doing here. Even if I wasn't exactly pleased about the mutiny, I wouldn't like to see you going astray."

When he'd first took me on, I'd told Rollick an abbreviated version of the history I'd recently shared with Quinn. It'd been reasonable for him to ask, since if there were any continuing grudges against me, that would affect him too. He'd never held my past carelessness against me, and the concern he expressed now sent an uncomfortable prickle over my skin.

Maybe it made sense for him to be concerned. He was only outside looking in on our strange relationship, and for most shadowkind, this sort of association with a mortal would have been more about getting off than anything else. Had I let my growing affection for Quinn distract me in ways that could get me—or her, or my squad—into trouble?

I couldn't think of any, but the implications lingered even when I tried to shake off his words. "I appreciate that," I said. "As well as your leniency as far as the mutiny went."

Rollick shrugged, the corner of his lips quirking upward. "Good help is hard to find. You're still the best lieutenant I've got in many of the ways that count most."

One of which was the fact that no one knew I worked for him, so I could investigate these other powerful shadowkind without them targeting him. Somehow I doubted he'd have the same confidence in me if he knew the full extent of the discussions I'd been having with Quinn.

Discussions we were going to continue now.

I made myself look at my boss—really look at him, both the shiny human-like guise and the demon I could sense lurking within. He was striding forward as he always had, bolstering his power, protecting his empire. I couldn't blame him for that. Just as he shouldn't really blame me when I made whatever moves I needed to in order to defend what mattered to me.

A prickle of discomfort was spreading through my calves. I shifted my tentacles against the floor, looking forward to the reprieve of diving back into the shadows. "I do my best. Thank you for your trust." Even if I was going to betray it again.

It was a short trip down through the gloomy innards of the building to Rollick's personal suite one floor below. There was something to be said for being able to simply step out of the shadows right next to where Quinn was already lounging in the living room rather than needing to go through the song-and-dance of pretending to be the wind tapping on the windows.

Lance and Crag had already arrived. Lance had plopped himself down on one of the armchairs and collected Quinn on his lap, where she was laughing as he gave an account of his exploits that was ending with, "...and that was the last time they ever sold balloons at that zoo." The gargoyle, leaning against the entertainment unit a few feet away, gave a grunt that seemed to dismiss the story as frivolous. They all looked up as I emerged.

"The boss gave you a free pass too," Lance observed

with a grin. "I'm starting to think our mortal is even more tricksy than he is."

Quinn snorted. "I'm working on it." She gave him a peck on his cheek—which he answered with a pleased growl and a nip of her neck—and then got up to wrap me in a hug. "It's good to see you."

Something about the press of her arms around me suggested that she needed this embrace more than her breezy words implied. I hugged her back, a mix of worry and anger rising in me as I wondered what had happened to her in the past couple of days to shake her up. There was a slight catch to her breath, a tiny tremor that ran through her limbs that I only picked up thanks to the sensitivity of my suction cups, that spoke of a vulnerability I hadn't sensed in her the last time we'd spoken.

"Are you all right?" I asked quietly, letting my lips brush her hair and inhaling the freshly sweet scent of her.

"Yeah. Pretty much. I mean, it's not the greatest situation still, right." She eased back and seemed to gather herself. "There are some things I'd like to talk about. Maybe we should go out on the terrace. Rollick said he doesn't have cameras in here, but the only place I'm pretty much sure of is outside. For more private matters."

I tipped my head toward the wall. "We can't make use of any of the nearby guestrooms today, unfortunately. Someone's checked in—"

"We couldn't anyway," Quinn broke in with a grimace. "He—he set us up. He recorded everything that happened in there."

Oh. *Oh*. Fury seared through me so abruptly and forcefully my vision briefly hazed red. My jaw clenched.

Rollick had given no indication of it when we'd spoken... Well, why would he? I doubted he wanted to chat with me about what he'd witnessed if he'd decided to dismiss our flouting of his unstated rules.

It shouldn't have surprised me. I'd even thought to check for recording devices—I just hadn't done a thorough enough job of it, obviously. I hadn't managed to protect Quinn in that most basic way—he'd watched her, maybe even enjoyed seeing her pleasure when it hadn't been meant for him at all...

Quinn grasped my arm, bringing me back to the present. Lance had sprung off the chair with a snarl; Crag had marched forward to grip Quinn's shoulder, his gaze searching the room.

Our woman glanced around at all of us. "I'm okay. He and I... hashed it out, as well as it could be hashed out. I'm not happy about it, but it's already happened, and... and if everything works the way we hope it will, then soon it won't matter. So don't go rushing off to defend my honor or anything. I'd rather you were here with me."

"I should skewer him," Lance muttered, waving his claws through the air. "Turn him into a demon shish kabob."

"Easier said than done," I replied, understanding Quinn's request. We wouldn't gain anything by taking Rollick to task for it, not anything that would help her. We might very well end up shish kabobs ourselves. "Come on, let's go get some fresh air. And I'll make a particularly careful sweep of the terrace before we talk further."

It felt strange, stepping out into the warm mid-morning brightness outside. I didn't normally take on physical form outside in a setting like this by daylight. A burst of laughter carried up from the beach far below; faint strains of animated chatter filtered from the rooftop lounge. But no one could see me and my monstrousness in our current perch.

I made good on my promise, scanning every part of the terrace and its furnishings with both my eyes and my tentacles. When I was satisfied that even Rollick couldn't have concealed a device anywhere nearby, I sank down onto one of the loungers to rest my now-aching legs.

Lance paced around the terrace, leaping into a handspring with his usual agility but an energy that was more restless uneasiness than his usual buoyant spirits.

"What do we do now?" he said. "Less than two days before the deal ends and Rollick gets to make more demands. What is he going to want next?"

"Everything we find out about our enemies makes it clear how much of a menace they are," Crag rumbled. "I don't think we'll be able to destroy them quickly."

Quinn sat down on the chair next to mine and reached out her hand to rest it on one of my tentacles as easily as if she'd been taking my hand. I wasn't sure when I'd get used to her easy affection toward every part of me.

"Not if we're trying to do it using Rollick's subtle methods," she said. "I think we need to put the plan we talked about before into action. The morning when the ten days will be fully up—a little less than forty-eight hours from now. Let them deal with each other."

She spoke with a firmness she hadn't shown before. Her recent interactions with the demon had obviously solidified her resolve. I felt no desire to disagree with her after what she'd just revealed about him.

I pushed myself up straighter, letting my tentacle loop around her arm. "We still need to balance the factors carefully."

Quinn nodded. "I've been thinking about that. I have a couple of things I can 'hide' in the apartment that will show that I've been there, and I think I know where to put them that Rollick won't notice them ahead of time. And once we've delivered the message, you can keep watch and recognize when the other shadowkind are acting on it. If you 'warn' him just a little before they get here, we'll have time for him to approve of a plan to get me to a different safe spot and gather his defenses, but not enough time for him to head them off completely."

"Then they smash each other!" Lance said, his eyes brightening as he smacked one fist into the other palm.

My chest constricted. "We can't cut it too close. If they catch one glimpse of you leaving—or if Rollick's no longer bound by the deal and decides it's safer to simply remove you more permanently—"

Quinn gave me a reassuring squeeze. "It'll be better if it's earlier in the morning anyway, before it's at all light out, when there aren't any people around. Crag can offer to fly me to wherever we'll be going—that'll be the obvious strategy anyway. And by the time Rollick is finished dealing with the rest of them, we'll have vanished."

She glanced at me. "Can you find someplace where we'll be able to get by at least until we take stock of how the clash turned out? I'll wear my vest the whole time, so we don't have to worry about anyone tracking me from my sorcerer energies."

She was putting so much trust in me—in all of us—to pull this plan off. For a second, my throat closed up.

There wasn't anything to be ashamed of in the devotion that'd kindled in me, more with every moment I spent with her. She'd earned it far more than Rollick ever had. Let him deal with the consequences of the conflict he'd gotten himself wrapped up in, not her. That was justice, not indulgence.

"I can manage that in the time we have," I said. "But— what you really wanted was to get back to your parents and your studies..."

Quinn's mouth tightened, but she held her chin steady. "I did, but if that needs to wait so that we're all safe and the people back home are too, then that's how it needs to be. I'll be one step closer to being really free. I can't complain about that."

Well, she could. She just wouldn't, not with that fierce stubbornness to survive that'd already kept her going so long.

I couldn't resist tugging her to me, slipping my arms around her again. Quinn tipped her head against my shoulder, melting into my embrace.

"He's going to be even more mad at the three of you," she murmured. "You were lucky he mostly forgave you the first time..."

I cut her off before she could follow that train of thought any farther. "Let him be angry, then. I'd rather deal with that than see him keep you on a leash."

Crag let out a thrumming sound of agreement, and Lance hissed through his vicious grin.

We were really going to do this. We were going to screw over one of the most powerful shadowkind in the realms in epic fashion...

And I didn't feel the slightest doubt about my decision, not while I held this strange and wonderful mortal woman in my arms.

CHAPTER TWENTY

Quinn

I was examining the frame of the bed when the rasp of footsteps in the living room reached my ears. I leapt to my feet, my pulse stuttering, abruptly overwhelmed with gratitude for my past self's wisdom in keeping the bedroom door shut so my visitor couldn't have seen me in that odd pose.

I opened the door to find Rollick on the other side, about to reach for the handle. He didn't look at all startled by my abrupt appearance, stepping forward to glance past me into the room with an upbeat but oddly intense air. "Do you still have the wig and the dress I had you wear for your arrival?"

My pulse hiccupped to even greater effect. "Of course," I said. "Why? Do I need to leave?" Had the plans we'd made been thrown off just a day before we'd meant to carry them out?

But Rollick took in my reaction and smiled in his

annoyingly charming way. "Don't panic. You wanted to see more of the hotel. I might not be able to offer you a view of your parents anymore, but I'm giving you the chance to stretch your legs, so to speak. In a less precarious way than previously."

I blinked at him, taking a moment to process the words. "You're letting me go out into the rest of the hotel? But—"

He raised a hand dismissively. "I know what I said. I have a very good memory. That's why we're having you put on your fancy vest with the dress to hide it, and the wig to disguise your looks even more. And we'll stick to parts where you won't be available for close inspection, at least to begin with."

Why was he offering this gesture *now*? My heart thumped faster again, but this time it was more in anticipation than fear. I might get the chance to learn something that would strengthen our plans or help us stay ahead of the demon if he gave chase afterward. No way could I pass up the opportunity.

"All right," I said, managing to smile back. "Thank you." I grasped the door handle and looked at his position right on the threshold. "I'm going to close the door before I get changed. Just because you got a show without my knowing about it doesn't mean I want to do a repeat performance."

A bit of an edge crept into my voice with those words, but Rollick took it in stride with a chuckle. "Your maidenly honor is perfectly safe," he said, and turned on his heel.

As I pushed the door shut and turned to riffle through the wardrobe to figure out where I'd stuffed my previous disguise, Rollick started to hum a jaunty little tune to himself. At first, I thought he was trying to irritate me. Then a thought occurred to me that was startling enough that I froze in place.

He was making noise so I'd know for sure he was out there and not spying on me from the shadows in here. I hadn't really thought he would, but it'd been important enough to him to confirm it for me all the same.

I didn't know how to feel about that consideration.

Well, I'd known he *could* be considerate, or at least act like it, when he wanted something. He was still trying to win me over like he had been all along. He'd just learned more about what tactics I'd appreciate.

I couldn't trust a single thing the demon did, not really.

Finally I dug out the dress and wig from amid the heap of clothes Rollick kept in his bedroom for purposes I could only speculate on. There were women's and men's things, but I knew the shadowkind could conjure their clothes around their physical bodies as they took on concrete form. Mementos from past "guests"? Spare clothes in case those guests needed a change of outfit? Stale perfume clung to a few of the items, suggesting they'd been worn at some point.

I tugged on my silver-and-iron vest with a soft hiss of the beads and then layered the loose dress on top of it. Studying myself in the mirror, I adjusted it until I was sure it didn't reveal any odd bulges when I shifted my position. Then I pulled my hair into a quick braid so I could tuck it under the wig.

I'd left the makeup bag on the vanity, untouched since my arrival. I dabbed on some lipstick for good measure, deciding not to bother with the bronzer. It would probably look too obviously fake if I did end up passing close by anyone. I was no makeup genius.

When I emerged from the bedroom, Rollick stopped his ambling circuit of the room and his humming to look me over. I expected to cringe under his attention, but his gaze felt more assessing than leering. He gave a brisk nod of approval and motioned for me to join him.

"You should keep quiet unless I indicate that you should speak," he said as we headed out and up the stairs that led to his office level. "For your own safety. It's not likely we'll end up in a situation where we'll be chatted up anyway, but just in case."

"I get it." A nervous shiver rippled through me. As much as I wanted a better understanding of my luxurious cage, I couldn't help asking, "Are you sure this is a good idea?"

"I wouldn't be doing it if I wasn't," Rollick said smoothly. He shot me another smile. "You know, I didn't shut you away in my suite for any reason other than your own protection. I'd happily have given you free run of the hotel if I thought there wasn't a danger in it."

Yeah, I believed he would have. He'd have trusted that I wouldn't make a run for it because I'd have known how quickly he could track me down—and the consequences that I and the people I cared about might face for my defiance. My lungs tightened as I thought of my parents back in Florida—

No. If we escaped his clutches, if he had no idea where we were and was busy licking his wounds from a battle with my other enemies, threatening my parents wouldn't do him any good. And if I didn't get free before he arranged another deal, I might lose what little protection I'd already arranged, as well as my chance to escape.

We stepped onto the elevator, which whirred down to the second floor. It opened to a narrow hall where bass pounded through the walls. Rollick led me down the shadowy space to a door he unlocked with his thumbprint.

He slipped through the doorway first, paused, and gestured for me to follow. As I crossed the threshold, the music washed over me with a reverberation I could feel down to my bones.

We were in a room about the size of the bedroom upstairs, with a couple of small tables surrounded by sleek but cozy armchairs in the same wine-red as much of his other furniture. A window that filled the entire opposite wall let in multi-colored strobe lights and a view of the club beyond.

It wasn't that late, only around nine at night, but dancers already undulated throughout the space, both on the floor below us and on the second level of the club that stood across from Rollick's private, enclosed room. The strobe lights wavered over them, shifting to a green and blue that made their bobbing forms look as if they were rolling in the ocean surf. The boldest dancers—maybe they were trained professionals—gyrated on a low stage at the back of the room.

"Are all of these people staying at the hotel?" I asked, staring out at them.

Rollick came up beside me and shook his head. "Hotel guests get special benefits like a free drink, but the club area is open to the general public. It's quite popular. People line up for over an hour to get in. There've been catfights over the guest list."

I turned to face him. "Am I supposed to be impressed by that?"

"I suppose you wouldn't be." He swept his hand toward the hundreds of people enjoying the club. "It means something to all of them, though."

"So this is your grand achievement?" I asked, unable to restrain a note of skepticism. "You've spent millennia building up your power and influence so you could give people a place where they can party?"

The demon shot me a look that was both amused and baleful. Then he sank into an armchair that was just a couple of feet from the glass. He patted his knee. "They can see us too, if not in much detail. They should think you're 'entertaining' me if we want to keep up appearances. Come sit."

I balked. "Please tell me this isn't the real reason you wanted me to come down here. I'm going back to the suite —*alone*—if you're just looking to cop a feel."

Rollick laughed. "I promise I can keep my hands to myself. Just perch there; it won't kill you. I'd like to show you something—about the club, not anything perverse."

He sounded relaxed enough about the situation that I relaxed too. I didn't want anyone looking up and thinking Rollick had brought a woman around who was acting strangely. If suspicion somehow came down on him before we were ready, that could be disastrous.

Tentatively, I walked over and lowered myself onto his lap, trying not to look awkward about it while staying perched a few inches away from the rest of his well-built body. No way was I going to lean right into him like I was actually cuddling up with the demon.

Rollick let out a soft chuckle and set his hand on my waist to steady me. It stayed there, a mild warmth seeping through my clothing to match the warmth of his thigh beneath mine, and didn't venture anywhere more sensitive. Still, every nerve in my body was on edge.

"There," the demon said. "That isn't so horrible, is it? I can behave myself when I need to."

I ignored both him and the thrum of tension that had formed between my legs at the feel of him beneath me, focusing on the dancers beyond the window. My stance swayed a little with the rhythm of the music. "What is it you wanted to show me?"

"All work, no play." Rollick tsked teasingly at me, his thumb tracing a careful arc over my side. "Take a look at all those people out there. Notice anything unusual?"

I frowned and leaned forward, squinting through the uneven patches of light. At first, I had no idea what he was talking about. The dancers shimmied and swiveled in their club clothes—a little fancier than I typically saw at the club near the university that I occasionally popped into, but that was the only difference.

Then a few details here and there caught my eye. A guy near the platform adjusted the hat he'd left on, and I'd swear I caught a glimpse of a shape like a small horn above his ear. Another man deeper into the crowd twisted in a way that brought out the impression of small spikes down his spine pressing against his shirt just for an instant. And a woman near him spun with a flash of red in her eyes.

If I hadn't known the shadowkind existed, I might not

have noticed those glimpses at all or would have assumed they were tricks of the light. But I did know now, and I also knew who this club belonged to.

"You have shadowkind patrons too," I said.

Rollick hummed in agreement. "It's hard for all of them to stay completely under the radar to someone alert. But if they can pass, they're welcome. Nearly half of the beings here tonight are shadowkind, like usual."

"*Half?*" I stared at the dancers again, picking out a few more figures who looked supernaturally attractive or graceful or whatever—though not so much that I'd have thought they were anything other than exceptional humans before. Others, I had no idea which might be mortal and which were simply pretending at it.

"Why do they all come here?" I asked. "I mean, I'm sure you're a great host and all, but they really care about dancing that much?"

"It's not just about the dancing." Rollick gazed past me out the window in a moment of unusually pensive contemplation. "You took a jab at me about what I've built over all this time. I've built places where the shadowkind who feel more at home in this realm than our own can enjoy everything it has to offer while knowing their interests will be protected, and I'll continue to build more every time the currents shift."

I cocked my head. "Do they really need protecting?"

"Does Torrent?" Rollick asked simply. "Or Lance, or Crag? You seem to think they do, and there are plenty of beings down there less capable than they are. I'm not going to deny that there's a tendency in us toward aggression and brutality. There's a reason mortals have labeled us monsters on the rare occasions they've stumbled on us. But plenty of us aren't interested in indulging in those urges unless forced to, and I keep those who'd want to hunt and exploit out so they can't bother anyone. I lay down rules so less experienced or... intelligent beings don't make any mistakes that'd come down on the rest of us."

He made it all sound so fair and even generous. The impression didn't sit totally right with me. "What about all the mortals down there? Who's protecting them?"

"Don't you worry about that," Rollick said with another stroke of his thumb. "I might not always have enormous respect for humankind, but I have nothing against them. Some of them are amusing or charming in their own ways." He tapped his fingers against my side as if to count me in that number. "They get to have a good time within the rules I've laid down too, no one harmed or disturbed. Unless they try to play predator themselves, in which case I think a little terror is good for them."

I couldn't say he was wrong. I glanced over my shoulder at him, my skin increasingly flushed from our closeness. "Why did you get started on this mission of yours?"

Something shuttered behind the demon's dark blue eyes. He gave me a lazy smile. "That's a long story and not particularly interesting. I just thought it might help you in arranging your priorities to know more about who you're working with. What I stand for. What I'm trying to preserve from idiots who think they can rearrange the structure of both the realms."

The mark he was leaving on society, whether most of us humans had any clue or not. The thought tugged at me in a way that hollowed out my stomach.

Maybe he *had* built something impressive, something admirable, whatever his reasons were for doing it. He'd gotten thousands of years to lay the groundwork, and he probably had thousands more to repeat his successes.

My own life felt as miniscule as a handful of sand, the grains currently slipping through my fingers too quickly for me to catch them.

A sudden melancholy swept over me, dulling the energetic beat of the music as completely as if someone had tossed a thick blanket over my head. My throat tightened. All at once I wanted to be anywhere but here. And definitely not with the company I currently had.

"All right," I said, with conscious effort to keep my voice even. "I've seen it. Can we go now? It's probably better if I'm not on display for very long anyway, right?"

If Rollick was bothered by my abrupt request, he didn't show it. He gave me a gentle nudge, and I stood, folding my arms over my chest and holding back from outright hugging myself. He set his hand on the small of my back to guide me out of the room, and I didn't argue. It was all for appearances anyway.

"There's one more thing I'd like you to see," he said as we walked down the hall to the elevator. "It won't put you on display at all."

"All right," I said, not wanting to make a big thing of my mood—not wanting to invite questions.

We got off at the top floor by his office, but instead of turning to the stairs that led to his private suite, Rollick ushered me in the other direction, to a different flight that went up. We stepped out into cooling night air onto a patio scattered with empty tables and a shadowed bar area beyond them.

"The rooftop lounge is closed for 'maintenance' tonight," Rollick said in a dry voice, and motioned me over to the wall at the opposite end of the bar. As I approached it, my heart somehow soared and plummeted at the same time.

The only view I'd gotten from the hotel before now was the vast stretch of the ocean. This was the city side.

Before me sprawled Los Angeles. Beneath the sprinkling of stars, the buildings glowed with vibrant colors: purples, blues, ambers, and here and there a gleam of hot pink. Cars wove between the buildings, casting the streams of their headlights in front of them. It was an immense urban jungle, but a gorgeous one.

My fingers curled around the railing at the top of the wall, clutching it tight. More pressure filled my throat and formed behind my eyes. I felt as if I were clinging on against nearly as stark a fall as I'd faced yesterday morning.

"I thought you'd appreciate seeing the city from up here," Rollick said, leaning against the railing a few feet away from me. "What with all your architectural interests. There aren't many vantage points as good as this."

He spoke casually with no hint that he saw the gesture as anything momentous, but his words broke a crack in the dam I'd been holding against my emotions. Before I could catch myself, a sob burst from my throat. I clapped my hand over my eyes as tears gushed out faster than I could blink them back.

Shit, shit, shit. I sucked in a shaky breath, swiping at my eyes, struggling to get control of myself. He must think I was pathetic. How could he possibly understand the fears I'd been grappling with most of my life, the sense of loss that was growing with every day that slipped through my fingers because of this stupid magic I'd never wanted inside me?

It would have been hard enough to make my own mark on the world before my time was up and my heart gave out even before the latent sorcerer powers had kicked in. Now... now I had no idea if I'd ever finish another project for class, let alone see one of the breathtaking skyscrapers I'd imagined brought to life.

Every time I tried to steady myself, another wave of anguish rocked me. I gulped and sniffled, turning away so at least the demon wouldn't get to witness me falling apart— but then Rollick's hand was on my shoulder, light but solid, easing me back around toward him.

"Hey," he said, sounding a little bewildered but not at all mocking. "I didn't mean to upset you."

"It's not— You weren't—" I couldn't quite choke out the words to form any kind of explanation. "I'll be fine." Couldn't he just bring me back to the suite and be done with it?

Apparently not. He leaned closer and wiped a tear I'd missed from my cheek with his thumb, his expression almost inquisitive, as if I was displaying a rare phenomenon he'd never witnessed before. "You're not fine right now. What can I do for you?"

He could give me my life back. He could make everything go back to normal. Except he couldn't actually do either of those things. He couldn't do anything at all— he wouldn't even if he could—*he* was part of the problem.

I shook my head, still struggling to get a grip on myself. The flood of tears had slowed, but they were seeping out in a trickle, my breath hitching.

Rollick gave a thoughtful hum and glanced past me toward the view. "It's a very sad thing if you like *Jacksonville* so much that the City of Angels disappoints you."

The remark was so wry and ridiculous that a laugh tumbled through the gloom that'd been wrapped around me. I sputtered something not quite a giggle or a sob and found I could take my next breath without it catching in my throat. "As always, you think very highly of everything to do with you."

"Only because I have ample evidence that it's deserved," Rollick replied with total assurance, a subtle smile returning. "But I suppose we all have our own tastes, as wrong as some of those might be."

I managed to glower at him, and he shot a full grin back at me, and suddenly my balance felt steadier again. I didn't exactly feel *good*, but I wasn't on the verge of a total breakdown, so I'd call that a win.

"Agree to disagree," I muttered at him.

He chuckled. "Fair enough. May I escort you back to the suite, Quinn? I'm sure you've had enough of my company for tonight."

I'd had enough of his company for a lifetime, but it seemed rude to point that out when he was being so gracious about the whole situation, pretending I hadn't just fallen apart in front of him when he could have been heckling me about my mortal sensibilities or something.

I simply nodded and walked with him back to the suite. He saw me in with a promise that we'd "have more fun tomorrow" and a onceover that was only slightly more pensive than usual, and then he let me be.

And as the door shut behind him, I found myself weirdly glad that he'd been there when I'd had the meltdown. That I hadn't been on my own, drowning in the emotions with no one to snap me out of them.

A prick of guilt formed in my gut. I scowled and strode through the suite to toss myself onto the bed.

I wasn't going to have any regrets about doing whatever I had to do to escape this place and the demon who'd brought me here. Even when he was theoretically being kind, it was always for his own benefit.

Nothing was going to sway me from making whatever desperate grab I could at reclaiming the life I was supposed to have, short as it might be.

CHAPTER TWENTY-ONE

Quinn

On my tenth night in the Sunshine Sin Hotel, I had to pretend to sleep even though my nerves were jittering too hard for me to do more than doze for short spells. Maybe Rollick had been telling the truth when he'd said there were no cameras in the suite, or maybe he'd been trying to lull me into a false sense of security. I wasn't sure I could take anything he said at face value.

And the last thing I wanted was for him to suspect at all that I was anticipating what was going to happen in the wee hours of the morning.

After hours of lying there with a knot in my stomach, enough exhaustion finally closed in on my mind that I actually did drift off. I woke up with a start at the sound of my name.

"Quinn!"

The voice was so brusque I didn't recognize it as

Rollick's until I'd jerked upright with a jolt of my heart. The room was still dark, only a thin wash of moonlight spilling through the tall windows. The demon was standing in the doorway, his handsome face gone taut with more tension than I'd ever seen on it.

I was groggy enough from my interrupted sleep that I responded exactly the way I should have, not yet remembering the full situation. "What's going on?"

"It seems the fiends who want you have somehow gotten wind that I might have taken an interest as well," he said, still terse, striding into the room. He opened the wardrobe and grabbed the wig and discarded dress from inside, then spun to scan the rest of the space. "We need to get you out of here, temporarily at least. And remove every trace that you ever were here."

I blinked at him and pushed myself off the bed. There was a real urgency to the moment even if I'd been ready for it. Things wouldn't go well for me if I wasn't gone in time.

"Can't you fight them off, Mr. Powerful Demon?" I asked, because it seemed like the sort of thing I would have said if I hadn't been counting on him not doing that until his hand was forced. I grabbed my backpack and started stuffing in the few belongings I'd left out so that it wasn't obvious I'd packed for this moment.

"That would only confirm to them that I have something to hide," Rollick muttered. "A being who has no idea what they're nattering about would graciously allow them to search the premises for you in case you snuck in without my noticing, as if that's possible. Put on that vest of yours—we don't want them catching wind of you once you've left the shielded section of the hotel."

I yanked the vest out and tugged it over my head. Then I pulled on an extra T-shirt for good measure, because I already knew what answer I hoped to get to my next question. "Where am I going?"

"Crag will fly you to another secure location until I let him know it's safe to return," Rollick said, to my relief. "It's dark enough that he should be able to avoid notice, and our unwelcome guests haven't gotten close yet. But they're coming on fast, so move quickly!"

Everything had worked out. Well, so far—I couldn't count my chickens until I was actually out of here. I yanked on my shoes and stuffed my phone into a pocket on my bag, purposefully steering my gaze clear of the places around me where I'd stuffed a couple of things I didn't want Rollick seeing. They were tucked away well enough that he shouldn't catch sight of them just looking around in a hurry, but we were counting on the shadowkind searching for me digging a little deeper.

Tucked between the mattress and the box spring but right near the edge was a folded sketch that I'd signed *Quinn* and an unreadable last name on. And I'd slid a hair elastic with a few blond strands clinging to it behind the TV. Not places Rollick would expect me to have accidentally left something behind, but telltale giveaways if the intruders stumbled on either or both. The message my men had passed on should encourage the other shadowkind to pry.

As I swung my pack over my shoulder, Rollick prowled around me, his eyes taking on an eerie glow in the darkness. I suspected he could see in it much better than I could, but he was brisk in his perusal. He crouched to look under the furniture but didn't jostle anything around.

"Good," he said, guiding me out of the room with a hand on my back. "I trust the gargoyle will put as much effort into keeping you safe as he has so far, and the rest of your devotees will meet up with you at the safehouse. Nothing to worry about; just a small kink in our plans. We can get on with your training soon."

"Wonderful," I murmured. It wasn't as if he didn't already know I was hardly the most enthusiastic student. Then we reached the terrace doors, and Crag wavered into being from the shadows there in full gargoyle form.

My heart leapt at the sight of him. I'd have flung myself into a tight embrace if Rollick hadn't been standing there. It seemed wisest not to do anything that might provoke the demon in the middle of our precarious plan. Instead, I walked over to the gargoyle and lifted my arms so he could easily scoop me up in his preferred carrying position with me tucked against his broad, stony chest.

"Do *not* be seen," Rollick said in one final warning, and Crag dipped his head with a grunt to the affirmative. Then he took off into the air.

The gargoyle soared so high so fast that I lost my breath, staring up at the distant stars. I guessed the point was for us to be swallowed up into the darkness of the sky so no one all the way on the ground could make us out while we were still near the city. I leaned my cheek against the planes of Crag's chest and then tensed a little.

"I put the extra shirt on so the vest isn't pressing against your skin directly. Is it helping?" I could remember far too clearly how he'd started to struggle with the toxic metals burning him when we'd fled my attackers ten days ago.

"It's still not an enjoyable sensation, but it's less intense with the barrier," the gargoyle said with another swish of his wings. His voice came out in a deeper, rougher rumble than usual in this form. He started flying out over the ocean instead of up into the sky and lowered his head to brush his lips against my hair. "Are you comfortable?"

"I'd rather be here with you like this than anywhere else I've been all week," I told him, and kissed his shoulder. The combination of the granite-like texture of his flesh with the living warmth that emanated from it was strangely thrilling. "How far are we going?"

"Rollick thinks we're heading to a property of his out in the desert," the gargoyle said. "Torrent was able to locate a small island where he's stashed some supplies—nothing there for Rollick to connect to us. No other shadowkind around. As long as you have your vest on, no one should be able to find you there."

I wouldn't let myself question what would happen after, not yet.

We flew on and on. Dawn light started to turn the horizon gold, but we were far out enough over the ocean now that I couldn't even see the mainland. Crag started to drop. I twisted my neck and made out a splotch of land amid the deep blue water, like a birthmark on the ocean's surface. As we glided toward it, I saw palm trees and a wooden shelter that wasn't much more than a rough shack, large, jagged rocks catching the spray from the waves along one side and seaweed-mottled sand along the other.

Crag set me down on the sandy ground outside the

shack, which only had three walls but held a few bundles of the supplies Torrent must have brought. I stepped away from the gargoyle quickly so that he could get some distance from my vest and then glanced around. With the brightening sky and the warm breeze rustling through the palm trees, the island looked like some kind of paradise.

"It's our very own desert island," I said with a little laugh. "And I didn't have to go through a shipwreck to get here." Relief surged up through me, stretching my mouth into a broad smile.

I was free. For the first time in ten days, I was out of Rollick's clutches. For the first time in nearly three weeks, there was no immediate threat of attacking monsters. They had no way to find me.

I couldn't stay here forever, obviously, but for the time being, it was a paradise in every possible way.

I set down my backpack in the shelter of the shack and then walked down to the water. The waves lapped at my toes, refreshingly cool in contrast with the already-rising heat of the tropical sun.

Crag followed me. He'd stayed in gargoyle form, either because he wanted to be sure he wouldn't need to whisk me away again or it simply hadn't occurred to him to shift back when I didn't mind him like this. I had to assume *he* felt more comfortable in his actual shadowkind form than the human guise he squeezed himself into.

"Is this the kind of place you'd want to fly out to when you weren't busy with some job for Rollick?" I asked, trying to picture his life before it'd gotten tangled with mine. How often did *he* get to feel free when he had to hide his true self so much of the time? "No humans so you don't have to worry about spreading your wings. Plenty of fishing opportunities."

The gargoyle let out a low rumble of a chuckle. "Maybe because of my nature, I'm usually drawn more to rocky terrain. Rushing up and down the slopes is quite a sensation."

"I bet it is." The thrill-seeker in me leapt in eager anticipation just imagining it.

"And there can be good hunting on mountains too." He flexed his clawed fingers with a satisfied expression that brought more warmth into my chest. Then he paused, seeming to feel the need to clarify, "I only hunt what I can consume—or for others, like when I brought fish to you. I don't enjoy slaughtering every creature in my path. Unless those creatures are vicious beasts trying to attack you."

"I think in that particular situation, it's understandable." I tucked my hand around his elbow. "What's best for hunting in the mountains?"

Crag tipped his head in a thoughtful way. "It depends on where the mountains are. There's a kind of horned sheep I'm very fond of. We could bring Lance along—you liked how he cooked the fish with his fire. Roasted sheep would be even better."

He spoke so easily about us traveling together, experiencing more of the world together without having to worry about fiends giving chase, as if he wouldn't allow there to be a future when that wasn't possible. Right now, with my newfound freedom stretching out in front of me like the vast sprawl of the sea, I could believe it too.

Tears sprang to my eyes. Crag peered at my face as I

brushed my fingers across my eyes. "Are you all right? If you're not happy here—"

"No, I'm good," I said quickly, swallowing the lump that had risen in my throat. "They're happy tears. It's just amazing not to have so many threats hanging right over me." I still had things to worry about, I had no idea how our plan would pan out in the long run, but we'd won this part of the game. We'd managed to beat Rollick this once.

The exhilaration of the knowledge sent me back toward Crag. I grabbed him in a hug, meaning to keep it short because of the vest I had to keep wearing, but he wrapped his bulging arms around me and squeezed me back.

"Thank you," I said. "I know you've basically screwed yourself over with him. You could have kept working for him—he'd forgiven you—"

"That doesn't matter to me," Crag said in his usual gruff way. "I'm yours. You're my Softness. I'm only glad I could be a part of getting you free."

My throat tightened with emotion again. I lifted my head and bobbed up on my feet to press my mouth to his.

We'd never kissed while he was in gargoyle form before. I'd felt the sensation of his stony lower lip before thanks to his jaw that never shed its rocky quality, but the texture of both together and the brush of the fangs that protruded at the corners of his mouth sent an eager quiver through me. Heat flared between my legs.

There were no cameras here, no unwanted figures watching us. I was free in that way too. I could welcome this monster I'd fallen for without any fears that our intimacy would be violated.

But a second later, the body I was hugging contracted a

few inches, the fangs vanishing and part of the mouth mine was melding with taking on the more pliant feeling of human flesh.

I pulled back to find Crag nearly human-like again, his skin bronze-brown other than his jaw, his horns and wings vanished, his facial features smoothing out, and his body shrinking just a little more into its still large but not monstrously massive stature. I stared at him, confused, and then understood.

He thought I wouldn't want to be kissing the "monster." That I'd rather have him like this. But it was the monster who'd saved me—now and many times before. Didn't he know by now I didn't see anything horrific in his natural form?

I raised my hands to rest them on either side of his jaw. "I like you this way, but I like seeing you as you really are too. I like... *feeling* you as you really are. I've gotten to enjoy your gargoyle tongue. Will you share the rest of you with me?"

Surprise flickered through Crag's expression. "Are you sure? I—it's more likely I could hurt you by accident. And... it's not as if I'm the most attractive man even in human form, but at least—"

My heart wrenched. I pulled him into another kiss, which turned firm and hot enough to make my knees wobble when he kissed me back. Then I eased away just far enough to say, "I think you're amazing in every form. You've been the gargoyle with other shadowkind before, haven't you?" He'd admitted to me that while he'd never taken a human lover before me, he'd had flings with shadowkind women in the past.

Crag's grunt told me I was right. "That's different. You're different."

"Maybe, but I want everything they got." I peered up at him, giddy with the glow of the dawn and the wild terrain all around us. "Give me the gargoyle, please?"

CHAPTER TWENTY-TWO

Crag

How could I deny this woman, mortal or not, when she looked at me like that? When she *spoke* like that, with longing humming through her words?

And an answering desire thrummed through me as I gazed down at her—to possess her as fully myself, as no other being had ever taken her. To feel the softness of her mortal body against and encompassing the hardened planes of my true physical form.

But there was a brutality to that hunger, to the craving to claim and possess. I'd never experienced the urge this strongly with any of my shadowkind lovers, as little as I'd known or cared about them beyond the brief release of the encounter. That was exactly why I couldn't give the beastly part of my nature free rein.

She was mine, but I had to preserve her as well as claim her. I couldn't let her tenderness be damaged.

I was a monster, but I was *her* monster.

I bowed my head over her and let my gargoyle self rise to the surface. My skin tightened and toughened, my wings flared from my back, and my face sharpened. My ears lengthened alongside the horns that poked above them up into the warm air. My largest fangs jutted from the sides of my jaw.

I was a beast in every sense of the word now. I'd used this form to terrify more beings both mortal and shadowkind than I could count.

I was good at that. It was what I was made for. I had trouble imagining how Quinn could look at me and see something to appreciate.

But she did. She smiled up at me and trailed her hand down the side of my face, tracing the ridges of my brow and cheek. Then she hooked her fingers around my jaw and tugged my mouth back to hers.

Her lips felt even softer than usual against my stony ones. I kissed her back carefully, only giving myself over to my eagerness bit by bit, increasing the passion of the embrace. When my lips parted, my fangs sliding against her skin, she gave a quiver that would have worried me if she hadn't tugged me even closer an instant later, giving every appearance that she was reveling in the sensation.

I hugged her to my chest as I kissed her harder, but the impression of her vest through her shirt sent a prickling over my skin that was much less enjoyable than the rest of this experience. She couldn't risk taking it off, even out here.

So I'd just have to bring her as much pleasure as I could around it.

I laid her down on the sandy ground and braced myself over her so we weren't pressed quite so closely together. With that bit of distance, the effect of the silver and iron was only a faint niggling I could tune out. It faded away completely when I captured her mouth again.

Quinn hummed encouragingly, her mouth slipping open so her tongue could twine with mine. As I teased my sinuous gargoyle tongue past her lips, she reached up to curl her fingers around my horns. Her grip on them, gentle and yet determined, inflamed me in ways I hadn't expected.

I wanted every part of her. I wanted to show her I could bring her to the same heights she'd reached with my companions all on my own. I couldn't resent the enjoyment and devotion they'd offer her, but right now she was only mine.

I let out a soft growl and trailed my fangs along her jaw to the side of her neck. Quinn whimpered and tipped her head back to allow me greater access. I had the urge to nip her to the point of drawing blood, to mark her and let the spark of pain fuel more pleasure the way Lance did, but I didn't have the dragon shifter's fiery breath to seal the wound.

Quinn was strong, but she was also fragile in ways even most mortals weren't. The illnesses of this world could affect her so much more easily than most. I would ravage her, but never to the point of threatening her.

As I slicked my tongue over her throat, Quinn let out an impatient murmur and ran her hands down my chest. She couldn't quite reach the fitted canvas shorts I normally wore in gargoyle form, but the arch of her hips toward mine told me exactly what her goal was. Her thigh brushed the erection already straining at the fabric, and I groaned.

I wanted to feel her on me, around me, everything—but she wouldn't be ready for me all at once. We'd had to take it slowly even in my human form, and I was even larger now.

Besides, there were other parts I wanted another taste of now that I'd discovered just what a delicious delicacy my mortal woman was.

"I'm going to get you good and ready," I murmured against her skin, and eased down her body to grasp her own shorts. Quinn squirmed out of them and her panties with my tugging fingers for help, and for a moment I just gazed down at her most intimate parts, the pale downy hair and the glistening folds that I was honored to witness.

A flush crept across Quinn's pretty face. "I can handle you," she said. "I'm sure I can. It just might take some... warming up."

"I'm only admiring you," I told her, which made her blush deepen. "But you'll definitely be warmed up when I'm through."

I bent down to lap my tongue over her slit. Quinn gasped, her hips bucking upward so I could devour her even more thoroughly. I gripped her hips, careful not to let my short claws dig into her skin, and lapped my long tongue right into her the way she'd enjoyed so much a few nights ago.

An even needier sound burst out of her. I drank in her tangy sweetness, like nothing I'd experienced with the few shadowkind women I'd dallied with, and my cock stiffened to the point of aching.

I was going to make her come at least once before I attempted to push *that* inside her. Let the rush of bliss relax her, and then we could find more delight together that much easier.

Lance had said once that it was easy to tell what would satisfy our mortal from her cues, and he'd been right. Quinn urged on every flick of my tongue and graze of my lips that inflamed her with her cries and growls and the swaying of her hips. She reached for my horns again, not holding on to them now but simply stroking them in a way I hadn't realized could provoke such pleasure in myself.

I plunged my tongue deeper, pressed it against the spot that brought out the most sound in her, and rubbed my upper lip across the little nub nestled in her folds that gave her such pleasure. Quinn came with the most beautiful noise, a choked moan that reverberated through her whole body as it quaked around me.

My wings flexed over me in response, her bliss radiating through my own body. I was on the verge of exploding just like that, but I wasn't going to rush this.

As she sagged back against the sand, I eased away only far enough to caress her with my hand now. Her muscles were looser with the release, but not quite enough that I was sure I wouldn't hurt her.

"Fuck, that feels good," she panted as I slid two fingers inside her. "I want all of you."

"Soon," I said, the word coming out in a hungry growl. "I'm going to stretch you so it's good all the way through."

I spread my fingers to stroke them around her channel, encouraging it to accept more and more pressure. Quinn sputtered another curse and rocked her hips, her juices coating my hand. I had the feeling that if I swiveled my thumb over her nub, she might come again just like that. But the next time she found her release, I wanted to be inside her properly.

Her overlapping shirts had ridden up to expose her stomach. I bent my head to kiss the soft skin beside her belly button as I continued working her over.

The swell of her breasts was too tempting even with the noxious materials that covered them. I couldn't resist. I slipped my other hand under the fabric of her tank top beneath the vest, ignoring the sharper pang of discomfort, and reached up to cup one of the silky slopes.

Another moan tumbled out of Quinn's mouth. She outright writhed beneath me, caught between my hand above and my stretching finger below. I massaged her breast and skimmed a claw over the nipple the way I'd seen Lance do to impressive effect. The gasping reaction I got was the perfect reward.

Her channel was so slick against my other hand, the muscles lining it gone increasingly pliant with each rotation of my fingers. I forced myself to stroke her a few more times before bringing those fingers to my lips and licking her arousal off them.

Quinn shifted up on her elbows with a ragged breath. "Kiss me again."

I was more than happy to oblige. Our mouths melded together, our tongues tangling, and her hands skimmed over my chest. Then I drew back to yank off my shorts.

Quinn's gaze followed the movement, her eyes widening with obvious eagerness as she took in my thick shaft.

She showed no hesitation at all, spreading her legs wider in invitation, but I couldn't help halting just to check. "Are you sure?"

This couldn't have been how she'd ever imagined her encounters with men would go. When I had only my rock-like jaw as a reminder of my true nature, I was nearly as human as any of them. But like this...

"Right now, there's nothing in the world I'm surer about than the fact that I want all of you inside me immediately," Quinn grumbled.

There was no denying how much she meant that statement. A relieved chuckle spilled out of me. I tucked a hand under her hips to lift her to meet me and lined myself up.

Her channel expanded again to encompass me. Every inch I penetrated her, more pleasure raced through my own body, until I felt as if I were on fire with a heat I'd have happily burned up in.

Quinn groaned, pushing herself toward me as her fingers dug into the sand. The joy that washed over her expression and reverberated through her panting breaths set off a fresh flare of need in me.

I thrust into her, slowly at first and then with increasing speed as she showed no sign of pain. The sounds breaking from her throat now were nothing but gleeful. Sweat beaded on her forehead and glistened on her collarbone. I bowed over her to lick it off with a swipe of my tongue, and she clutched at me, holding me with her.

I kissed her on the mouth and then her neck, bucking

into her even faster. A wild keening reverberated from her chest. She bucked in time with my rhythm with increasing wildness, her fingernails scraping over my stony skin, her breath fragmenting more and more. Pressure built at the base of my cock, but I held myself focused on her reactions, her pleasure, holding off my own final bliss until—

Her sex clenched around my cock, and a shudder ran through her body. It was as if she were wringing my own release out of me. With a groan, I spilled myself into her softness.

Quinn shivered again with a giddy grin. She held my face, gazing up at me with affection shining in her sky-blue eyes, and beamed as if she were the sun itself. As I eased out of her and gathered her against me, a strange sensation wrapped around my heart.

I wasn't ashamed of what I was, not generally speaking. I'd put my monstrousness to use to serve all kinds of needs. When things had gone wrong... it hadn't been on purpose, and I'd made what amends I could. Every advantage had its downsides.

But I couldn't say I'd ever felt outright *proud* to be the monster I was before this moment, holding Quinn in all her combined strength and fragility, knowing how much she trusted me to look after her. I would serve her for as long as she'd have me, and I'd put all my bulk and brutality toward ensuring she got every bit of life she deserved.

CHAPTER TWENTY-THREE

Quinn

The second time I woke up that morning, it was on the floor of the island shack, sprawled on the sleeping bag Crag had unfurled for me. From the angle of the sun and the small shadows cast by the men standing over me, it was nearly noon.

I pushed myself upright, rubbing at my eyes, and took in the newer arrivals. Torrent and Lance showed no sign of recent injuries, so they must have gotten clear of the hotel without any problems.

Lance dropped down onto the floor of the shack next to me with his usual carefree grace, and I motioned for Torrent to sit at my other side, mindful of the strain standing put on his legs. Crag stayed on his feet, alternating between peering over the ocean and glancing at us, but when our eyes met, a tingle shot through me in the memory of how we'd celebrated my newfound freedom.

Lance tucked his clawed hand around my elbow, and

Torrent rested one tentacle against my back. I was left with the sense of being perfectly contained between my three monstrous men. We fit together so easily. Maybe having them in my life would be harder if I ever got to go back to a regular one... but with the harmony I felt in their presence, I had to believe we could make it work.

"How long have you been here?" I asked Torrent.

"We just arrived," he said. "I had to pull a small craft along with me over the water to carry the dragon shifter." He shot a wryly baleful look at Lance.

Lance let out a playful huff. "If you'd gotten a boat big enough to hold an engine and not just a shadow, I could have driven it myself."

"But we didn't want any chance of the wrong person spotting us. It seems that we got away clear." Torrent took my hand and ran his thumb over my knuckles in a way that provoked another tingle. "I know this place isn't up to the standards of your previous accommodations—I didn't have much time to work on it—"

"Wait, you built this?" I stared at the building around us. Yes, it was roughly made, but I hadn't realized it was a recent construction. Because the wood that made up the small structure was weathered... but not by the actual weather, I realized. They were pieces of driftwood, some of the ends ragged—mostly flat boards, but ones that had ended up in the sea one way or another.

When I squinted closer, I couldn't make out any nails or screws. The boards had been wedged against each other in a careful configuration that kept them stable, some of them presumably braced against the boulder at the rear of the building. Some kind of thick tarp or treated fabric had been wrapped over the roof to cover any cracks.

"It's amazing that you put this together at all," I said, taking in the details with an architect's perspective. It might not be the kind of structure I'd dreamed of designing, but it was sturdy and functional in its simplicity. Staying up and doing what it was supposed to do were the most important qualities for our purposes.

Torrent's mouth curved into a small smile. "I've sometimes enjoyed making sculptures and other fixtures along the beach for people to find. It's a way of staying present in the mortal realm even if I can't really show myself. I've picked up a few tricks over the years."

"Well, it worked just fine for me to catch up on some sleep." I yawned and stretched my arms over my head, but curiosity was already gnawing at me. "Did you see what happened at the hotel? Was there a fight? Has Rollick reached out?"

"We stayed behind watching long enough for the big bad beasties to show up," Lance reported, drumming his other claws against the floorboards. "All human-like, so we're not sure what kind of beasts they are."

Torrent nodded. "And they found something they didn't like. The window to Rollick's suite was smashed just as we were taking off. It seemed like it'd get dangerous to stick around anywhere nearby at that point."

My pulse hiccupped. If my monstrous stalkers had been busting up Rollick's suite, then they must have found at least one piece of evidence I'd left that'd convinced them he was lying about not knowing where I was. But in my focus on getting *me* out of the hotel, I'd forgotten— "What about the other guests —the human ones? If the other shadowkind attack Rollick and his people, will the mortals around be okay?"

"These beings have still mostly been keeping up appearances in their other activities," Torrent said, squeezing my hand. "I doubt they'd want to show off their monstrous forms in front of downtown Santa Monica. Both sides will want to keep the conflict contained away from mortal eyes."

Lance tugged at his ear. "I think I heard a fire alarm going off as we were zipping away. That'd clear out the building nice and quick."

Relief rushed through me. "Okay. But we don't know yet how the fighting turned out? Whether either side took significant damage?" As monstrous as Rollick had proven himself to be, he was still more on my side than the creatures who were going around eating sorcerers and trying to kill my men so they could enslave me. I couldn't help hoping that he'd come out of the clash better off than his opponents.

Torrent shook his head. "Rollick said he'd contact me by phone when everything was settled. I haven't heard from him yet, and no missed calls or messages from when I wasn't available to answer. We couldn't risk getting caught up in the skirmish by staying."

"Of course not. I'm glad you're okay. Both of you." I gripped his hand tighter and leaned against Lance's shoulder. A sigh slipped out of me.

The dragon shifter peered at me with a mix of concern and eagerness before reaching toward one of the bags of supplies. "Have you eaten yet? We made sure to grab many things when we were setting up."

"I remembered the snacks you like best," Crag put in with a pointed rumble.

Lance waved him off carelessly. "Yes, yes. But she needs all the vita-whats and so on too." He plucked out an orange and started carving it into slices with his claws without waiting for my answer.

My stomach did gurgle then. I'd been so tense from our escape and then exhilarated that we'd succeeded that hunger hadn't crept up on me before I'd dozed off. All I'd had was the gulp of water with my morning pills. "Thank you," I said, reaching to accept the slices from the dragon shifter.

As the tartly sweet juice filled my mouth, Lance rummaged around in the bag, partly shredding the thin plastic with his claws, and pulled out a chocolate bar. "There, you can be helping keep her fed too," he said, wagging it teasingly at Crag before handing it over.

It was actually my favorite type of bar—I must have mentioned that to the gargoyle sometime in our travels. I beamed up at him. "Thank you too. You all made this place perfect."

But the world beyond this island was far from perfect. I took another bite, more pensive thoughts creeping up over me. "So, I guess now we just wait and see how things pan out, and then we'll figure out where we go from here?"

I expected Torrent to agree immediately, but instead he paused as if debating whether to say what he was thinking. I straightened up to catch his gaze. "What?"

He tipped his head to the side, his mouth twisting at a crooked angle. "I did have a thought—something we might want to investigate while the shadowkind who've been searching for you are distracted."

"Okay, and what's that?"

He motioned in what I assumed was the direction of the mainland. "When I was scouting out enemy activities for Rollick, I came across evidence that there's a sorcerer family in Arizona that our enemies were trying to track down. I've spent some time in that area on other missions for Rollick before, and I think I know exactly where the family is located. From what you've told me about the sorcerer Rollick brought to talk to you before, this bunch is more experienced and has more power."

"I think most would be," I said. "He seemed like his talents were pretty weak. But why would that matter right now?"

"You still need to sort out the problem of the magic in you—understanding how to work with it or even getting it out of you, if that's possible," Torrent said. "We could try to talk to them today. Heading to their little settlement here, we wouldn't need to go anywhere near L.A."

Hope trickled up through my chest. "Do you really think they'd talk to me?"

Torrent shrugged. "I don't see why not. I'd imagine they'd have at least a little sympathy for your situation. If not, then we just leave, no harm done."

Lance had tensed a little at my other side. I glanced over at him, my stomach clenching. "But we don't know how they'd treat the three of *you*."

The dragon shifter put on a grin that only looked a little stiff. "We've got you to vouch for us, baby girl. And we can always stick to the shadows farther out if we don't want to tempt their voodoo."

Torrent tapped him with a tentacle. "*You* should definitely stay well back—you can keep watch over the road leading to their settlement. It'd be hard for them to affect any of us—from what I've seen before, only one might be powerful enough to even attempt to coerce a higher shadowkind of our power—but after you've had your mind muddled with sorcery once, you're more susceptible."

Lance gave a snarl but didn't argue. Crag drew himself up even taller, still in his gargoyle form, and spread his wings. "Torrent and I can keep a closer watch over Quinn. We won't let her be harmed."

"It'll still be a little risky for *you*," Torrent said, searching my gaze with his sea-green eyes. "There's always the chance of shadowkind noticing you and passing on word. You're safest here."

I dragged in a breath. "But I need to figure out how to leave here eventually, and the longer we wait, the more chance there is that some other beings will go after those sorcerers and kill them. It's better that we go now while we know the ones hunting me and them are distracted, like you said. Just a quick conversation, see if there's anything they know that could help. If you're all in."

The men around me inclined their heads without hesitation. I pushed myself to my feet, ignoring the nervous twist of my gut. "All right. Let's find out what these sorcerers can tell me."

CHAPTER TWENTY-FOUR

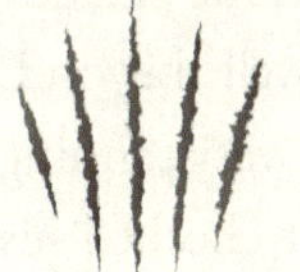

Quinn

Just this once, Torrent let me drive. I couldn't really see that as an act of faith when he hadn't had a whole lot of choice in the situation, but having my hands on the steering wheel and my foot on the gas pedal reinvigorated my sense of freedom.

I was tracking down answers, maybe even a full solution to my problem. What the people I was going to see could tell me might give me *complete* freedom from the problems that'd been dogging me for the past few weeks... From the monsters that'd been attempting to claim me as their meal or their tool.

The desert landscape whizzed by on either side of the lonely road: plains of rippled orange-brown earth dotted with scruffy shrubs leading to ruddy cliffs that rose in the distance. There was no sound from outside other than the whistle of the wind over the jeep Torrent had acquired for us somehow or other. The air conditioning blasted a steady stream of cool air over us, but I could see how hot it was outside from the shimmer on the pavement ahead.

The sorcerers had their sort-of ranch in a secluded valley just beyond the nearest of the cliffs ahead of us. We'd already left Lance in the shadows about a mile back, watching the road well beyond the influence of any enslaving magic. Crag was scanning the landscape from the backseat while Torrent checked his phone next to me and nodded to the road ahead.

"The road will be pretty rough since no one but them comes out here, hardly a road at all, but the jeep should be able to handle it. I don't think whatever shadowkind guards they have posted around the settlement will stop you when you're alone in the car. You know what to do if the sorcerers turn out to be hostile."

I nodded, my chest constricting a little. I might enjoy the chance to take the wheel, but I didn't love the fact that none of my men could stay right by my side for this meeting. Sorcerers saw shadowkind as enemies at worst and slaves at best, not as friends or lovers. They'd be even more wary of my men if they'd heard about the recent killings like the guy I'd talked to before had. If I turned up with a couple of shadowkind companions, they'd *definitely* be unhappy.

"Shout really loud," I said. "I think I can handle that."

"And we'll keep watch from our vantage point," Crag put in. "We'll be able to tell if anything's really wrong."

"As long as I don't go inside." I thought I should be able to manage that. How likely were the sorcerers to want a stranger poking around in their homes?

"If you get a bad feeling, you can just leave," Torrent

reminded me. "We don't know for sure this group will be able to help you at all. There's no point in taking any more of a risk than you already are just by coming out here."

"I know."

It was late in the afternoon now, the shadows stretching long, and he still hadn't gotten any word from Rollick. I didn't know if that was a good sign, meaning the demon and our other enemies were still totally occupied with their clash, or a bad sign, meaning the other shadowkind had managed to batter him beyond capability of communication.

Either way, no one would be expecting to find me out here. If we faced any danger, it'd come from the sorcerers and the shadowkind *they* commanded.

As the cliffs loomed closer, Crag stiffened in the back seat. I eased up on the gas before he'd even spoken.

"There's a being up ahead," he said. "I can only sense it faintly from here. It's staying still—I think it's a lesser shadowkind, but it feels large and strong."

Torrent made a face. "They have guards, as we expected. I was hoping not so far out, but I guess it's not surprising."

I pulled over onto the side of the road and stopped completely. "Will you still be able to get close enough to see what's happening?"

He studied the sheer hills that framed the shallow valley we couldn't yet peer into. "There's a lot of high terrain. I think we should be able to find a spot where we can look down into the valley from the shadows while avoiding any sentries. But it might take us a minute or two to get to you from there." He paused and glanced over at me, his eyes darkening. "We don't have to do this. We can go back to the island and make other plans."

I inhaled slowly and touched my pocket with my old multitool, the one that'd helped me fix so many problems much smaller than the one I was currently facing. I had that. I had the steak knife I'd stolen from one of my hotel dinners and my silver pen-dagger in the other pocket. I had the moves ingrained from my self-defense classes.

And I was wearing my silver-and-iron vest, concealed by a fresh tee, which would make it difficult for any lesser shadowkind and even most higher to hurt me. Torrent had said it should block any persuasive vibes if the sorcerers had managed to enslave a being like a succubus or the siren who'd manipulated me on the hotel roof.

I'd spent the past ten days hiding away in Rollick's luxurious hotel, accomplishing nothing except putting on an inadvertent porn show for my captor and tapping into skills I didn't really want. I *had* to do something, had to try to take control over my life again, or what was the point in having gotten free at all?

I couldn't expect my shadowkind men to take all the risks on my behalf. That wasn't remotely fair.

"This is our best chance," I said. "And we don't know how long the shadowkind after me will be distracted for. Anything we do after today will only be more dangerous."

Torrent didn't argue with any of my points. He simply waited for me to work through my thoughts, easing one of his tentacles over to hug my knee. I rested my hand on the sinuous limb.

"We could try to hide in the vehicle, make ourselves as inobtrusive as possible," Crag said abruptly.

I glanced over my shoulder, raising my eyebrows. "As much as I'd like to bring you with me, I don't think *inobtrusive* is a word that could ever describe you." I turned to face the cliffs again. "These sorcerers have managed to avoid getting attacked so far. They must have a pretty good security system. I'll go in alone. They can't do anything *worse* to me than the monsters chasing me want to do."

They had no reason to want to hurt me, after all. I was just a fellow human seeking help.

"Then we'll part ways here," Torrent said, but he reached for me first, his fingers sliding along my jaw and tugging me into a kiss. The press of his mouth against mine felt like a promise and a plea that I'd return to him safely. I kissed him back hard, a sudden swell of emotion nearly overwhelming me.

There was a lot wrong with my life right now. There were so many things I wanted to fix. But somehow in the middle of the chaos, I'd found these three brutal but incredible men who'd lit me up inside and followed me into every challenge we'd faced.

Crag grunted from behind me, where he couldn't easily mimic Torrent's farewell gesture, but he took my hand and kissed the knuckles briefly. Then they both vanished into the shadows. I knew they'd have leapt from the car immediately to dart as quickly as they could over the landscape, avoiding the sorcerers' enslaved shadowkind guards.

I pushed on the gas again with a growl of the engine. The increasingly imperceptible lane led straight ahead between the two jagged hills and then downward with a slight curve into the broad, shallow valley between them.

The jeep's wheels jostled over potholes and bumps, but the vehicle managed all right. Torrent had picked it well.

As I came around the bend, four single-story adobe buildings came into view around a larger two-story structure, all of them blending into the orange-y earth around them.

I hadn't seen any sign of sentries myself, human or monstrous, but probably some shadowy presence had taken note of me, decided I wasn't a terrible threat, and simply informed the inhabitants of my approach. I was still at least a hundred yards away from the nearest building, dust spurting up from under the tires, when a few figures emerged from the homes and headed up the road toward me. One of them raised her hands for me to stop.

Easing my foot on the brake, I ground to a halt there on what was pretty much just bare dirt at this point and put the jeep into park for the time being. Then I got out, grabbing my messenger bag and slinging it over my shoulder automatically, staying close to the vehicle. Even with the sun having sunk behind the western hill, the air was hot enough to bring sweat beading across my skin.

It was an older woman, her coiled hair a mix of white and steel-gray, and a younger couple who'd come out to meet me. The older woman, who was the one who'd motioned to me, appeared to be the leader. She strode a little closer with the man and the other woman, who I figured were in their thirties, following just behind.

"What are you doing here?" the first woman asked in a dry but commanding voice, squinting at me.

My pulse thumped faster. This was the deciding

moment—whether they believed my story would determine whether I got any help from them at all.

"I heard that there were people who lived out here who had certain... skills. Skills I'd like to learn about, because I didn't get a chance to from my own family before I lost them."

It was a simplified version of the truth, because the last thing I wanted was anyone talking about a visit from a girl with a transplanted heart. The full story was too complicated anyway.

The man folded his arms over his chest. "*Who* told you that?"

"It was... it was in some notes my parents left behind," I lied. I wasn't going to tell them a shadowkind had directed me here. "I know about the rifts, and the monsters that come through them, and that it's possible to control them. Sometimes I feel like I should be able to, but I didn't have anyone to teach me. I don't even know if I *want* to do that —I just need to understand this power I've got so I can figure out what to do about it."

The three figures shifted on their feet, obviously uneasy. But their sentries hadn't given them any reason to worry about me, and from what I'd heard from and about other sorcerers, my story was plausible. The only question was whether they'd want to bother spending the time talking with me.

Before they could answer, a little boy came running across the uneven terrain. He couldn't have been more than four. He grabbed the younger woman's leg and stared at me, then up at the others. "Mommy, Daddy, who's this lady?"

My gut twisted with guilt at the lie I was about to tell, but I grabbed the opening he'd given me. These were people who stole the free will of shadowkind beings and forced them to do their bidding. I shouldn't feel bad about manipulating them just slightly in turn.

"I was about his age when I lost my mom and dad," I said, letting my voice turn rough with all the losses I had actually faced.

I could tell the tactic landed as I'd intended. The young woman's face fell. She squeezed her son's shoulder. "Go back to the house, Jonah. Ask Grandpa to read you a book." As the little boy scampered off, she returned her attention to me. "Your parents were sorcerers."

I nodded. "But I haven't been able to piece together much... I only just found some of their writing that made a little more sense of things I heard and saw when I was a little kid. My memories are all kind of a blur, though, and the journals didn't give many details."

The three sorcerers exchanged a glance. The older woman took the lead again. "This isn't a good time for pursuing an interest in the magic of the shadows. There are monsters hunting people like us. You'd do better to forget about it."

I folded my arms over my chest. "I don't think I can. I have this strange... feeling inside me. It's been getting stronger. Maybe if I could just get rid of it—is that even possible?"

She frowned and rubbed her mouth. "There is... Overseas, out where there are times when the sun never rises for days... Norway, I think? I've heard there's an enclave for sorcerers there, a place where those without power go when they're hoping to spark it in themselves. I don't personally know anyone who's taken that route instead of having it through their family line, though, so maybe it doesn't work. But if it does, it's possible someone there would know how to snuff out a power that already exists too."

My heart leapt, although I wasn't sure how I was going to get all the way to Norway. Minor details. "Okay. I guess that's a start. I don't know how soon I'd be able to actually look into that, though. Since I'm already here... is there anything you'd be willing to tell me about how you work with and control your power?"

The older woman sighed. "Since you *are* already here, I suppose we could talk a little. I'm not sure how much we could tell you, but you could ask a few questions. Come over to the courtyard." She motioned to the man, who from the similar dark eyes and hooked shape of their noses I suspected was her son. "Ivan, bring some lemonade or something. It's hot enough to invite the devil out here."

I followed the three sorcerers into the circle of their houses on cautious feet, hoping my shadowkind protectors still had me in their sights.

CHAPTER TWENTY-FIVE

Lance

Quinn needed to be here. She needed to know about the foreboding energy that'd gotten all twisted up inside her heart. I reminded myself of that as I twined through the shadows along the road.

I needed to keep watch. I was the first line of defense if anything ominous came this way. But my whole being itched with the uncertainty of what might be happening to Quinn off where she'd gone, down into the place where the sorcerers lived. What might those sinister mortals with their warped minds decide to do to her?

Was the real danger away from here or in the direction she'd gone?

The buried memories rattled at the inner cage I'd stuffed them into. Slivers of groans and agonized winces trickled out despite my best efforts. I flexed my shadowy sense of my claws, longing to dig them into the firmly packed soil, to gouge my presence, my *survival*, into this landscape.

No. I could already imagine what Torrent would say. We didn't want anyone knowing we'd come here. We didn't want to lead the monsters who'd claim Quinn to these other sorcerers even after we'd gone.

Even if these particular mortals would deserve whatever fate they met from the fiends.

The sun had dipped below the hills. Its glow still spilled over the sky and lit the clifftops, but gloom swathed the ground. I leapt and darted from one side of the road to the other, spinning this way and that, working the restlessness out of my being as much as I could without any real muscles to stretch.

So strange that I felt more at home in the physical body I pulled together out of the materials of this foreign realm than I did in the darkness now. The concreteness of it, the certainty of it, appealed to me in a way I couldn't put into words.

I liked that I could put my *claws* into it—there was the thing. What was the point of having claws if you couldn't slice and dice with them? And fighting was much more satisfying with bodies colliding than when tangling with another being while you were both wisps of essence that barely had a presence at all.

The car had vanished into the valley some time ago. Ten minutes? An hour? I didn't have much of an internal clock at the best of times, and this was definitely not the best.

What would the sorcerers tell Quinn anyway? That she should order around all the beasties like Rollick had her doing? That she should try to command all of us?

Well, maybe I wouldn't mind if she threw some of that power at the monsters who wanted to sink their claws and fangs into *her*. It would serve them right. Fighting back wasn't the same as hunting down beings who'd never done a thing to you. Quinn would use the magic in her properly. Quinn understood how awful it was—the things the other sorcerers did.

But I couldn't say the thought that they might know how she could toss the power away completely didn't wake up a flicker of joy in my chest. She could be rid of it, not a sorcerer at all. Then none of that taint would remain, and none of the others would want to steal her away, and she could be only mine.

All right, Crag's and Torrent's too. They'd stood by her when she needed them like I had. I would just have to steal her away for my own self, only the two of us, as often as I had the chance. I shouldn't have to share *all* the time.

A creeping sensation wavered over my body. I spun again, my focus sharpening. Was something—or someone —coming? From which direction? Maybe it was simply Quinn returning. I could hope for that.

The impression faded as quickly as it'd risen up, but I didn't think it'd come from the sorcerers' valley. I studied the more distant bulge of reddish rock that jutted from the ground and the bristly plants that dotted the flatter soil near me. I couldn't see anything traveling in the gloom, but I wasn't as sensitive to movement as the gargoyle was.

It could be just a tiny beastie. Maybe even one of the sorcerers' dupes patrolling farther. If I stayed still, it wouldn't think I was of any concern all the way out here.

Or it could be nothing at all. Just my nerves jumping because of the memories churning inside me.

I bared my teeth as if I could scare that possibility into submission, and snapped them a few times for good measure, but in the shadows they didn't make the satisfying gnashing sound. No, physical form was much better. I couldn't wait until we could leave here and I could stretch my limbs out properly.

A pebble rattled. I whipped in the direction of the sound, my ears pricked, my eyes narrowing. The tufts of coarse grass waved in the breeze. Somewhere off on the other side of the road, a rabbit hopped behind a bush.

Just a mortal beastie. Even less of a threat than a shadowkind one. Humph. Rollick would have chuckled at me. Maybe even Torrent would have laughed. Not Crag—most of the time he didn't really get even actual jokes.

And not Quinn. Quinn would have told me it made sense that I was uneasy. She'd be hurrying out of the valley as quickly as she could. She knew those sorcerers were no—

The surge of energy walloped me, so suddenly and with so much force that I tumbled right out of the shadows. I sprawled on the dry earth with my scales scraping the scattered stones and my thoughts whirling in my head. Panic flashed through them, jumbling them even more. That'd felt— It was too familiar— No, no, I couldn't let—

I reached to leap back into the shadows instinctively, and another wallop smacked into my body. I could practically hear my brains jostling inside my skull. The energy crackled through my mind, digging in like dozens of tiny claws. I couldn't move, couldn't speak, could hardly piece together coherent thought. What— How—

Another presence loomed, still far but large enough that I felt it even across that distance now. So powerful. So determined. And others—other shadowkind rippling into my awareness as they charged ahead of it.

They'd come. The ones we thought were busy with Rollick—they'd found the sorcerers too. They'd come. And Quinn was still there. I had to—

I was moving, but not because I'd decided to. My body morphed back into its shadowy state and lunged forward across the desert plain alongside the other racing creatures. An urge gripped me way down in the center of my being, with words I couldn't remember hearing with my actual ears reverberating through me.

Find all the sorcerers. Slash their throats. Leave the rest to me.

No. I couldn't do that. Especially not while Quinn was there.

I tried to fight the compulsion, but its claws had stretched into threads that wound all through my essence, gripping every particle of me.

Just like before—just like when the ones who'd kept me in that cage had given their orders.

A cry burst from my throat, silent to the outside world as the gloom swallowed it up. I strained at my limbs, but they kept hurtling forward, toward the place where I knew the sorcerers lived. The ones who were strangers to me... and one other besides. One lovely woman I'd sworn to protect, who, yes, was a sorcerer too, whether she wanted to be or not.

Icy panic washed over me, but it didn't dislodge the hold the magic had on my will. It simply closed around my gut with a queasy lurch. I couldn't give in, couldn't let this fiend control me. I had to break the spell, somehow…

But I'd only broken it before by getting my captor to let down her guard. I didn't even know where the being who'd compelled me was now. Somewhere behind, lurking while we ran ahead to carry out the most dangerous work. Driving us forward in front of him like a herd of deer ahead of a wolf.

Except we weren't the real prey here. The mortals with their tender flesh were.

I wrenched and flailed at my body as it whipped toward the valley, but nothing I did made the slightest difference. The command laced all through my being urged me on and on with visions of human necks sliced open, blood splattered across the ground.

Some part of me *reveled* in the thought, and I couldn't even tell how much that was the magic and how much my own fury at the humans who imprisoned our kind this way.

For a few fleeting moments, my anger seared through all my resistance and my horror. I would tear into them and let their lives leak out into the earth. They would never twist another being's will to their own again. I—

The image flashed before my eyes of a very specific pale neck I'd become familiar with, pale blond hair falling around it beneath a delicate chin, and another smack of cold nausea broke through the stirred-up rage.

Not her. She didn't count. She wasn't like them. I had to defend her.

Find all the sorcerers. Slash their throats.

The other beings around me didn't know Quinn was in the valley. I was abruptly certain of that. The immense being who'd given the command would have instructed them to leave her alive if it'd realized.

But I knew. And the compulsion in me demanded that I end her life too, that I serve the master who'd caught me in his leash to the full extent of my ability.

I'd been able to fight the hold the sorcerers of the past put on me a little—to delay, to bend their instructions in tiny ways. I'd never felt an iron grip quite like this.

Because my enslaver now was shadowkind. The compulsion came with an understanding of my nature no human could have held, as if the being that'd given its orders saw me and knew me inside out. How had any human even come near that kind of recognition to command shadowkind to their will?

That brief question fled as I flung myself down into the valley and the buildings came into sight up ahead in the fading sunlight.

There was the jeep I knew Quinn had arrived in. Even realizing it was probably empty, my fangs jutted with the impulse to leap inside and shred whatever was within.

No, no, *no*.

My agonized protests made no difference to the movements of my body. I leapt over the jeep, a glance through the window confirming no one was inside and allowing me to race onward. Then I burst out of the shadows in full dragon form, snarling and flexing my claws.

Other creatures were leaping from the darkness all around me. A few had already stormed into one of the houses, a shriek and frantic yelling spilling past the bashed door. The horrible, unshakeable tug inside me drew me past the buildings, following a trace of scent I couldn't stop myself from recognizing, from knowing that the woman attached to it was technically one of the sorcerers I'd been commanded to destroy.

There she was. The first glimpse of her bright hair and frightened face just about tore me in two, wanting to run to her and shield her, knowing my claws and fangs would rip into her of their own accord despite my wishes.

I cried out again, attempting a warning that snagged in my throat. Every bit of determination in my body rallied in resistance, straining against the magic propelling me onward—but it wasn't enough.

Crag was sweeping her up in his arms. He was going to carry her away, and the orders driving me toward them refused to accept that, as much as the rest of me wanted to shout for joy at her potential escape. I couldn't stop myself, couldn't do more than growl in a mix of rage and anguish as I threw myself at the two of them.

"Lance!" Crag roared in protest, whipping himself around so that my claws sank into his stony flesh instead of gouging Quinn's. Small mercies. I recoiled inside at the smoky blood that gushed from my friend's wounds, but my limbs and teeth slashed on.

No, no, please, no...

The protest turned into a silent wail inside my head. It didn't help me. Nothing could drown out the commands ringing through me—to stop the gargoyle, to savage him until he fell and I could wrench the woman from his grasp to claim her for the being that'd made himself my master.

CHAPTER TWENTY-SIX

Quinn

The lemonade cut through the worst of the heat, the perfect mix of sweet and sour as it slid down my throat, but it left my mouth sticky. I swallowed, looking around at the three sorcerers who'd offered it to me.

Ivan had stuck close to his wife, who'd introduced herself as Jenny. The older woman—the apparent matriarch over this small community—was Victoria. A few other figures had emerged from the buildings to listen in on our conversation, but they hadn't bothered to introduce themselves.

I still didn't feel exactly *welcome* in their midst. I clutched the strap of my messenger bag with my free hand, fretting briefly that my vest was showing under my shirt and they'd wonder about my weird fashion choices, as if that was what really mattered.

"Is this normal?" I found myself saying, thinking of my

donor's family with their house in the Florida wilderness. "All of you living off in the middle of nowhere together? Doesn't it get kind of lonely?"

Victoria shrugged. "We have other properties in other places, in cities and towns or at least closer to them. This spot was meant for when we're harnessing a new demon and making sure they're fully under control, or simply to gather the extended family together. But with recent events... We've felt it's better to stay here where we can be more sure of our safety for a while."

"Where are you from?" Jenny asked, watching me curiously. I wondered if she'd ever met a sorcerer who didn't understand their powers before me.

It seemed unwise to mention my actual home state in case these people had heard about all the chaos shadowkind had been creating over there. "California," I said instead, which was at least true of where I'd most immediately come from. "Near L.A."

Victoria hummed to herself. "I don't know of any major established families operating around that city, but there are a lot more small-time practitioners who don't mingle much with the community. Although I wouldn't have expected you to have trouble with an emerging power you hadn't meant to call on if your parents weren't particularly skilled." Her eyes narrowed.

"Is it about skill?" I asked quickly. "From the things they wrote, it sounded like it's something that just... wakes up in you and almost tells you how to use it. Which sounds really weird. And I still don't know what I'm doing."

"There are strategies for getting more in touch with the

power," Ivan put in. "Meditation and that sort of thing. And also..." He paused.

I focused on him, hiding my eagerness. The other sorcerer had already mentioned meditation to me, but maybe this group knew something more. "Also?"

He glanced at his mother, and Victoria gave a short laugh as if amused that he was deferring to her. She gave me a thin smile. "You do understand exactly what it is that we do, don't you?"

"You... you get control over the monsters that can come out of the shadows," I said. "You can tell them what to do, and they have to do it. Make them use their supernatural powers for your benefit and things like that."

"That's the gist of it. Well, this won't matter until you're confident enough to fully harness one of those monsters. And many practitioners dismiss this aspect because they feel it's abasing ourselves when we should hold ourselves much higher than the creatures we command. But we've always found, and I know other families who feel similarly, that you can wield your power much more effectively the better you've familiarized yourself with the demon."

I held my eyebrows from rising. "Familiarize yourself how?"

She waved a hand carelessly as if it didn't matter much. "Oh, however makes you feel you're developing a better understanding of them. When I've taken on a new subject, I'll spend hours in our training room with it, giving it free rein other than making sure it doesn't harm me, watching its behavior. Ivan takes his on hunts and shares the meal with them. Jenny likes to draw and paint hers. There's a sort of closeness that can develop that seems to bring forth more of the power."

Huh. I hadn't tried communing with the creatures Rollick had brought around. But then, neither he nor I had known there'd be any point in trying. The first sorcerer hadn't mentioned that strategy. "So that just works for the one creature you're studying, right?"

"That's where you'll see the greatest effect," Ivan said, his tone getting more enthusiastic. "But we've found that making those sort of connections makes it easier to control others as well. Partly because you need less effort to keep the ones you've developed a deeper understanding of under your control so you have more energy to expend elsewhere, but I think also because you understand monstrousness in general better."

"I'm not so sure about the last part," Jenny said, giving him a teasing nudge of her elbow before meeting my eyes again. "It definitely helps just in freeing up energy, though."

Interesting, even if it wasn't advice I ever expected to put into practice. "Thank you," I said, riffling through my thoughts for the next question I'd want to ask. "Is there any—"

Victoria stiffened so abruptly that my mouth snapped shut around the words I'd been going to say. Her head jerked around, her gaze darting across the terrain beyond the settlement, around where I'd parked the jeep. I swiveled, following her gaze.

The landscape was draped in shadows cast by the tall cliff to the west. I couldn't make anything out, but Victoria had obviously sensed something.

"Into the houses," she shouted abruptly. "Everyone, *now*. Call whatever creatures you can to our protection."

With the last words, she was already racing toward one of the buildings, Jenny and Ivan right behind her. The other sorcerers darted off toward their own homes. I hurried after the three I'd talked to, but as I reached the door, Victoria spun around, motioning her son and daughter-in-law past her.

"*You* brought them with you," she hissed. "They followed you here. How else could they have found us right now?"

"What? I—"

Then the first shadowkind beasts lunged out of the shadows at the edges of the courtyard. As the monsters charged toward us, Victoria slammed the door in my face. The other doors had already banged shut all around me.

My stomach flipped over. I couldn't tell her that the monsters who'd been killing sorcerers had already been close to finding her before I'd ever come here, or I'd have to explain how I knew that, and I didn't think knowing I was chummy with some *other* monsters would endear me to her either.

There was no point in running toward the jeep. I'd have to push through a horde of shadowkind to get there, and they didn't look at all friendly. My heart thudding, I shoved myself around the side of the house. The lemonade glass slipped from my hand and shattered on the ground, but I didn't have time to think about that.

A shovel was leaning against a shed around the back. I dashed to it and grabbed it, knowing it wouldn't give me much protection but that it might at least buy me a minute or two in fending the creatures off. The shed itself was locked, so I braced my back against it, brandishing the shovel with one hand and groping in my pocket. Would the larger steak knife or the smaller silver blade offer more protection? I had no idea.

Had my monstrous men seen the coming onslaught? Were they on their way to get me out of here, or was I completely on my own?

How the hell was I getting out of this if they couldn't make it to me?

I clenched my jaw even as my pulse thundered past my ears. I wasn't going to be a useless mortal. I'd fend for myself as long as I could. I dug the silver pen-dagger out of my pocket and held it and the shovel ready.

The monsters that'd surged into the courtyard hardly seemed to notice me back by the shed, though. Hinges squealed and doors groaned as they hurtled themselves at the entrances to the houses. I flinched at the resounding crashes as one and another door fell. Someone inside one of the homes screamed.

Shit. I didn't want to see another family murdered. But I wasn't even sure I could defend myself, let alone the sorcerers who'd left me to my own devices.

A few smaller creatures veered my way. One that was shaped like an armored greyhound sped toward me with teeth gnashing.

As it reached me, I swung the shovel at its head and sent it flying across the dusty ground. Another beast leapt at my elbow, I whipped around to bash it away—and brawny arms with the feel of sun-warmed granite wrapped around me from behind.

"I've got you," Crag said in the deeper, gravelly rumble of his gargoyle voice. It was the most welcome sound I'd ever heard in my life.

I leaned into him, dropping the shovel and letting him take my weight. He hefted me against his chest, pushed off the ground—

And a bright green blur of motion launched itself at us from around the side of the building.

Crag yanked himself around before I could fully comprehend what was happening. His body lurched, and the grunt that jolted out of him told me he'd been hurt by whatever had hit him. It'd almost looked like—

"Lance!" he roared, and I choked on my own spit. How could the dragon shifter be attacking him—us. He would never—

The gargoyle jerked and growled, striking out with one arm while the other held me close. The answering snarl was far too familiar. A chill rippled through me as I remembered Torrent's remark about how it'd be easier for the sorcerers to bring Lance under their control because he'd been affected by that kind of magic before.

Easier for them... and easier for the shadowkind beings now wielding sorcerous magic too?

"Lance!" I cried out in an echo of Crag's protest, as if my voice would be able to penetrate the spell.

Crag tried to lift off the ground again, only to stumble with a ragged breath. When I looked up, I saw his smoky blood streaming off him like when the beasts had attacked us in the sky before. More shrieks and ragged shouts were carrying from the buildings near us, but all I could focus on was my wounded gargoyle and my dragon shifter turned rabid.

A sob caught in my throat. This couldn't be happening. Was there anything I could do to stop it?

Crag staggered, nearly dropping me. As my feet hit the ground, I clutched his neck to make it easier for him to sweep me up again if he could. Then a sinewy appendage whipped past us with a fleshy smack.

Torrent had emerged from the shadows to fight alongside us. Crag pushed closer to the shed, turning around enough that I made out Lance in his dragon form snapping and raking his claws across the tentacles Torrent had flung at him. The other man had even transformed his arms so he could maneuver four tentacles at once while two continued holding his legs steady.

One lithe appendage smacked the dragon shifter into the ground, but Lance rolled and sprang back to his feet in an instant, nimble as ever. A burst of flame erupted from his lips, and Torrent flicked one tentacle to the side before it was totally charred. The burgundy skin bubbled with a fresh burn.

Crag took in our surroundings and set me down. "Stay here," he growled. "Call for me if any more come." Then he leapt in to help Torrent subdue Lance.

He wasn't quite fast enough. Just before he pounced, the dragon managed to clamp its jaws shut on the end of one of Torrent's tentacles. The sinuous flesh ripped with a meaty sound that made my gut churn.

"No!" The protest burst from my mouth, and I was darting forward before I could think better of it. Torrent wobbled backward with smoke gushing from his mangled tentacle, Crag pummeled Lance into the ground, and the dragon shifter let out a screech as if the gargoyle was crushing his chest.

But it was still him. It was still *Lance*. It wasn't his fault —they couldn't *kill* him.

"Lance!" I shouted, my hands waving through the air like some kind of maniac. "Lance, it's us. We've got you. Just—if you can just stop fighting—"

I was maybe five feet away when the dragon somehow managed to squirm out from under Crag's massive body. He threw himself straight at me, eyes searing and jaws snapping.

I teetered backward, and Crag hurtled between us with a roar. One thick, rock-like hand whipped toward me to shove me to the side and clocked me across the face.

I crashed to the ground, blood bursting from a split lip, pain radiating through my jaw and cheekbone. Crag pounded Lance with his other fist, ramming him in the opposite direction. He pinned the dragon shifter down, and Torrent rushed over as fast as his unsteady legs could carry him. He whipped one tentacle against the top of Lance's skull, and the dragon finally sagged, temporarily knocked unconscious.

"We have to get out of here," Torrent said roughly, twining another tentacle around my waist and yanking me to them. Crag flung Lance's limp body over his shoulder, snatched me from Torrent, and sprang into the air as the tentacled man vanished into the shadows again.

I could barely think as the ground fell away beneath my feet and the wind gusted over my bruised face. The screams behind me had stopped—when had they petered out? I couldn't hear anything now except faint snaps and snarls.

Crag dipped and bobbed in the air, obviously struggling, but before I'd gotten my thoughts totally straight, he was landing on a ledge partway up the nearest cliff. The yawning darkness of a narrow cave loomed beyond him. He set me down in a sitting position and then really looked at me for the first time since the fight had started.

Unmistakable horror flashed across his monstrous face. He shifted back into man-like form in a blink, kneeling beside me. "Quinn, I—I didn't mean to—"

"I know," I said, and winced at the brush of my split lip against the upper one. I pressed the side of my hand to the wound and swayed to my feet. "I'll be okay. You—he really went at you—"

"It'll heal," Crag muttered, still looking agonized by my minor injury even as more smoke wavered up off his own back. Then Torrent reappeared behind us in the thicker darkness of the cave.

"We need to make sure Lance is restrained in case the effect of the sorcery hasn't worn off when he comes to," he said, his voice taut with strain. "Quinn, watch for any shadowkind coming this way. I don't know if they noticed us leaving—they seemed... occupied."

I whirled toward the mouth of the valley, backing into the shadows at the mouth of the cave as I did to reduce the chance of being seen. My messenger bag still hung from my back, and I clung to its strap across my chest with both hands. I'd lost my silver pen-dagger somewhere in the chaos, but it hadn't helped much anyway.

The other shadowkind couldn't sense me here, not with my vest on. That might be the only reason I was still alive. Lance had known about the magic I possessed, and those few minor beasties who'd come at me must have gotten it into their heads to attack any human who might interfere, but all the others had been focused on the sorcerers they could detect.

Most of the shadowkind from the attack must have merged back into the shadows. I couldn't make out many moving bodies in the courtyard through the dimness of what was now approaching twilight. Light streaked over the darkened ground from a few windows on the houses, but no forms moved through that illumination either.

A sickly chill wrapped around me like a wet sheet. They were all dead. Victoria, Ivan, Jenny, their relatives whose names I'd never gotten. Even the little boy, Jonah. Slaughtered by those creatures.

I knew the men shuffling around in the cave behind me might not mourn them. They'd hardly been kind to me as soon as trouble had arrived, and they'd been a human sort of monsters to the shadowkind they'd enslaved. But I couldn't shake the horror creeping through me.

They'd never be as monstrous as the actual monsters because they could simply never wield as much or as many different types of power. And now our opponents had merged the one human supernatural skill with all their innate abilities, to the point that they'd managed to control even Lance. I swallowed thickly.

Then something prickled through my senses, making me go perfectly still without understanding why. I peered through the valley for several seconds before the feeling became solid enough for me to focus on its source.

Something was coming. Something I couldn't see but that made the energy embedded in my heart jump and stutter like never before. Instinctively, I pulled the vest tighter against my chest as if that could ensure nothing out there picked up on my reaction.

There was another shadowkind down there, one that had only just arrived. One powerful enough to set all my nerves jangling. It must have slipped into one of the houses, because all at once a huge silhouette formed by one of the windows, blotting out most of the light.

The massive shape bent down, and the fleshy tearing sound that followed was violent enough that my ears caught a trace of it even across that distance. Or maybe I only imagined I did, knowing what must be happening.

That was one of the ringleaders. One of the powerful shadowkind Rollick had warned me I might have to face was devouring the sorcerers' organs and absorbing their powers, like it must have many before. A shiver passed through me, and I cringed deeper into the cave.

I couldn't tell how quickly the being passed from building to building, but I never got the impression that it so much as looked our way. I hadn't left anything behind except for the jeep, and maybe it would assume that'd belonged to the sorcerers living there. I didn't think the shadowkind invaders had followed us, because then they'd have focused on capturing me, not killing everyone else. It'd just been horrible luck that they'd managed to track down the sorcerers' settlement so soon after the attack on the hotel.

Or maybe this group had never been involved in that attack to begin with. The men had figured that there were at least two beings in charge. One could have gone to confront Rollick while the other continued searching for more sorcerers to snack on.

Just when I thought I couldn't get queasier, a shrill weeping that I definitely wasn't imagining split through the evening. I leaned forward again, my heart in my throat, squinting at the settlement.

A mostly human-shaped being, though not the huge one I'd seen in the houses, was dragging a small, squirming form out of one of the buildings. I swallowed thickly, my stomach heaving.

It was Jonah. I didn't need to make out the details of his appearance to be able to tell from his size and his alternately sobbing and pleading voice. That was the house Jenny had sent him into.

The shadowkind attackers hadn't killed him. They were *taking* him—carrying him away now as they hurried at a brisk lope up the road. What the—

Rollick's words came back to me. These fiends had wanted me because I was a human with sorcerer powers they could hope to influence, one who hadn't already been taught to ward off the shadowkind. Were they planning on using that little boy the same way they'd hoped to use me?

Someone moved beside me. I startled in the instant before I realized it was Torrent. He stopped next to me and stared out over the valley.

"They're leaving," I said. The ominously large presence I'd sensed was fading away, and the few shadowkind still in physical form were scurrying back the way they'd come. "They took the little kid. I think—I think they're going to try to make him their pet sorcerer like they wanted to do with me."

Torrent's mouth twisted. He reached for me as if automatically and then caught himself. I glanced over at him, and my chest hitched.

His hand. His right hand—the smallest two fingers were torn right off. The other two and the thumb were a mangled mess, distorted above the mashed mess of his palm. Even his wrist looked battered.

"You—" I stared with a fresh rush of anguish.

Torrent jerked his hand out of view. "It can't be helped," he said sharply. "I've made other accommodations. I can deal with this."

Lance had done that. Lance had mutilated Torrent's human-like body even more than it already was when he'd torn into his tentacle. Oh, God.

These men had come out here for me. They'd come out here to help me get answers, and now Lance's mind had been stolen from him all over again, Crag had been forced to hurt both his friend and me to get us out of there, and Torrent had lost even more of his ability to interact with the mortal realm the way he'd used to.

And that poor little boy...

Tears welled up in my eyes. A wrenching but undeniable certainty filled me.

I'd thought I might be able to run away from this horrible situation. To let my problems rip each other apart, to ask some sorcerer expert to carve the power out of me. But every time I tried to escape, the people I cared about got hurt even more. I couldn't let anyone else suffer on my behalf.

It was my battle too now, as much as I hated that. Which meant I had to face my enemies and fight, or I'd lose even more than I already had.

As that horrible revelation sank in, the faint thrum of an engine wavered through the valley. Torrent frowned, looking toward the road as I did. A dark car had just driven into view from between the cliffs. Even though we were both hidden by the shadows at the cave entrance, we both drew back a little farther, watching warily.

No beings attacked the car, but then, I hadn't seen any hanging around for at least a few minutes now. It parked next to my jeep. The figure that got out was mostly lost in the thickening darkness, but something about it and its movements struck a chord of recognition in me.

I stared as that figure headed across the terrain, not toward the buildings but toward our mountain. He glanced at something in his hand. I couldn't quite believe what I was seeing until he halted about twenty feet from the foot of the cliff and peered up at us with a wry tip of his head.

"Quite the mess you've managed to get yourselves into this time, my mutinists," Rollick said.

CHAPTER TWENTY-SEVEN

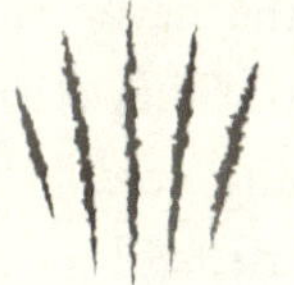

Rollick

For the first several seconds, if I hadn't known exactly where Quinn and therefore the three men who'd dedicated themselves to her cause must be, I'd have thought I was talking to thin air. The cliff above me was a mass of shadow-swathed rock.

I kept my arms folded loosely over my chest, my stance casual. No outward sign of the emotions roiling inside me. No indication of the wounds now sealed but still faintly throbbing on my back and thigh. You didn't get very far in our world if you couldn't disguise your weaknesses.

Sometimes even from yourself. I'd thought I'd known approximately how this reunion of sorts would go, but I was unprepared for the jolt of relief that hit me when Quinn's pale form eased into partial sight overhead. She was standing on two feet, both arms appearing to be attached—whatever carnage the fiends who'd reached this spot before me had carried out, she'd escaped it.

She was whole and well, and it was hard to say which of my conflicting impulses was stronger. Definitely the two strongest were the one to yank her into my arms as if I could hold her together longer that way and the one to tear her apart myself for the havoc she'd created back at *my* primary home, as much as they clashed with each other.

"What are you doing here?" she demanded in a voice that only wavered a little, still mostly cloaked in darkness. "What do you want?"

"Strange questions from a woman who just this morning agreed that we'd be meeting up again as soon as I took care of the little problem at the hotel," I said. "Well, I'm not waiting for an engraved invitation."

"You—"

Before she could say anything else, I stepped into the shadows and rushed up through them to the outcropping where she was standing. Before I'd even emerged back into physical form there, I could sense the long stretch of gloom in the cave where they'd taken shelter and the impressions of my three unreliable employees, although Lance's presence felt unusually subdued. Had *he* been injured?

Then I pulled my human guise together and looked Quinn straight in the face from just a few feet away, and every thought and emotion burned away in a blaze of fury that I hadn't been any more prepared for than I had the relief.

This anger wasn't directed at her. Her upper lip was split on the left side, blood marking it and the skin above it, where a bruise was also blooming across her cheek. My claws poked from my fingertips unbidden. I caught myself an inch from spitting out my conjured veneers and snapping my true, fanged teeth.

My voice came out in a rough hiss. "What wretched being did that to your face? Because when I get my claws into him—"

Crag pushed into view, strangely halting with an arm's length of distance between him and the mortal he so exalted —or maybe not strangely given what he said next.

"It was me," he said in a raw rumble. "I—I was trying to keep her out of the way—"

Quinn whipped toward him. "It wasn't your fault. You were protecting me as well as you could with so much going on."

She took a step toward him, reaching out, and froze when he jerked himself farther away. The gargoyle closed his hands into fists and stared down at them before taking in her injuries again.

Even if I'd still wanted to flay the perpetrator alive after finding out the circumstances, I couldn't imagine any punishment I could have visited on Crag that'd hit him harder than the guilt he was already clearly flagellating himself with. My own hands clenched. Seeing her lovely face marred still made me want to hit *something*.

Why should it? I should be furious with *her*. It was her own fucking fault. Her fault my hotel had been stormed. Her fault the four of them weren't securely tucked away in my safe house.

I was furious about that too. My jaw clenched against the acidic words I wanted to toss at all of them. But damn it if there hadn't been a swell of awe mixed with that searing rage from the very first moment the invaders of my hotel had snatched a sketch from beneath the mattress in my suite's bedroom.

She'd played me. This mortal woman who was barely even an adult by human standards had played *me*, a being who'd roved this realm for thousands of years. It was ridiculous and awful and impressive all at once.

She was lucky that I had been around long enough to see plenty of businesses rise and fall and to know how easily I could rebuild from the rubble, or I'd have been a lot more pissed off about the fact that the Sunshine Sin Hotel might never re-open. I certainly couldn't go back there for as long as these assholes were continuing their rampage.

And she hadn't even done all that just to get away from me. She wasn't sticking her head in the sand and hoping she could play house with my traitorous employees while the rest of the world went to hell around her. The very same day she'd escaped me, she'd come here searching for answers.

It was just too bad our enemies had arrived with bloodier interests at the same time.

Of course, she hadn't been clever enough to *completely* foil me. I wasn't an idiot; I'd known she might fly the coop like she'd taken off on me once already. I'd also noticed how closely she guarded the messenger bag she kept her most essential possessions in. It hadn't been any trouble at all to sew a GPS tracker into the lining where she'd never notice it.

Not that I was going to tell her how I'd found her so easily. Let her believe it was my amazing powers of perception or some supernatural skill I'd worked that she could never avoid.

Another figure stirred deeper within the cave. Torrent. "He's waking up," he called to Crag, and I knew immediately he was talking about the dragon shifter. My once-loyal lieutenant glanced at me from where he was crouched, his tentacles oddly stretched across a limp form I realized was covered in green scales. It looked as if he were... holding Lance down.

A hint of my confusion must have made it onto my face, because Quinn spoke quietly in explanation. "One of the beings that's been taking in the sorcerer powers was leading the attack. He must have gotten Lance under his control. He made him attack us."

My body tensed, a jab of worry lancing through my gut. Our enemies had gotten awfully far with the hearts and livers and so on that they'd already devoured, then. To sway a shadowkind as sharp as Lance, even if he'd been prey to sorcerers before... And that'd been before this being had gulped down the innards of the dozen or so magically inclined humans living here. How much might the idiot be capable of now?

This was not good at all.

The scaled body shifted, and a thin whine seeped from its mouth. Then the serpentine figure seemed to crumple inward into the smaller, human-like form that would allow Lance to actually speak. He coughed. "Torrent? I—they—sorcerous shadowkind—"

The last words cut off with a snarl and a gnash of his teeth. Torrent eased back his tentacles. "They're gone. It looks like their influence has left you too. They didn't try to bring you totally under their control—small mercies."

"They came up on me so fast. I didn't even know they

were there before that one caught me up..." Lance swayed
into a sitting position, hanging his head. "I—I'm sorry. I
would never—I tried so hard to stop it—"

"It's not *your* fault," Quinn said emphatically, hurrying
over as if she had no further concerns about my arrival. "We
know you didn't want to hurt us."

His gaze darted up, and his stance went rigid. "You're
bleeding. I could have—" A low, ragged groan rippled out
of him.

Quinn's face twisted as if she were just as agonized as he
sounded. She dropped to her knees in front of him and
gripped his arms. "I'm okay. You can—you can heal it up,
and I'll be good as new."

The dragon shifter eyed her with an air of
bewilderment as if he couldn't totally believe she meant it
—that she'd trust him to take care of her. But when she
turned her head to offer the cut on her lip to him, he leaned
forward and exhaled a flicker of his fiery breath over that
patch of flesh.

Watching him flick his tongue over the spot afterward,
almost a kiss, made my hands clench all over again in a way
that didn't make any particular sense. I'd already observed
her with all three of these men getting far more intimate
than that gesture, after all.

The second he'd treated her wound, Lance swiveled
away. He tipped over, slumping and stretching at the same
time into his dragon form, his head swerving away from the
rest of us to press against the rocky wall.

Quinn hesitated and then set her hand on his scaly
shoulder. When he didn't shake her off, she leaned in,
wrapping her arms right around his sinewy frame and

resting her cheek against his scaled neck. She'd been the one who'd nearly died, and there she was offering *him* all the comfort she could, even while he looked as far from human as he could get.

She really didn't mind, did she? It wasn't just getting off on an unusual situation or exotic anatomy. It wasn't imagining away the full extent of their monstrousness. She saw him as being as much of a person as anyone else she might have cared about regardless of how inhuman he appeared in that moment.

Suddenly I wanted to rip him apart, which wasn't a reasonable reaction either. I spun on my heel with a brisk gesture toward Torrent for him to join me.

As I stared out over the darkness now blanketing the valley, he came up beside me at the mouth of the cave. He'd retracted all but his usual two supporting tentacles now.

"So," I said, "should I even bother asking what you're doing out here rather than at the meeting spot we agreed on?"

I wasn't going to admit that I'd realized they'd betrayed me to a far worse extent than that. I still needed Quinn—needed her on my side more than ever, if what had happened here today was any indication—and for now that meant I needed these unreliable underlings too.

My lieutenant lowered his head. "You knew how to contact me," he said with typical terseness. "We thought we'd have the chance to find out something useful about her powers while the other fiends were distracted. You *want* her to get a better handle on her sorcery, don't you?"

Oh, he figured he could turn this around and make it sound as if it'd been a favor to me, did he?

I held in a snort. "I would have preferred it if that training didn't come with a heaping side of bloodshed, FYI."

"We got her out of the way as quickly as we could—and it doesn't look like the other shadowkind even realized she was here."

"Dumb luck." I exhaled sharply and turned to him, just as he adjusted his arm at his side, and the remark I'd meant to make next fled my mind. I stared at his mangled hand—if it could even be called a hand now. Different words tumbled out. "Some part of *you* didn't get out of the way fast enough."

If he hadn't made it clear his loyalties lay elsewhere, I'd have winced a little at the insensitivity of that spontaneous comment. I knew how tormented he was by the infirmities he'd already had when he came to me. But maybe he deserved having the results of this misadventure rubbed in a little—just how badly his choices had gone for him.

It seemed my mutinous followers had gotten punished quite thoroughly before I'd even arrived.

Torrent tucked the damaged hand under his uninjured arm, his voice dropping. "Lance. When I was trying to keep him off Quinn. You know how fierce a fighter he can be."

I did. I hadn't expected him to ever turn those talents against his own squad, though. Fucking sorcerer-scheming shadowkind and their new brainwashing abilities.

I couldn't ignore the opening, though. "It doesn't seem to be working out so well for you—this whole playing guardian angel to the mortal thing. How many losses are you willing to take before you decide it's time to cut out?"

Torrent answered without missing a beat. "I knew there

were risks in this line of work, and I knew there were risks in taking her side. I have no regrets. Not like I would have if she'd ended up in those assholes' hands."

I'd thought he'd been that unshakably committed to *me*. If he was even more devoted to her...

I glanced back at where Quinn was still snuggled up to Lance and caught her watching us in the fading twilight, her gaze lingering on Torrent's back, her expression strained. Her eyes darted away at the turn of my head, but I recognized the horror I'd seen written there. And suddenly I understood where I'd gone wrong.

This wasn't the right direction. There were fault lines in the unusual relationship my trio had formed with the budding sorcerer, but if I wanted to crack their unified front, I needed to push from the other end.

And the catastrophe they'd brought on themselves had given me my perfect point of leverage.

CHAPTER TWENTY-EIGHT

Quinn

The light of the electric lantern wavered off the walls of the cave, which we'd ventured deep enough into that little of the glow should show in the valley. It felt weird to be sticking around the place where our greatest enemies had just carried out a massacre, but the fact was that they believed they'd gotten everything they could out of this place. They hadn't noticed me while I was here, and no one outside the valley knew I'd come. This was the last place they'd return to.

I couldn't imagine bedding down in one of the blood-splattered houses, though. I hadn't wanted to face the carnage at all. I'd stayed up here while Crag and Rollick had gathered the lantern and a bunch of blankets to act as a makeshift bed.

We'd spend the night here, and then... Then we'd have to figure something else out. I assumed Rollick had ideas about that, but he'd stayed focused on our immediate situation so far.

My own mind was still a blur of shock and guilt, but I knew I couldn't just go back to being his caged sorcerer.

I sat down against the cave wall, ignoring the gurgle of my stomach. Crag had flown back down to the houses to see what food he could scrounge up. He seemed intent on taking whatever tasks he could that would keep him away from me, which only made the guilt wound through my gut grip me harder.

I rested my hand on my messenger bag, the one certainty I'd clung on to since the first shadowkind attack. Although my phone couldn't place calls and I had no desire to sketch, so its contents were becoming increasingly useless.

The phone alarm went off, and I reached for my pills automatically, chasing them with a gulp of water from my bottle. My heart thumped on in a heavy but steady rhythm. A ripple of energy passed through it.

Somehow it was getting hard to believe that the transplanted organ was my weakness and not the strongest thing in me—strong enough to transform me into a person I'd never have wanted to be.

The other shadowkind had all faded into the shadows, but Torrent wavered into view as I put away the pill case. He sank down next to me, keeping his ruined hand close by his side where it wasn't as noticeable.

"Managing okay?" he asked, his eyes searching mine. As if *I* were the one who'd been permanently mutilated today.

My throat constricted. "I should be asking you that."

Torrent's eyes narrowed, but his even voice came out in

the gentler tone I'd only heard him use with me. "I've never wanted your pity, and that hasn't changed." A wry note crept in. "I've still got five fully functional limbs, which is more than humans even start with."

The fact that he could joke about it comforted me only a little. "I guess you can't just swap out which is which." Or he'd already have done that with his legs.

He shook his head, lifting one of his usual tentacles to slip around my shoulders. "There's a certain synchronicity between our shadowkind and human-like forms. I couldn't make this tentacle into an arm or a leg any more than Crag could convince his wings to sprout from the top of his head."

He lifted his wounded arm, considering its mangled state with a contemplative air. The flesh had all melded back together with those special shadowkind healing powers, if into a form that no hand or wrist should look like. "I might chop it right off. Then I could conjure some kind of fixture to work in its place like I do with my foot." He flexed the thumb and the two remaining fingers at their awkward angles. "I'll have to see how well I can still work with this in its current state."

His voice stayed calm, but I knew him well enough by now to catch the jump of a muscle in his jaw, the slight flattening of his lips after he stopped speaking. It hurt, moving that hand, just like standing on his battered legs did. The arm might hurt for the rest of his life even if he amputated the worst of it.

He'd only met me a few weeks ago, and our association had already amplified the pain he'd been enduring for decades in a way that might never leave him.

Torrent glanced at me, forcing his mouth into a crooked smile. "At least now you have confirmation of just how effectively Lance can defend you when he's in his right mind."

"I think I already had plenty of confirmation of that," I muttered, and then Rollick blinked into being near the cave entrance.

"Unwilling sorcerer," he said, brandishing what looked like a balled-up dish towel. "I brought something for you."

I pushed myself to my feet, all my nerves immediately going on the alert. Rollick hadn't accused us of anything other than taking off on an unexpected side-mission, but I had trouble believing that he *hadn't* put the pieces together that I'd purposefully left evidence of my presence in his suite. He was smarter than that. But also smart enough not to bring it up if rubbing our faces in the betrayal didn't suit his current purposes.

"What's that?" I asked, eyeing his supposed gift with skepticism. "You want me to do some washing up?"

He chuckled and walked over until he was closer than I really preferred. Torrent got up too, standing to the side and watching the interaction warily. He'd intervene if he thought he needed to, but I wasn't sure how much he *could* do against Rollick directly.

The demon simply raised the dishtowel to the level of my face, smiling one of his charming movie-star smiles. "The dragon shifter couldn't do anything for the bruise. It occurred to me that a little ice is good for mortal injuries."

"It's okay," I said, pulling back, but Rollick grasped my arm carefully but firmly and brought the chilly fabric to my cheek. From the texture of the lumps, I could tell the thin towel was full of ice cubes.

"It's not okay," he said, with a dark note under the silky quality in his voice that I didn't think was aimed at me. "I'm meant to be seeing to your safety. And I don't imagine any of your devotees likes seeing you looking battered either."

He glanced at Torrent. "Speaking of safety, while Crag is being a perfectionist about what constitutes an appropriate meal, why don't you keep watch over the road into the valley? I'll send the gargoyle to relieve you when he's back."

Torrent's shoulders tensed, and he caught my eye as if seeking my permission. He wanted to know if I actually felt safe with the demon looming over me.

"Go ahead," I said. "I'm sure if Rollick was planning on carving me up, he'd have gotten on with it already."

The demon snorted, but he didn't argue. Torrent nodded and vanished into the shadows.

I turned my focus back to Rollick, wishing his considerate gesture didn't require him to be standing just inches away from me, his stunning face filling almost my entire vision. Wishing he wasn't being so gentle about it. If he'd been raging at me, it'd have been easier for me to keep seeing him as the enemy.

I reached toward the balled towel with its icy filling. "I can hold it myself."

Rollick tsked his tongue and ignored my hand. "For some strange reason, I feel the need to ensure this task is seen through to my specifications. You have a continuing habit of improvising."

I couldn't easily deny that. "You're not obligated to protect me anymore," I reminded him. "The deal was only for ten days."

He shrugged. "I thought I made it pretty clear that I'm not keeping you alive and well simply because of a few words we exchanged. If anything, today's events have only convinced me more how important it is that you stay out of the grasp of those fiends. They're wreaking enough havoc as it is."

I didn't really want to know, because it'd make the guilt inside me swell even larger, but I couldn't help asking, "What happened at the hotel?"

Rollick's expression barely flickered. He did know how to keep up a poker face. "I was visited by many higher shadowkind, though all minions, as far as I could tell. They were convinced I knew of your whereabouts, and they attempted to force me to cough that information up. I made them regret trying. Unfortunately, I had to evacuate the hotel in the process. As far as anyone knows, there was a gas leak that's being investigated. It may need to continue being investigated for quite a while, since I don't think I can safely reopen until this other problem is dealt with."

He shifted his weight on his feet, and I thought I caught the faintest hint of a wince. How many of those minions had he needed to fight off on his own?

"Are you okay?" I asked before I could think better of the question.

"I heal faster than you," he said, which wasn't really an answer. And then, "The scar you gave me is still the most impressive one of the bunch. None of them were wielding silver or iron."

I bit my lip, restraining a wince of my own, but he didn't sound accusing about it. Was it possible he really didn't know we'd set him up? Maybe the other shadowkind had been so convinced by the message Torrent had passed on that they hadn't even looked for evidence, just gone straight into shaking Rollick down.

"What do we do now?" I said. That was the more important question.

Rollick cocked his head. "Did you find out anything useful from that bunch down there before they became monster food?"

I thought back to my truncated conversation with the sorcerers. "Not really. There might be some kind of enclave of sorcerers in Norway that has a better understanding of how powers can develop at all. And I'd have an easier time controlling the ones we're up against if I knew them better, which seems pretty unlikely to happen when they make their followers do most of the actual work."

The demon hummed thoughtfully, but my mind had darted to my last memories of the battle. To the little boy that one minion had dragged off. Jonah.

My mouth went dry, but the vague conviction that'd been sitting like a lump in my stomach took on a clearer form.

"We need to get the kid back," I said.

Rollick blinked at me. "What?"

"The little kid they took. We told you about that. They probably think they can use him the way they wanted to use me. Or they'll realize he won't be powerful enough in time and eat him too. But they kept him alive. We can save him."

"We're having a hard enough time saving you," Rollick

said dryly. "One sorcerer kid won't make that much difference—in the near future, anyway. The only thing I agree with these pricks about is that the fewer sorcerers are in existence, the better. Present company excluded, of course."

His casual dismissal rankled me. I pushed aside his hand with the icy towel, my cheek already numb, and stepped farther away, folding my arms over my chest. "No. He's just a little kid. *He's* never done anything to shadowkind, and he doesn't have any family left to teach him to anyway. And he wouldn't—"

My throat choked up abruptly. I was *not* going to cry in front of Rollick again. I dragged in a breath, willing down my emotions, while he studied me.

"He wouldn't what?" he asked.

"He wouldn't have been taken if they hadn't gotten the idea of having their own sorcerer because of me," I said quietly. "Or if they'd managed to catch me. They took him because they *haven't* been able to capture me." Whatever ways they were tormenting him already, it was in my place. I hadn't wanted to make that kind of trade.

The demon studied me. He lowered his voice to match mine. "And now you want to stage some kind of rescue attempt? Don't you think your devotees have gone through enough just looking after you?"

He said it almost sympathetically, but the words hit on the main source of my guilt so dead on that I felt as if he'd punched me in the gut. I squeezed my arms tighter around myself. "I didn't want any of that to happen."

"Of course you didn't," Rollick said. "It's only a natural consequence of your precarious situation. Which is why you really shouldn't go running off on unplanned missions like this one. They're clearly going to follow you to the ends of the earth as long as you'll still have them."

Was this his way of trying to talk me out of wanting to rescue the kid? No matter where we went, I didn't know how to protect the men who were so determined to protect *me*. Torrent maybe would have stepped back if I could have convinced him that I really didn't want him around, but I had the feeling Crag and Lance would stalk me from a distance as long as I was still breathing, determined to make up for the fact that they'd been partly responsible for dragging me into the danger to begin with.

I wouldn't let the demon distract me. "Lance found a place in this part of the country where these shadowkind seem to be operating from, didn't he?" I said. "In Utah, I think he said? That's probably where they'll have taken the kid, unless you think they've got a hideout in every state."

Rollick let out an amused huff. "I agree that would be the most likely place, but that doesn't mean we should pay a visit."

I frowned at him. "It could be for more than just rescuing him. We need to know more about what kind of shadowkind we're up against anyway if I'm going to stop them, and that seems like the best place to look for evidence. You're a super powerful demon. Are you telling me you can't pull this off?"

"I'm telling you I don't see the point, and that I doubt it'll go well."

"Only if you don't pull your weight," I shot back, my annoyance at his callous refusal overwhelming all my other emotions. I paused, remembering the sense of foreboding that'd risen up in me right after the slaughter in the valley below. "I know I have to tap into my powers now. I know I can't just stand by and let these fiends do whatever they're hoping to do. I'll train or work with you however you want—but you have to help me with this."

I needed to start standing up to the monsters right away, or what was the point in taking a stand at all? Jonah needed me *now*, even if I couldn't do much more than snatch him from their grasp. If I'd been more willing to join the battle and work toward stopping these fiends before instead of putting all my energy into running away, maybe the villains never would have made it to the settlement to begin with.

I could fix this one thing. I wasn't backing down until I did. How could I live with myself if I gave up a literal child to be enslaved by fiends in my place?

Rollick arched an eyebrow. "Or what?"

I gazed steadily back at him. "Or I'll go off on my own again and probably get myself killed, and we'll see how well your plans work without me."

I didn't know if I'd have actually taken that risk, not with so much at stake, but the demon clearly didn't know either. He eyed me warily and then let out a huff of breath. "You do drive a hard bargain. We will see what we can find out and whether the attempt has any chance of success—"

"Figure out how to give it a chance," I broke in, picturing little Jonah again. "I'm not doing anything with you, not making any deals or helping with any of your plans, if you're going to let a preschooler die just because of what his parents did."

CHAPTER TWENTY-NINE

Quinn

Before Rollick could respond to my declaration, Crag arrived near the mouth of the cave. It appeared he'd assembled some sort of sandwiches, a little awkwardly with dents in the bread from his broad fingers, which kind of made it more impressive that he'd managed at all. He'd brought a whole heaping plate of them as if I had enough room in my stomach to gulp down five. Or maybe he'd figured all of us would dig in.

"I wasn't sure what to do with the other food in the kitchens, so I went with this," he said gruffly, setting the plate down by the lantern. Not even handing it right to me, as if moving that close could somehow damage me.

"Thank you," I said quickly, shooting him a bright smile even if I couldn't make it totally authentic when he was so obviously struggling with what had happened earlier today. I sat down by the plate and motioned to him. "Are you going to have one? This is way more than enough for me."

Crag shook his head with a jerk. "They're all for you. I wasn't sure what you'd like most."

Maybe I could have come up with something to say to make him feel better, but Rollick snapped his fingers, capturing the gargoyle's attention. "I need you standing watch by the entrance to the valley. I can't imagine our main enemies would head back this way, but we don't want any wandering shadowkind or humans stirring up trouble while we're still here. Tell Torrent he can take a break." The demon cast a downward glance my way. "And I need to go see about a few things, since my would-be sorcerer is as stubborn as ever."

My spirits lifted a smidgeon despite the possessive "my." Did that mean he was seriously considering launching a rescue effort for the little boy?

He didn't clarify, only stepped into the shadows a second after Crag had, leaving me apparently alone. The demon hadn't even bothered to tell me not to go wandering off myself—but then, I couldn't really wander anywhere when I had no way of getting off the cliff without Crag carrying me in flight.

I examined the sandwiches and determined that the gargoyle really had put together a wide variety. One was ham and cheese, another what looked like turkey or chicken along with a few leaves of lettuce, another roast beef with mayo. There was even an egg salad one, from egg salad I had to assume had already been mixed up when he'd found it. I couldn't picture Crag boiling eggs and then carefully cracking and dicing them.

He must have gone through more than one kitchen to find all that. Working so hard to make me happy. How happy had being with me made *him* today?

I swallowed the lump in my throat and forced down the sandwich with lettuce after it, since I figured getting a little bit of vegetables in the mix was probably a good thing. My doctors really would not have been pleased with the majority of my recent diet... other than the hotel meals Rollick had provided.

The thought of the hotel brought my spirits low all over again. Our plan hadn't worked, not really. Rollick had destroyed some minions—great. He hadn't even gotten the chance to take on the real threat, and they hadn't slowed him down much. And he'd found us again so easily.

Maybe he'd spent enough time around me that he could track me just by my general vibe now, regardless of the vest. Or he knew how to trace one or more of the men. It would make sense for him to have some secret way of keeping tabs on his own minions.

My brief stint of freedom had only gotten me a little more information that I had no idea how to use, as well as put all three of my boyfriends through various sorts of trauma. Wonderful. I didn't know if we'd have been better off staying at the hotel, but it couldn't have been that much worse.

I was just finishing the sandwich when Torrent returned, emerging from the shadows with his usual stiff gait.

"Any sign of trouble?" I asked.

He shook his head. "Not a single vehicle within sight, and no shadowkind came anywhere near while I was out there. I think we'll be safe enough here for the night. Are you going to get some rest?"

"Soon," I said. I didn't think I'd be able to sleep just yet with all the anguish churning inside me. I looked down at the sandwiches and thought of Lance's enthusiasm for mortal food. "Where did Lance go? Maybe he'd like a little dinner too."

Torrent tipped his head toward the far end of the cave. "He slunk off through the shadows that way. You could take the lantern and go look for him. I don't need it. It might be good for him to have some company."

"Yeah." My throat tightened all over again. I got up, picking up the plate with one hand and the lantern with the other. "There's plenty to go around if you wanted to eat."

I wasn't surprised when he shook his head. Torrent had generally skipped our group mealtimes.

"I'll be here if you need me," he said. "Just call."

He'd already faded back into the nearest patch of darkness before I turned to venture deeper into the cave.

I crept onward cautiously in the glow of the lantern light. The rocky walls veered to the left and closed in until I could barely walk without brushing my shoulders on them. Then the cave widened again into a space about as big as the hotel suite's living room.

A blanket Lance must have grabbed from the heap near the entrance lay rumpled on the floor off to the side, but there was no sign of the dragon shifter himself.

"Lance?" I said tentatively, holding up the lantern and peering into the shadows. "Are you here?"

His human-like form wavered into being sitting cross-legged on the blanket. He gazed up at me with a somber expression that didn't look right on his normally eager face.

"Are we leaving?" he asked.

"No, not yet. Not for a while, I don't think." I sat down across from him, not sure how close he'd want me to get. He'd accepted the embrace I'd offered him after he'd first become conscious, careful as I'd had to be to avoid pressing my vest against him through my other clothes, but I hadn't been able to tell whether he'd taken much comfort from it. And then he'd slipped away to come over here, apart from all of us.

I set the plate on the uneven floor between us. "Crag made sandwiches. I've already had enough, so I wanted to see if you'd like anything."

Lance considered the clumsy sandwiches, and a small but sly gleam lit in his violet eyes that sent a surge of relief through me.

"The gargoyle is good for hunting," he said. "I don't think we should appoint him head sandwich-maker."

My lips twitched toward a smile. "Maybe not, but they taste perfectly fine. I'm sorry there wasn't any ice cream."

Lance hummed to himself and picked up the ham and cheese. He took a few careless bites, his gaze drifting across the cave as he chewed. Then he dropped the sandwich and shoved the plate away. "I don't really want this."

He fixed his attention on me instead. I saw the moment he started studying the bruise on my cheek in the tightening of his stance. "It still hurts?"

"A little," I admitted. "But I've gotten bruised before. I'm used to it. It'll heal up in a week or so."

Lance raked his hand through his black curls, which looked even wilder than usual. "Torrent won't heal."

I couldn't lie to him about that. He knew what shadowkind were and weren't capable of way better than I did.

"He isn't mad at you," I said instead. "And neither am I, in case I didn't make that clear enough earlier."

Lance let out a sound that was closer to a grunt, as if he didn't totally believe me. Watching him, I couldn't help thinking of bodily activities he'd enjoyed even more than eating. I hesitated and then scooted closer to him, touching his cheek with my hand. Maybe this was what he needed.

"I trust you," I said, stroking my fingers along his prominent cheekbone. "What happened today had nothing to do with *you*. I know when you want to put your dragon claws and fangs on me, I never have to worry."

Lance met my gaze again. For a few seconds, his expression looked torn between conflicting impulses while he held perfectly still. Then he reached out and teased the tips of his claws over the bare skin of my lower thigh below the hem of my shorts. "You still like the claws, huh, baby girl?"

A quiver of desire raced through me despite my concern for him—or maybe because of it, seeing how my admission had started to revitalize him.

"Always," I said, and leaned in to kiss him.

He might have been a little more tentative in the strokes of his claws than he'd normally been before, but he claimed my mouth with total enthusiasm. He grazed the sharp tips up and down my legs and then across my stomach below the base of the vest. I pressed closer to him with a giddy shiver and then eased back an inch both so the metals weren't so near his body—and so that I could run my hands up under his shirt to explore his smooth skin in turn.

Lance gave an approving growl and vanished for a split-second, which was all it took for him to shed his clothes. He captured my mouth an instant later, flicking his tongue between my lips and reaching for the waist of my shorts.

He might not have been interested in the food, but he was definitely hungry. The furor of his response was getting me all kinds of heated up too. It could be we both needed this, a hasty passionate collision to jolt ourselves out of the melancholy that'd fallen over us.

"My woman," he murmured, nipping a path along my jaw. "My Quinn. Always."

I squirmed out of my shorts and panties. Lance fingered the bottom of my shirt with a grumble, knowing as well as I did that we couldn't risk removing the vest.

To distract him from that minor setback, I clambered right onto his lap, nudging him down onto the blanket at the same time so I could take in his full naked glory sprawled beneath me.

At least, that was the idea. As I straddled him with my hands splayed against his chest, pushing him downward, Lance's whole body went rigid with a sudden flinch. His own hands shot to snap around my wrists as a hiss that sounded like a deadly warning rasped out of him.

It happened in a flash, and then his grip on my arms was already loosening, though he didn't quite let go. Anguish filled his expression again.

I scrambled off him to kneel beside him instead, and he released me then. "I'm sorry," he said roughly.

"You didn't hurt me." I showed him my unmarked wrists. An inkling crept into my mind of what the problem might be. He'd held my wrists before when we'd hooked up, though he'd been on top of me then. It'd turned out I liked the restraint, but at first he'd done it because of memories lingering in his head.

The only humans he'd really interacted with before me had been the ones who'd enslaved him.

"You felt trapped," I suggested. "I know you don't like that. I should have realized—"

"No," he interrupted, with a scowl I could tell was directed at himself rather than me. He shoved himself into a sitting position and pulled me tight against him, heedless of the vest. "I shouldn't be afraid with you. I know *you* wouldn't hurt me. You had nothing to do with those other ones. It just—my body reacted..." He trailed off mournfully.

I nestled my head next to his, pressing a kiss to his shoulder. We were even more entwined than we'd been a minute ago and almost totally naked, but the mood had shifted in a way I wasn't sure we could get back. But talking this through was more important.

"It makes sense," I said. "People like me were horrible to you. And you were just reminded of that time in the worst possible way today."

"They were *nothing* like you," Lance snarled, and hugged me even tighter.

I returned the embrace, wishing I knew how to heal the wounds inside him as easily as he could seal the ones I'd taken.

"Will you tell me about it?" I asked tentatively. "What

happened back then? Maybe I'll be better at not stirring up those memories if I totally understand."

Lance let out a wordless mutter and tucked his face into the crook of my neck. It felt like a refusal, but then he turned me in his arms so my shoulder rested against his chest and his breath ruffled my hair.

"It isn't a very interesting story," he said.

"I'd still like to hear it, if you're okay with telling me. I want to know *you* as much as I can."

He made a noncommittal sound, but then he started talking. "I wandered through a rift into the mortal realm. I hadn't been here before, and it was overwhelming—and then this magic wrapped around me, like it was putting a cage around my thoughts and moving my body for me. The sorcerers must have lived near the rift, watching for beings they'd like to use."

He paused and then went on. "They kept us in cages. There were four of them and seven of us. All of us higher shadowkind. Those sorcerers were ambitious. But they didn't want us roaming around when we weren't following their orders, so, the cages. They would weaken us too. Jab us with silver and iron things. Make sure we were never at our full strength." He shuddered.

I slipped my hand around his arm and squeezed gently. "That's awful."

"It wasn't even the worst for me. I was the strongest because I was the newest. The others had been through much more. The sorcerers would send us out to take things or kill people... mortals who were always weaker no matter how we'd been weakened... I don't know what the sorcerers wanted, really."

"But you got away from them," I said.

The dragon shifter nodded, his chin brushing my temple. "I thought I would get us all out—all of us shadowkind they'd trapped. We all wanted to leave. The others were older—they had more that they missed—they would talk about it sometimes when they weren't feeling too badly... They would try to reassure me that I wouldn't be locked away there forever. They were right about that."

He stopped for a moment, and I gave him the space to find his next words. He kissed the top of my head.

"The sorcerer who'd put her magic around me—she liked how I looked. Maybe she wanted to know how my claws would feel too. I just knew... I had a little bit of power there. So I pretended that I wanted her too. To get her to open my cage. To let me touch her, when normally we couldn't. And when I did..." His lips drew back in a snarl, and he lifted one hand away from me to make a savage swiping motion through the air.

"She deserved it," I said without hesitation. After the description he'd given of his treatment, the knowledge that he'd murdered his captor didn't bring even a flicker of discomfort.

"Yes. But the others... I got their cages open, and the other sorcerers realized, and they had a strong hold still. Me and one other, we were bound by the woman I killed, and when she was gone we were free, but the rest—"

He stopped for a moment, his head drooping. "The sorcerers ordered them to attack each other. They weren't sure who was even under control then, they just wanted us all dead. I tried to kill those sorcerers too, but by the time I slashed the last throat... the other shadowkind with me, they'd torn each other apart."

Tears had welled up behind my eyes. From what I'd seen, I didn't think all sorcerers were quite that vicious, but it was easy to understand the shadowkind's immediate animosity toward them if any at all acted like that.

"I didn't save any of them," Lance said quietly. "They all died by their cages. I don't know—if I'd picked a different moment, or gone after the other sorcerers before letting them out, or—" A tremor ran through his body, and then his muscles stiffened. "Those mortals call us monsters, but they couldn't let us go even then. They'd rather see us die!"

I reached up to loop my arm around his neck, hugging him as well as I could in our current position. "And you can't blame anyone but them. You did everything you could —and you shouldn't have been in that position to begin with. And it was still... It was still helping the others a little. At least they knew someone cared enough to try to get them out. And they didn't have to go through any more of the torture."

"Maybe," Lance muttered, sounding unconvinced. "If I could tear those sorcerers apart all over again..." He growled in frustration.

My earlier guilt congealed in my stomach. "I'm sorry," I said, my voice faltering.

Lance pulled back far enough to see my face, his eyebrows rising. "You don't need to apologize. You didn't have anything to do with it."

"I know, but—I got you into the situation we're in now. It's because of me that you had to go through something like it again, having your self-control stolen from you. Bringing sorcery back into your life."

"No." In one swift movement, Lance flipped us. I found myself sprawled on the blanket under him, staring up into his flaring eyes. He braced his hands on either side of my shoulders and his knees by my thighs, gazing down at me. "Never apologize for that. I got you. I *have* you. I've never—you're the only being—I didn't know how much I was missing. I would go through all of the awfulness a hundred times over again if it meant keeping you safe and with me."

My pulse stuttered at the determination in his words. "Lance—"

"I love you, Quinn," he broke in. "That's what humans say when they feel like this, isn't it?"

I blinked at him, twice as startled as before. It'd never occurred to me to wonder whether the shadowkind could even feel love the way people thought about it. "I don't know."

He snorted and leaned in to nuzzle my face with a flick of his tongue along the tender underside of my jaw. "I want to be with you all the time. To hear you talking, to see what you'll do, to feel you next to me." He lowered his body so it rested against mine, his eyes peering into mine from just a couple of inches away now, his heat engulfing me. "I would go anywhere and do anything if it helped you. Isn't that what humans call love?"

I choked up for a completely different reason than before. I suspected that for an awful lot of people, love didn't extend even half that far. Who was I to tell him what he felt couldn't be called that?

And an ache had formed around my heart at the same time with the knowledge that I felt the same way. If he'd told me there was something all the way on the other side of the world, through deadly landscapes and past brutal enemies, that could protect him from the influence of sorcery or heal his guilt over the lives he'd failed to save, I would have jumped to get it for him without a second thought.

"I love you too," I said, almost as surprised by my words as I'd been by his. The emotion had been creeping up over me without my noticing, but the declaration felt so right.

Lance beamed at me, his previous somberness falling away. He lifted one hand to tease his claws along the side of my neck and bared his teeth with his dragon fangs glinting. "Do you? And not just my claws and fangs and—"

He rolled his hips, the erection I'd only been vaguely aware of before sliding against my sex. A whimper spilled out of me at the abrupt rush of pleasure, but I held on to my voice.

"All that stuff is very good," I murmured. "But I also love how adventurous you are, and how you can see the fun side of everything, and how you question things instead of just accepting them. You're brave, and you stand by the people you care about even when it's hard—not just me, but Crag and Torrent too."

A rumble vibrated through Lance's chest. "When they deserve it. You always do. My Quinn. All mine." He captured my mouth again then, stroking his cock over my clit until my hips canted upward in a plea. Then he plunged right into me, drinking in my gasp, sighing his own satisfaction with a tinge of fire.

As I lost myself in the rising wave of bliss our bodies kindled together, one clear thought penetrated the haze.

I loved all three of my shadowkind men, didn't I? I wanted to protect them as much as they'd protected me. But what had I really faced, what had I really risked on their behalf?

Lance had said he'd do anything for me, and I believed him. Shouldn't I be willing to go just as far to save him and the others?

CHAPTER THIRTY

Quinn

I woke up next to a warmly scaled body. Lance had stayed with me the whole night in the cave's deeper room, but sometime while I'd slept he'd morphed back into his dragon form.

I didn't mind. For a supposed reptile, he was awfully hot-blooded, and his scales were so smooth they felt almost silky against my skin. In his longer body, he'd been able to curl himself right around me, spooning me from behind with his tail tucked around my front so that I was completely engulfed in his affection.

I had about ten seconds to appreciate the peacefulness of the moment before Rollick's lilting voice echoed from the other end of the cave. "Any mortals around here who wanted to run a rescue mission should probably stop sleeping in."

Lance stirred as I sat up with a jolt. The demon was

agreeing to go after Jonah? I didn't want to give him time to change his mind.

The dragon shifter stretched cat-like while I yanked my panties and shorts back on, and then sprang up into his human-like form. He grabbed me to press a quick kiss to the crook of my jaw with a much more upbeat energy than he'd shown yesterday. Maybe our talk... and all the other things we'd done... had helped him even more than I'd dared to hope.

"Who are we rescuing?" he asked as I tugged him with me toward the entrance to the cave.

He'd slunk off before the rest of us had discussed that part of the catastrophe. "The sorcerers had a little kid," I said. "The shadowkind that attacked yesterday took off with him, probably to try to make him work whatever magic he's got on other monsters. We can't let them do that."

Lance let out a humph that I couldn't decipher. He might not have been keen on doing anything that helped a sorcerer, child or not, but he wouldn't want our enemies using the boy either.

We found Rollick standing near the mouth of the cave, looking ridiculously dapper in his tailored suit in the middle of the rugged environment. I'd have thought he might have adjusted his fashion sense a little to fit the setting, but then, maybe it fit his personality to refuse to bow to his surroundings. My men seemed to wear pretty much the same thing all the time, so maybe shadowkind had particular clothes they found most easy to conjure, whether because of their nature or out of habit it was hard to say.

The demon motioned to a plate next to the heap of blankets that'd been supposed to serve as my bed, and I realized someone had gone down to the settlement again to make me breakfast. Scrambled eggs, a piece of toast, and an apple waited for me.

I didn't know whether Crag had gotten more ambitious with his culinary skills or if one of the others had taken a stab at feeding me. It was hard to picture Torrent working over a stove with his tentacles serving in place of his wrecked hand, but even harder to imagine Rollick lowering himself to playing cook for a mortal.

"What's the plan for the rescue?" I asked, sitting down on the blankets and wielding the fork.

Rollick propped himself against the rocky wall, alternating between watching me and peering down into the valley. "I've been able to confirm that the kid was taken to the camp of sorts that those idiots have set up in Utah— the one you found." He tipped his head to Lance. "I've set up a few distractions that I believe should draw the ringleaders away for long enough that we can crash their party without having to do battle with them directly."

Somehow that information both relieved and unnerved me. "Are you sure you can't tackle them head on? We could end this whole thing today if you took them down." Or was he still avoiding showing how invested he was, even now that they'd chased him out of his home?

Rollick's grimace suggested he wasn't happy about the situation either. "They're clearly powerful beings with a lot of powerful underlings, and they've already advanced their human-style sorcery beyond what I expected. I don't think I'd win against all of them on my own or even with just the four of you backing me up. Maybe if I summoned an entire army... but that would take days to organize, and they'd almost definitely catch wind of the activity, and then they'd stash the kid somewhere even harder to find. Which I don't think is what you want?"

"No." I swallowed a mouthful of eggs, finding my mouth had gone dry. "But is that what we'd do next—after we get him out? Raise a whole army?"

"I don't know," Rollick admitted. "I'm only going along with this whole rescue effort so I can get a better read on what we're up against. If we can simply pick them off using more cleverness than might, that's vastly preferable to staging a full-out war. To both me and you. There's no way there wouldn't be a lot of mortal casualties if it got to that point."

Lance's good spirits had dampened as we'd talked. He adjusted his weight from foot to foot restlessly. "Is it a good idea for me to go with you? If they work their new magic on me again..."

Rollick focused on him. "Do you have any reason to believe the being that imposed their power on you was a shadowkind on a similar level as yourself?"

Lance shook his head. "I didn't see him, but whoever it was, he felt very... large. And old. Heavy."

I remembered the sense I'd gotten of the being that'd arrived at the settlement after the other shadowkind had killed the sorcerers. "That's got to be the one that came to collect the organs."

Rollick nodded. "It seems doubtful that the ringleaders would be letting any of their underlings partake. They want as much of the ability as possible for themselves. So if we've diverted them from the camp, then you won't have anything to worry about." He splayed his hands, offering a crooked smile. "And if we don't manage to divert them, then we're most likely screwed anyway."

"Very comforting," I muttered.

"Take comfort in the fact that I know what I'm doing, and I've been pulling off whatever I want to for thousands of years," Rollick said, and turned back toward the valley. "Torrent and Crag are searching the sorcerers' houses in case there's anything in there we can use. I'd like to move out as quickly as possible, but since I'm not letting you out of my sight again, stubborn sorcerer, I'm hoping we can find a thing or two that might allow you to defend yourself a little better during this escapade."

I guessed the steak knife I'd still managed to hold on to wasn't likely to cut it. I sat up a little straighter, swallowing the last of my eggs and stuffing the apple into my messenger bag for the trip. "Definitely. If there's any way I can hold my own without the rest of you worrying about me, I'll take it. We can head down there now. I'll eat the rest of my breakfast during the drive."

Rollick shot me an amused glance with a brief flick of his gaze toward Lance. "Somehow I don't think there's anything you could do to prevent a whole lot of worrying from your devotees. But at least having you armed may mean they can focus *slightly* more on the task at hand rather than protecting that mortal body, as lovely as it is."

I hid my wince at the guilt his casual remark provoked. He was right, but I didn't know how to change that. I'd already tried running away, doing whatever I could to escape our enemies and this situation, and it hadn't kept them safe. Was there anything that could?

It seemed more and more certain that the only way I could really protect them was by stopping the fiends that were after me, whatever it took. And this rescue was the first step toward doing that.

As I got up, Crag appeared on the ledge outside the cave in gargoyle form, his wings already unfurled. "We've got something that might be useful," he told Rollick. "Can't handle it easily ourselves, though."

I stepped toward him. "Bring me down, and I'll take a look."

It killed me that he hesitated before reaching his arms out to me, as if he thought the simple embrace he'd used to save me from danger more than once might now injure me. I wrapped my own arms around his neck and tucked my head beneath his chin. "I'm okay. Let's go find whatever I can use to make sure I stay that way."

He grunted, but there was no denying the tenderness with which he held me against him as he lifted into the air. He didn't say anything as we glided down to the courtyard where I'd spoken with the sorcerers yesterday. When we landed, his hold on me tightened for an instant before he let go. "It isn't pretty. They left the bodies."

I got a preview of what he meant before I'd even moved away from him. By one of the bashed-down doors, a body was sprawled, the arm slumped across the threshold. Blood splattered the doorframe. A meaty scent already tinged with a hit of rot carried on the warming morning breeze. The sound of buzzing flies made me shudder.

Torrent materialized in a different, less bloody doorway

nearby. He beckoned us over with his good hand. "One in here was using a weapon I think you should be able to handle. It worked decently well for her. She took down a few of the creatures before they overwhelmed her."

As I headed over, Rollick and Lance appeared alongside us after their slightly slower journey from the cave through the shadows. I braced myself before stepping into the house.

The smell got thicker, but at least it wasn't quite as putrid as the lingering stench in the sorcerers' house back in Florida. I averted my eyes from the stream of blood that'd trickled across the floor from the doorway to the kitchen and followed Torrent to what appeared to be a family room at the back of the house.

Another body was sprawled there, a woman whose face I vaguely recognized from the silent bystanders yesterday... and whose torso was gouged open from throat to pubic bone. Her chest was a mass of shredded tissue. I caught one glimpse of it and jerked my head to the side, my stomach flipping over.

Oh, God. And they must all look like that—Victoria and Ivan and Jenny, and all the others who'd never introduced themselves. Would the monsters decide to do the same to Jonah after all? They might have already...

With my hand clamped to my mouth, it took me the better part of a minute to get my nausea and horror under control. My gaze settled on a crumpled heap in another part of the room that was steaming dark smoke. Torrent stepped over to it.

"This is one of the shadowkind she shot," he said, and held up a contraption about as long as his forearm. It was made of metal and wood and looked like a combination between a crossbow and a gun. "The bolts are half iron, half silver. There are a few scattered around here and more in a room in the basement, but I can't handle them easily."

"Of course not." I girded myself and stepped into the room to pick up the bolts he indicated, each like a shiny metal pencil with an especially sharp tip. When I'd stuffed the handful into my bag, he led me down a set of stairs to the basement, which was thankfully free of corpses.

The storage room he'd mentioned was stacked with dusty boxes. One shelf held a plastic carton that appeared to be full of more of those bolts. I grabbed that and spotted a dagger similar to the one I'd found in the other sorcerers' house.

"I'll take this too," I said. The last one had come in handy.

As Rollick obviously remembered. "As long as you don't stab that one into any of us," he said dryly from where he'd followed us to the doorway.

"Don't be too much of a jerk, and it shouldn't be a problem," I retorted.

My gaze fell on a few faded but relatively modern-looking notebooks stacked on a higher shelf. I picked one up and flipped through it. It appeared to be a journal, written in a messy but readable scrawl, the dates in that one from a few years ago.

"Maybe they knew more than they wanted to tell me," I said, stuffing those into my bag as well. "I'll read through their notes when I have a chance."

Rollick motioned to me. "Come on, let's make sure you're prepared to use that thing."

I couldn't get out of the house fast enough. We tramped over to the cliffside, and Torrent handed me the crossbow. It was heavier than I expected—I needed two hands to steady it—but the mechanism looked simple enough. Without help, I figured out how to arm it with three bolts, which appeared to be as many as it could hold at one time. Then I puzzled over how exactly to ready one to fire.

Rollick stepped closer, examining the weapon quickly and then showing me a metal fixture I needed to pull into place. "You'll aim using the sights here," he said, tapping a notch.

I held the weapon at eye level with both hands, curled one finger around the trigger, and squeezed hard. The bolt smacked into the rock just an inch below the darker spot I'd been aiming at. Not bad for my first try.

Now that I knew what to do, it only took a second to ready the next bolt. I fired off the other two in quick succession, managing to hit my target dead on the third time. My arms were aching a bit from the strain of keeping the crossbow aloft and still, but that was a small price to pay for self-defense.

"It'll be harder with moving targets—and when you've got to worry about more than one," Rollick said. "You'll want to shoot at whatever's closest and keep your back to as much shelter as you can find."

"Right." I dragged in a breath and looked around at the other men. "Better than hitting them with a shovel, anyway."

Torrent cracked the smallest of smiles. Crag still looked intensely grave. Lance bounced over to point out where the bolts I'd fired had landed so I could quickly snatch them up. Their ends had blunted with the impact, but at that speed they'd probably still penetrate flesh. It seemed wiser to keep them just in case.

I didn't know how many battles I'd need this weapon for.

"Do you want to practice more?" Torrent asked, shooting a sideways glance at Rollick.

The demon had been hurrying me along, but I couldn't say he was wrong to. Every second we lingered here was another opportunity for the shadowkind marauders to decide the little boy was better eaten than enslaved. But I didn't want to falter in the middle of our raid either.

I reloaded the blunt bolts into the bow. "I'll do a few more rounds."

For several minutes, I went through the motions of readying and firing and reloading until the movements started to feel more comfortable and I could hit a head-sized target from several feet away while walking slowly. I doubted I was going to get much more competent than that in the limited time we had.

Rollick had apparently decided we were using his car. He'd already grabbed my backpack from the backseat of the jeep and tossed it in the trunk of his sedan. I guessed that made sense when the invaders had seen the jeep when they'd launched their attack, if they'd been paying much attention to it.

"Get in," he said after I'd lowered the crossbow, opening one of the back doors. "Crag, you stick close to her. We don't know what we might encounter on the way there."

I clambered onto the buttery leather seat, and Crag sank down on the other side, in human form now. He sat so stiffly that I was afraid to even reach over and take his hand.

I studied him as Rollick gave Torrent and Lance some instructions I couldn't hear. As the demon got in and started the engine, Crag's muscles tensed, and I was suddenly sure he was going to fade right into the shadows rather than stay where I could see him.

I caught his arm before I could second-guess the impulse and cringed inwardly at his immediate flinch.

"Don't," I said, unable to keep the pleading note from my voice. "I'm not scared of you, and you shouldn't be scared either. It was a lot better that I got a bit banged up than that Lance sank his claws into me."

Crag allowed himself to look at me as the sedan lurched forward over the uneven ground. Even with my voice quiet, Rollick must have been able to hear me, but he didn't offer any comment this once, thankfully.

The gargoyle's voice came out low but rough. "I don't like how easy it is to hurt you without even meaning to. I thought—I thought it wouldn't happen, but I still can. It could happen without me even touching you."

My chest clenched at his words, but I raised my eyebrows. "I don't think that's very likely."

He pulled his gaze away. "There was a woman once— she was stealing wallets at the hotel club. I went to frighten her into thinking better of doing it again. But she—when she saw my true form—it startled her so much that her heart failed. She died."

Oh, shit. Suddenly his reactions—all the way back to when we'd first been sparring, how careful he'd been of me, how long it'd taken before he'd let me get a clear look at his gargoyle body—made so much sense. And that moment yesterday had brought all his past anguish rushing to the surface just like it had for Lance.

"You know that won't happen with me," I pointed out. "I have no problems at all with seeing you as a gargoyle." But the reassurance sounded weak even to my own ears.

Maybe it wouldn't go quite like that, but I knew better than anyone how fragile my health could be. I couldn't promise him I'd live forever or that nothing we encountered together would push me past my breaking point.

Crag wrapped his fingers around my hand just for a second and then let me go. "I'll protect you in every way I can. But that also means it's safer for you if I keep a little distance."

I didn't know what to say to that at all. An ache clamped around my lungs like a vise.

These men cared about me so much, but it was getting harder to say that having me in their lives was all that good for *them*.

CHAPTER THIRTY-ONE

Quinn

We left the car near the base of the mountain, out of view in a stand of scrubby trees near the side of the road. After driving through the majority of the day with only a few brief pit stops, I had to stretch the stiffness out of my legs. Evening was setting in again, but having the cover of darkness for this raid would make it easier for us to sneak up on the camp.

I'd carried my messenger bag out of habit, slung over my back. Rollick eyed it. "You should leave that in the car. The less you have weighing you down, the better."

The thought of leaving behind my stash of medication —and my first aid supplies, and my water bottle, and all the other bits and pieces that went into keeping my health stable—made my pulse stutter. Although if we didn't make it back to the car, there was a good chance it was because I'd already kicked the bucket.

I tugged at the strap while holding on to the small crossbow with my other hand. "I've got the spare ammo in there."

"Stuff your pockets full," the demon said. "You've got a hoodie with your things somewhere, don't you? Put that on and fill those pockets too. They'll be easier to grab for quick reloading that way." He turned away without waiting for my response. "You'll need to wait here for a little while anyway. I need to make sure the coast is clear and interrupt that repulsing magic Lance noticed here before."

How exactly was he going to do that? Rollick didn't stick around to explain, vanishing into the shadows the moment he'd finished speaking. I hesitated and then popped open the trunk so I could dig my hoodie out of my backpack.

He did have a point. The crossbow put me off-balance as it was. And at this elevation with the sunlight fading, the air was already turning cool. I might appreciate the extra layer once we were even higher up.

Crag stood stoically but not too closely by while I rearranged my belongings. After a moment, Torrent and Lance emerged from the shadows they'd kept to for most of the ride. Torrent leaned against the side of the car and flexed his tentacles. I assumed he'd make most of the trip in shadowy form, but it was reassuring to see him again before we set off.

Lance prowled around the trees, his head tilting to one side and then the other in a way that reminded me of his dragon form even though he was in his human body. "They work too much unnatural magic in this place," he muttered. "More than tricksy. Sick."

Seeing his uneasiness made my gut twist. "You don't have to come," I started. "You could hang back and guard the car—"

He whirled toward me with an emphatic shake of his head. "They got me when I stayed back before. Not again. We need to tackle the beasties together. I won't let them get in my head, and I won't let them get yours."

He flashed his claws meaningfully with that last statement, but his eyes still looked wilder than I liked. This mission was only dredging up more of that old trauma for him. He might have made some peace with it when we'd come together last night, but not enough to put it completely behind him.

"Rollick will make sure the beings with the sorcerer magic aren't around," I reminded him.

He hummed to himself. "I'd like to show them a thing or two." He scratched his claws across a tree trunk, starting to carve one of his abstract designs.

Torrent reached for him with his mangled hand, caught himself, and switched to snagging Lance's arm with a tentacle. He wasn't used to the new disability yet.

Of course he wasn't. How long had it taken him to adjust to his injured legs?

"We shouldn't leave obvious signs that we were here," he said to the dragon shifter.

Lance snorted. "They're going to know we came. There'll be pieces of their minions all over the place to show for it."

"They won't know it was definitely *us*. You made those carvings all over the cabin—some of their followers will have seen them. It's better to leave as little trace as possible."

Lance growled discontentedly, but he lowered his hand. He stalked over to me instead and wrapped his arms around me from behind, burrowing his face against the side of my neck. After the confession he'd made yesterday, his touch set off both a flare of heat between my legs and a softer glow of affection in my chest. I was abruptly doubly glad for the extra layer of the hoodie, protecting him from the worst effects of contact with my protective vest.

Torrent watched us for a moment and then stepped closer to loop one tentacle around my forearm, as if he felt the need to stake his own claim. I brushed my fingers over the row of suckers, and his gaze momentarily darkened with desire, but we both knew this wasn't the time or place for any more intensive indulgence.

Crag stayed poised a few feet away, his gaze flicking to us but his stance rigid. Would *he* ever touch me again, for more than a brief moment or a necessary flight?

I tried not to think about that possibility, soaking in the tenderness two of my men were offering.

It felt like no time at all when Rollick reappeared. "All right," he said. "The camp looks pretty sparsely inhabited at the moment. My distractions were effective. Let's get moving before they peter out and the head honchos return."

"What exactly were your distractions?" I had to ask.

"Let's just say I gave them reasons to think you might be a few different places where you definitely aren't and that aren't all that close to here." He jerked his head toward the mountainside. "Are we rescuing this kid or what?"

I raised my chin. "I'm ready."

Torrent squeezed my arm one last time and slipped into

the shadows. Rollick followed him, but I knew even in the darkness that dappled the mountainside, he'd be leading the way for all of the shadowkind men to the spot where he thought we could best launch our attack.

Lance stepped away from me and shifted into dragon form. Crag shifted as well, his leathery wings sprouting from his stone back, and picked me up gingerly. As embarrassing as it was, I knew I was the slowpoke here. It didn't make any sense for me to insist on walking when the ascent would take us more than twice as long that way. Every minute counted.

I didn't want this expedition to turn into another disaster. We'd just grab Jonah, quickly observe whatever evidence there was to see about the nature of the fiends we were up against and their plans, and get out of there.

Crag took off into the air, staying close to the darkened rocky landscape as he flapped his wings. We soared up the slope at a more measured pace than I knew he was capable of, since he had to follow Rollick's course. I wanted to point out that I was perfectly safe here in his arms despite his worries, but after our conversation in the car, I wasn't sure if that comment would go over well.

It was probably better not to remind him of his fears right before we went into battle.

I hugged the crossbow to my chest so it didn't bump against him. "Are the bolts and my vest bothering you?"

"It's no problem for this short a flight," the gargoyle insisted in his gruff way.

Abruptly, he dropped to the ground by a scrawny sapling. He set me on my feet and glanced around, I assumed to check that at least one of the other men was in range to protect me. Then he lunged into the shadows.

I understood why several seconds later when he burst back into physical form farther up the slope, where I could only just make him out in the dwindling light. He had some kind of creature pinned to the ground for an instant before he ripped its foxlike head right off. Then he was diving back into the shadows with its smoking body, removing the evidence.

A sentry. We must be getting close. I peered beyond him to the jagged edge of rock between the two nearest mountain peaks. We seemed to be heading for that spot.

Crag returned to scoop me up again without another word. I heard a few more faint squeals and gurgles as we went, when one or another of the men on the ground must have dispatched other creatures they encountered.

Crag didn't come back to earth until we'd reached the ridge. I crouched down between two jutting spikes of rock and peered down toward the shadowkind camp.

The ring of mountains circled what looked like a massive crater with a rippling lake in its middle. A few rough buildings stood around it, maybe to hide supplies. Or maybe in preparation for housing me there. A sliver of ice ran down my spine.

A distant whimpering reached my ears a moment later. I stiffened, squinting at the buildings, but I couldn't make out any movement. Which one was Jonah inside? How many shadowkind were lurking in the gloom between us and him?

My companions emerged around me, studying the terrain equally intently. "I think there were more here before," Lance said approvingly. "We can handle this bunch. Slash and sever." He clicked his claws.

"Don't get too cocky," Rollick said, but his tone was languid, as if we were back in his hotel discussing dinner plans. Apparently he wasn't all that worried at this point either.

"Should we try to take any of them prisoner to question them?" Torrent asked.

The demon frowned. "I haven't seen any higher beings that'd be able to talk so far. It's mostly beasties they've left guarding the place. If you come across one and have a solid chance, go for it, but we don't want to leave ourselves vulnerable spending extra time scouring the place."

He motioned to the buildings. "We have a straight path to get to them but not much cover. Crag and Torrent will charge ahead and clear the way. Lance and I will hang back with Quinn. As soon as we reach the buildings, we check each one. Quinn cajoles the kid so he doesn't throw a complete fit, Crag picks up the two of them, and we get back to the car as fast as we can move. During all that, everyone keep an eye out for traces of the shadowkind who built this place that might be useful. Any questions?"

Torrent rolled his shoulders. "We go right now?"

"No time like the present." The demon glanced at me. "Assuming you're good to go."

It was hard to be offended by him singling me out when I was the least capable fighter among us by approximately ten miles. I brandished my loaded crossbow with all the bravado I could muster. "As good as I'll ever be."

Rollick flicked his hand, and Torrent and Crag leapt forward, Torrent vanishing into the darkness and Crag staying in his gargoyle form. As they barreled ahead of us, I heaved myself over the lip of the crater and dashed down the shallow rocky slope as quickly as I could while making sure I didn't trip on the uneven ground.

Lance's claws scrabbled against the stone surface behind me. I didn't look back, but I suspected Rollick had slipped into the shadows like Torrent had, though for different reasons.

Torrent could move much more easily that way. Rollick simply didn't want any witnesses that he'd been here.

How much would he intervene even if our lives were at stake?

I tightened my grip on the crossbow. I couldn't worry about that, only about doing whatever I could to ensure we didn't get to that point.

As the now-cool breeze whipped through my hair, the first wave of shadowkind creatures burst from the shadows to meet our charge. There were far fewer of them than we'd faced when they'd been the ones descending on us out of the blue, but my pulse still hiccupped at the sight of the unnerving shapes wavering into being as if from nothing.

One thing that looked like an elongated racoon popped into being right in front of me. My finger squeezed on the trigger once—twice. The second bolt caught the thing in the chest, tossing it backward with an agonized hiss and a spurt of smoky blood. As I ran on past its slumped body, Lance slashed through its neck to chop off its head for good measure.

Crag and Torrent caught most of the beasts before they got near me. Crag whipped in one direction and another, tearing through the shadowkind like they were made of tissue paper. Torrent didn't fully emerge, but his tentacles lashed out of the gloom to smash one creature's skull and hurl another all the way to the lake.

Feeling a little steadier after my initial victory, I fumbled in my pocket for more bolts and managed to fit one and then another into the crossbow while slowing my pace only a little.

A lizard-like being hurtled at me from the side, and I threw myself away from it, stumbling and landing on my butt. My shot went wild, but then a clawed, ruddy hand snatched out of the shadows and ripped its chest open.

Okay, so Rollick wasn't just hanging around watching the rest of us do all the work.

A bristly boar-like thing raced toward me, but I saw it quickly enough to aim properly despite my hitch of breath. I caught it square in the forehead. It tumbled over onto its back, and Lance finished that one off too with a triumphant snarl.

Shrieks and grunts were echoing all across the crater's sides now. Smoking bodies slumped everywhere I looked. I shoved myself to my feet and hurried on toward the semi-circle of buildings near the lake.

A sudden, sickening thought unfurled in my head, making my stomach clench. How many of these creatures even *wanted* to be fighting us? We had no idea how many were supporting our enemies because they believed in their cause or wanted to impress them, and how many had been forced into obedience with their overlords' new sorcerous powers.

It didn't really matter, did it? We had to get through them either way. If the shadowkind men around me felt any remorse about slaughtering beings who might be victims rather than villains, they weren't letting it stop them.

Torrent and Crag would have killed *Lance* to protect me yesterday if they'd had to. They wouldn't have wanted to, but they'd have done it.

For me.

That realization left me chilled from head to toe. I picked out my lovers' forms in the darkness: Crag rampaging across the landscape, Torrent flinging out his tentacles, Lance springing this way and that.

The gargoyle's face was set in a mask of grim determination. He was taking no pleasure or pride in this fight. Maybe he saw slaughtering as many of the attackers as he could as the only way he could start to make up for the minor injury he'd given me.

Torrent still hadn't completely emerged from the shadows. He was too wounded now to be able to fully fight, but he was still giving it his all because he refused to back down when my life was on the line.

And Lance leapt from place to place with his typical energy and grace, but I caught the nervous twitch of his head here and there as he cast quick glances around the crater. Afraid of who else might be lurking here and what they could do to him. How they might warp his mind so he barely belonged to himself.

My gut balled into a cold, queasy knot. Since I'd met these men, I'd lost a lot, but that was because of our enemies. The three of *them* had given me the chance to become something more than I'd been before. To discover new sides to myself, to recognize new skills and desires...

Right now, I was standing up to these nightmarish creatures like I'd never have believed I could weeks ago.

But what had I given my men in return? Looking at them now, I couldn't help thinking that I'd taken more than I'd given. I'd left them with less of everything except the damage they'd been dealt.

What kind of love was that?

A larger creature loomed over Lance from behind, and my arms reacted automatically. I shot it in the head and the chest, and it stumbled enough to give the dragon shifter time to whirl around and finish the job.

I could protect the men a little... but not half as much as they did for me.

Something clicked together in my head, fragments of ideas colliding into a picture that filled me with a sense of horrified resignation. That emotion solidified into resolve as it sank in my chest like a stone.

They were willing to do all kinds of horrible things to defend me. I'd already pushed away my own parents and every friend I'd had or could have had to spare them the trouble and pain that came from being close to me, even when the only reason was my uncertain health. I'd gotten by on my own, keeping the burdens of my life to myself as much as I possibly could, for years. Why wouldn't I do the same for these men when they were facing so much worse?

If I really cared about them, if I really wanted to protect them properly, then I couldn't shy away from being as monstrous as they were.

My throat had constricted, but I didn't have time to wallow in the discomfort of the decision. I shoved more bolts into the crossbow, shot another small beast that scurried toward me, and then my sneakers were thundering onto the flatter terrain near the lake to reach the closest building.

Crag pushed ahead of me, jerking around me with an awkward motion to make sure he didn't come close to touching me. He slammed the door open. A shadowkind creature sprang at us from inside, but he wrenched its body in two without missing a beat.

The small room inside the hut was empty other than a few crates marked with grocery logos. Food for the shadowkind who enjoyed it or for the mortal prisoner they'd planned to keep?

We dashed onward, and a sob reached my ears from a hut around the curve of the lake. I pushed myself faster.

Torrent made it there first, one tentacle yanking the door off its hinges, the other whipping inside to snatch at the shadowkind guarding the boy.

"What's going on?" Jonah wailed.

I lowered the crossbow to my side as I hurtled through the doorway. The little boy was crouched by the far wall on a thin mattress, shaking, his eyes red-rimmed. For a second, he stared at me with as much terror as if I really had been one of the monsters. Then his face brightened slightly. "You're the lady. You were talking to Mommy and Daddy."

"I'm here to bring you someplace safe," I told him, bending down, and to my relief he raised his arms to welcome my embrace. An instant later, Crag caught us up from behind.

Jonah squealed and squirmed, and I squeezed him tight, struggling to keep my grip on my weapon at the same time. "It's all right," I murmured. "This one's a friend. We're getting you out of here."

The boy whimpered but clung to me without further resistance. Another creature flung itself at me, and I had no way of fending it off now. Its claws raked through my calf in the instant before Lance slashed through it. Then we were hurtling off into the air, my leg stinging, the little boy shivering in my arms, and this one small wrongness made right.

We'd shown our enemies that they couldn't call all the shots. That we wouldn't always be running away from them while they pushed us closer and closer to the edge of destruction. I was pushing back now, and I intended to drive them right out of this realm if it was the last thing I did.

But first I was going to have to do a little destroying of my own to fix the mess *I'd* made.

CHAPTER THIRTY-TWO

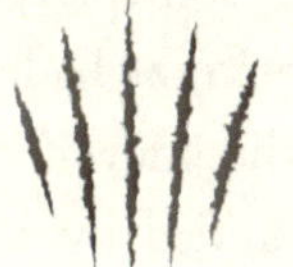

Quinn

The redhead set her hands on her hips as she looked down at the little boy in the thin dawn light. "You know, I never expected to be running a safe haven for sorcerer kids."

I rested my hand on Jonah's head where he was clinging to my leg. We'd met up with Sorsha, the shadowkind woman who'd given me and my men a hand when we'd been investigating the sorcerer killings in Florida a few weeks ago, on a desolate stretch of highway at the eastern edge of New Mexico. Apparently the RV parked behind her was able to travel a lot faster than Rollick's car thanks to some supernatural enhancements.

"I didn't know who else to ask," I said with an apologetic grimace. It'd taken some convincing just to get my shadowkind allies to agree that I should contact her, since we weren't totally sure of her or her companions' loyalties. But she hadn't betrayed us in any way so far, and she had offered her help if we needed it. And also... "You mentioned you'd taken in the daughter of the other sorcerers. He can't stay with us—he'd be in too much danger. I'm not sure how safe he'd be even if we dropped him off at Child Services someplace."

The sorcerer energy in me hadn't woken up until I was twenty years old, but who knew if it might be different for a kid who'd been surrounded by sorcerer family members from birth? Who was a sorcerer through and through rather than just having borrowed a heart from one?

I wouldn't have been surprised if Sorsha had washed her hands of the situation and told us to ship Jonah off someplace else anyway. But she cocked her head and then sank into a crouch so she was level with the little boy. She gave him a crooked smile that still managed to exude warmth.

"You must be having an awful time of it," she said. "I know how horrible some of those monsters can be. But if you come with me, you can make new friends. Including a little girl who's been through something a lot like what you've faced. She lost her family too, so we're building a new one. When you're ready, you might like being part of it with us."

Jonah pressed his face against my leg, and I stroked my hand over his short hair. It wrenched at me to send him away after we'd just rescued him from our enemies' clutches last night, but what I'd said was true. Those enemies would be searching for me even more vehemently now that I'd defied their attempt at replacing me. It was a fulltime job keeping ahead of them and working out ways to fight back without a little kid in the mix on top of that.

I wasn't that much less of a stranger to him than Sorsha was anyway. He'd seen me for all of a minute outside his house.

"She'll take good care of you," I told him. "Make sure you're safe. I know it's hard, but the monsters that came to your home have been coming after me too. You don't want to stick with me."

"I want Mommy and Daddy," he mumbled.

I swallowed hard. He knew they were dead, and I hadn't wanted to remind him of that fact any more than I needed to. I had no idea what else to say.

Sorsha glanced up at me. "Have you gotten a better idea what these fiends are after or what they even are?"

I paused, my gaze darting toward the shadows where I knew my men were lurking. They'd stayed mostly out of sight since we'd gotten back to Rollick's car and roared away from the mountain camp because Jonah panicked at any glimpse of their monstrous features. I'd told Sorsha that her more obviously shadowkind companions should stay in the RV for the same reason.

But Rollick, with his thorough disguise, had still driven us out here while I'd comforted Jonah as well as I could. He'd looked more pensive than usual. I had the feeling he'd seen something in the camp that'd gotten the wheels spinning in his head, but he hadn't shared his suspicions with the rest of us yet. He didn't appear to be inclined to with Sorsha either, since he didn't emerge.

Knowing his preferences for discretion, he probably didn't want her being able to identify him either.

"One of them has some kind of affinity to earth," I said. "I think that's the one that ordered the attack on Jonah's home. All I could tell about him is that he felt very big and powerful, which I know isn't super helpful. As far as what they're planning on using their new sorcery skills for, we haven't been able to figure that out either. But I'm guessing it's not anything good."

"Seems like a reasonable prediction," Sorsha said dryly, and sighed. "You'd think one psychotic megalomaniac shadowkind per decade would be enough. Are you sure *you* don't want to come back with us? There's plenty of room at the house, and we keep pretty tight security."

The offer tugged at my heart. Yes, I *wanted* to hole up somewhere safe and pretend none of this was happening. But the events of the past few days had made it amply clear that I couldn't run forever. And running to Sorsha and her companions would probably just bring my enemies down on them too.

I wasn't going to see anyone else hurt just so I didn't have to deal with this fate I'd never asked for but couldn't shake.

I shook my head. "I think I need to get ready to stand up to these monsters. We have a vague lead about a possible place in Norway where I could get a grip on my powers."

"I hope that works out for you. We'll keep our ears peeled as much as we can while we're settling this little guy in and let you know if we find anything else out on our end. And don't hesitate to call me if you need back-up." She gave me a firm look. "I mean that. I can be a lot more than a foster mom."

My cheeks flushed. "I'm sure you can. I just—we've had people we thought we could trust turn against us already—it was hard to know for sure who we could count on."

"Fair. I've seen that the shadowkind tend to be hesitant about joining forces in general." Sorsha scooted closer to Jonah and held out her hand to him. "You really should see the inside of the Everymobile. It's pretty amazing. And we picked up McDonalds drive-through on the way over. Do you like chicken nuggets?"

"It's okay," I told him, squeezing his shoulder. "See how nice she is?"

Cautiously, the boy detached his hands from my leg and took a step toward Sorsha. She scooped him up gently and pointed to the streamers waving along the side of the RV. "Check those out. Pretty cool, right? We've taken this thing through rifts a few times, and it always comes out a little more fun."

She tipped her head to me in farewell and carried Jonah into the RV, hugging him tighter when he started sniffling again. My hands clenched at my sides, but there wasn't anything more I could do.

I went back to Rollick's sedan to lean against the hood while the RV drove away. As it disappeared into the distance, there was a moment when it felt as if I were all alone amid the scruffy desert vegetation. There was no sound but a faint whisper of a breeze, nothing real but the hard-packed dirt beneath my feet.

Then the shadowkind men wavered back into view—all four of them, Rollick in front of me and the other three off to the side. Rollick folded his arms over his chest. "So you're wanting to jet over to Norway now?"

I opened my mouth and closed it again. The ache that'd formed in my chest as I forced Jonah to leave expanded, nearly smothering me.

I knew what I had to do. I'd known it since that moment during our raid on the mountain camp... maybe even before it, without admitting it to myself. The sorcerers had even given me all the information I needed to be sure I could do it.

But I didn't want to.

I closed my eyes. Was I going to be selfish, or was I going to show my love for the three men who'd offered theirs to me in every way they deserved, no matter how painful it was to *me*?

It wasn't even really a question. I knew the right answer. I hadn't been able to fix much in the past few weeks or to design anything worth admiring. Now that I had the chance to do something meaningful, something that showed what was important to me, I couldn't pass it up for my own comfort.

"I think looking for the sorcerer enclave in Norway is our best chance of figuring out how we can stand up to those fiends effectively," I said. "Unless you learned something in the camp that's given you some ideas?"

Rollick's mouth twitched with a hint of tension. "I have a few thoughts based on my observations, but nothing that comes with any obvious solutions beyond seeing you get a better handle on your powers. And it seems unlikely they'll be looking for us in Norway, which is a plus."

"Yeah." I sucked in a breath of the warm morning air. "But there's something I have to do first. It—it won't take long."

When I turned toward the other three men, Torrent gave me a quizzical look. Crag held himself with his usual stoic air, like he expected me to send him off on some new dangerous mission for my benefit. Lance beamed at me, equally ready to jump at my request. My resolve hardened.

I stepped closer to Torrent first, reaching up to caress the side of his neck with my hand. He wrapped his good arm around my waist, gazing down at me.

"I love you," I said. "I want to see all the other things you could make—I want you to get to make your mark on the world and enjoy every part of it that you can."

More confusion flickered through his expression, but it didn't diminish the fondness in his eyes. "Quinn..." He bowed his head next to mine, hugging me even closer despite my vest. "Love isn't a concept I've given much thought to. But I'd do anything for you—I can say that much."

I smiled through the pain radiating through my abdomen. "Then you'll understand."

Before he could ask *what* he was going to understand, I eased out of his embrace and moved to Crag. The gargoyle tensed as if worried that I was going to try to touch him too. I longed to give him one last hug, but I could tell he wasn't going to accept it.

"I love you too," I said, choking up. "You're so much more than a monster, and all the ways you've been here for me matter so much more than one little accident. I hope you can believe that."

Crag blinked, his forehead furrowing. "Softness," he said, his gruff voice unusually tender, but then didn't seem to know how to go on.

Lance's smile had faded as he watched, his mouth twisting with his own confusion. Maybe given what he'd been through he could sense where this was going even if he wasn't totally conscious of it.

"You know how I feel about you," he said when I moved to him.

"I do. And you know I love you too." *And I'm going to prove it*, I thought as I stepped in quickly to give him a tight hug. Oh, God, please let him understand.

I let him squeeze me back for just a few seconds before pulling away. I had to do this before my conviction faltered.

I gazed back at all of them, thinking of all the ways I knew them. Not just the way they moved or spoke, their everyday habits. I knew what they cared about, what made them smile and what made them hurt, how they reacted to a threat and how they celebrated a victory. I knew them in ways far beyond any connection the sorcerers I'd spoken to could have known the shadowkind they "harnessed."

So please, because I loved them, let this work.

I gathered all my agonized determination, all my fears, and all my love, and channeled it into my mouth alongside the energy that thrummed through my heart. The sorcerous magic sizzled through every inch of my body as a jolt of it shot into my voice, searing my tongue with its force.

"The three of you will go straight to the nearest rift and back to the shadow realm. You can go wherever you want from there, other than you'll stay far away from me, hundreds of miles, until the shadowkind who've been hunting me are no longer a threat. *Go*."

The words wrenched out of me as if tearing me into pieces bit by bit. The last emphatic syllable nearly cracked me right down the middle. I swallowed a sob at the expressions that crossed the men's faces: Torrent all shocked recognition, Crag's horrified consternation, and Lance's frozen in panicked anguish. I only got that brief glimpse of them before they were all swiveling around, leaping simultaneously into the shadows away from me.

It was only when they were gone that the sob burst out. I clapped my hand to my mouth and squeezed my eyes shut. Every part of me ached from my throat down to my gut. My legs wobbled, and I stumbled backward to catch myself against the side of the car.

Rollick stayed silent as the impact of what I'd done sank in. Some desperate part of me pleaded for it not to have worked, for any of the three to leap back out and declare that they weren't going anywhere, but when I forced my eyes open again, the desert landscape remained still and quiet.

It was done. I'd made sure they wouldn't be hurt any more in any way while they tried to do the same for me.

Maybe they would hate me for it. Maybe it made me as monstrous as the sorcerers they hated. But I'd have been even more of a monster if I'd let them keep hurling themselves into harm's way on my behalf, when this was my battle.

The fiends only really wanted me. And when they got me, I'd be ready to take them on... or I didn't deserve to live at all.

I expected Rollick to toss out some dry remark, but when he finally spoke, he simply held up his phone, his expression opaque, his voice carefully even. "Should I book us a flight to Oslo, then?"

If he was at all offended that I'd cared more about his underlings' safety than his own, he didn't show it. We both knew I wasn't tackling the monsters who wanted me completely on my own. But Rollick never had any problem looking out for his interests over mine. He'd intended to use me as a tool, and now in some ways, I'd be using him right back.

I lifted my head and clamped down on the agony inside with all the determination I had left in me. "Yes, I think you'd better."

ABOUT THE AUTHOR

Eva Chase lives in Canada with her family. She loves stories both swoony and supernatural, and strong women and the men who appreciate them. Along with the Heart of a Monster series, she is the author of the Gang of Ghouls series, the Bound to the Fae series, the Flirting with Monsters series, the Cursed Studies trilogy, the Royals of Villain Academy series, the Moriarty's Men series, the Looking Glass Curse trilogy, the Their Dark Valkyrie series, the Witch's Consorts series, the Dragon Shifter's Mates series, the Demons of Fame series, and the Legends Reborn trilogy.

Connect with Eva online:
www.evachase.com
eva@evachase.com